A CONVERSATIONAL KISS

It was scandalous that Gareth Rushton had actually kissed Selina—and even worse that she had not resisted. Now she had to set the matter straight before any misunderstanding led to further mischief.

"You think because I allowed you to kiss me . . ." she said, then began anew. "It gave you the idea I was . . . I'm not like that, Mr. Rushton. You are too accustomed to the morals of London society." Selin— —pped herself again. "No, i— ——ave you a mistaken i— ——will, of course, m— ——ink I should no—

To which R— ——be ridiculous. I— ——pt to kiss you again— without your permission."

A perilous promise indeed. . . .

SIGNET REGENCY ROMANCE
COMING IN FEBRUARY 1993

Katherine Kingsley
King of Hearts

Charlotte Louise Dolan
Fallen Angel

Laura Matthews
The Village Spinster

AT YOUR LOCAL BOOKSTORE
OR ORDER DIRECTLY
FROM THE PUBLISHER
WITH VISA OR MASTERCARD
1-800-253-6476

A CURIOUS COURTING

by

Laura Matthews

A SIGNET BOOK

SIGNET
Published by the Penguin Group
Penguin Books USA Inc., 375 Hudson Street,
New York, New York 10014, U.S.A.
Penguin Books Ltd, 27 Wrights Lane, London W8 5TZ, England
Penguin Books Australia Ltd, Ringwood, Victoria, Australia
Penguin Books Canada Ltd, 10 Alcorn Avenue,
Toronto, Ontario, Canada M4V 3B2
Penguin Books (N.Z.) Ltd, 182-190 Wairau Road,
Auckland 10, New Zealand

Penguin Books Ltd, Registered Offices:
Harmondsworth, Middlesex, England

Published by Signet, an imprint of New American Library, a division of
Penguin Books USA Inc.

First Signet Printing, January, 1993
10 9 8 7 6 5 4 3 2 1

Copyright © 1980 by Elizabeth Rotter
All rights reserved.
Originally published as *A Curious Courting* by Elizabeth Neff Walker.

Ⓡ REGISTERED TRADEMARK—MARCA REGISTRADA

Printed in the United States of America

Without limiting the rights under copyright reserved above, no part of
this publication may be reproduced, stored in or introduced into a re-
trieval system, or transmitted, in any form, or by any means (electronic,
mechanical, photocopying, recording, or otherwise), without the prior
written permission of both the copyright owner and the above publisher
of this book.

BOOKS ARE AVAILABLE AT QUANTITY DISCOUNTS WHEN USED TO PROMOTE PROD-
UCTS OR SERVICES. FOR INFORMATION PLEASE WRITE TO PREMIUM MARKETING
DIVISION, PENGUIN BOOKS USA INC., 375 HUDSON STREET, NEW YORK, NEW
YORK 10014.

If you purchased this book without a cover you should be aware that this
book is stolen property. It was reported as "unsold and destroyed" to the
publisher and neither the author nor the publisher has received any pay-
ment for this "stripped book."

For Laura and Matt, with love

ONE

"There's not an inch of Oak Park that's not entailed, and even if it weren't I wouldn't have the slightest desire to sell any of it. Why do you need some land for a hunting-box? You know you're always welcome to stay here." Sir Penrith Southwood dug his hands into the pockets of his buckskin breeches as he stood before the blazing fire thawing from the day's hunt.

"It never crossed my mind to suggest you sell any of Oak Park to me," his guest assured him, "and I appreciate your generous hospitality, Pen, but I have an itch to build something, and Leicestershire is the perfect spot. I've seldom had better hunting than these last two weeks."

"Lord, Assheton Smith does give one a good day, what?"

"He's one of the best masters I've ever ridden with. I thought the whole field would go round at that stile, but no, he took the bank and stile in two leaps."

"And you couldn't resist the challenge?" Penrith grinned.

"With him waving that handkerchief as though it were child's play? You know me better, Pen." Mr. Rushton stared meditatively at the hearth. "I wouldn't need much land. A few acres would do."

"You're not planning to build on the scale of Farnside?" Sir Penrith taunted. "You don't think perhaps you'll need twenty guest chambers and an equal number of reception rooms?"

His guest frowned momentarily, the black brows

drawn low over deep blue eyes. Sir Penrith instantly regretted his words, though he had meant nothing other than their surface quizzing. Not a month had passed since Julia Longmead had refused his friend's offer of marriage, and Sir Penrith was well aware that Gareth Rushton had anticipated adorning his ancestral home with that beautiful young lady, and filling it with their progeny. No, Farnside was a subject to be avoided. With a shrug Penrith cleared his throat and said, "Don't know as I've heard of any land for sale in the neighborhood. There might be a farm on the other side of Barton, but most of the land is held in large tracts. Would you care to ride into Barton to enquire?"

"Perhaps. I'd prefer to build something, but a farm might do. Had you heard of a specific one?" Mr. Rushton casually used the poker to restore a fallen log to its place in the fire.

"Some months ago. It could well have sold by now. Tidy little place with an older farmhouse that probably needs work. Devil of a nuisance to build something new, Gareth."

His friend gave him a sardonic smile. "I have nothing better to do with my time just now. The hunting season will be over soon, and I see no reason why I should not devote myself to architecture this spring. As I said, nothing on a grand scale. Have you never had the desire to plan a residence? No doubt it's all very well to accommodate one's self to the usages of the past, but frankly I had considered the merits of a little gem without smoking fireplaces and damp corridors. Farnside is all very well—such graciousness is somehow flattering to the ego—but I think it would give me pleasure to lay out the design of a modern building. After all, see what joy Prinny gets of it."

"Prinny! How he could take a modest farmhouse at Brighton and turn it into that monstrosity is beyond anything! Surely you have no intention of stuffing a hunting-box with fake bamboo furniture and painted dragons! Pagodas and palm trees be damned. Do you know what that place is costing him?" demanded the indignant Sir Penrith.

"I have a fairly clear idea, my dear Pen, but I have

no intention of creating a domed pleasure palace in the wilds of Leicestershire. A small villa, perhaps."

"No, by God, I don't believe it!" his friend protested before he noticed the other's laughing eyes. "Oh, you would roast me, would you? What do you know about architecture? For all the experience you've had, it might well turn out more on the order of a brothel. I can see the local linen draper talking you into lining the walls with silks and satins to complement the dainty little gilded chairs. Ugh! And perhaps some cupids to ornament the ceilings, or, for a more classical touch, paintings of naked Grecian maidens, or maybe some wood nymphs, to blend with the scenery." Sir Penrith glared ominously at his companion.

"You do have a vivid imagination," Mr. Rushton drawled. "Or perhaps that is your dream of the ideal establishment. Have you frequented so many brothels, then? I had no idea. Is that what they look like? I must certainly do some research." Toying with an enameled snuffbox, he pursed his lips thoughtfully. "I had something entirely different in mind, as it happens. The one room at Farnside in which I feel completely comfortable is my study, with its leather chairs and oak tables. You can kick off your boots and stretch your legs without fear of knocking over some spindly-legged table with its priceless Sèvres vase or Kakiemon bowl, to say nothing of a Chelsea dovecot potpourri vase balanced precariously on a side table. Not for the world would I think of removing the porcelain figurines that abound at Farnside. My mother has an admirable collection of porcelain in which she delights every bit as much as I do in my study.

"As a concession to me, she even has several Meissen groups of huntsmen with their hounds. No, no, I would never consider destroying the elegance she has created there for a whim. But sometimes I long for less . . . ah . . . cluttered surroundings."

Penrith listened in silence as his friend extolled the virtues of racing trophies and sporting prints over ormolu clocks and silver goatherds, bronzes of favorite hunters over fragile glass ornaments. Although he was basically in agreement with his friend, the underlying

9

cause of such a plan seemed very apparent to him. Before Miss Longmead's refusal, Rushton had never expressed such sentiments. Both from old and distinguished families, such elegant surroundings as Rushton described were their natural milieu, and they both moved in them with the greatest of ease—a handsome couple, the young lady as blonde as her suitor was dark, as delicately feminine as he was ruggedly masculine.

And it was all the more surprising that Miss Longmead had refused him when one was aware that he possessed not only a handsome person but one of the finest homes and fortunes in England. Although Miss Longmead's ancestry was impeccable, her family was generally acknowledged to be less well endowed financially than the position they attempted to maintain would suggest. Sir Penrith was no less aware than the Longmeads themselves must have been that Rushton had intended to come down generously in the matter of the marriage settlement.

Penrith's attention was recaptured when Rushton consigned plate-rooms and nurseries to obscurity in favor of gun-rooms, wood beams on the ceiling in favor of grotesque plaster vines intertwined with gilded birds. Mesmerized by such a vision of comfort, Sir Penrith could only murmur, "And you could clean your pistols in any room, or have the dogs about if you wished."

"Precisely. No schoolrooms, linen-rooms, and music-rooms. No solariums and summer and winter parlors." Mr. Rushton waved a languid hand about the room in which they sat. "Every room could be as devoid of feminine artifacts as this one. I cannot tell you how pleasant it would be to have no Rose Drawing Rooms or Green Writing Rooms. My dear Pen, I don't mean this place to be spartan by any means. No reason at all not to have the latest range for the kitchen or water closets in the house, and I've a mind to look into a system of heating I heard of recently. Now if I were to buy a farmhouse, I dare say I might eventually arrange it to my taste, but look at the possibilities of building from the ground up. One cannot wonder at Prinny's enthusiasm for building, merely at his lack of practicality and exotic taste."

Sir Penrith shook his head slowly as he stroked his moustache. "Sounds well enough, of course, Gareth, but you cannot have thought how much time it will take to plan and carry out the scheme. Why, I had to be right there every day when they put up the new stables. Hardly an hour without a decision to be made. And a house! Damme, if there wouldn't be a thousand times the number of questions constantly bombarding you. Say you found some land and spent a month or so in the planning. Just when it would be decent weather to start building, you'd be off to town for the Season."

"I have no intention of going to London this spring."

"Not go to London!" Sir Penrith was truly shocked. Another problem to be laid at Julia Longmead's door, he could not doubt. When speculation had been rampant in London over the possibility of the match, Miss Longmead had given every indication that she intended to have Mr. Rushton. The Season would have been more entertaining than ever in the ensuing activity, had the engagement taken place. Now this! Sir Penrith regarded his friend's impassive face with its heavy brows and determined jaw, the eyes coolly indifferent but the mouth firmly set. There was no talking to him of the matter; he refused, after imparting the blunt facts, to make any further comment on the matter.

Rushton sat casually in an overstuffed chair, his long legs stretched out toward the blazing hearth. In his hunting jacket and buckskin breeches he looked the picture of a sporting gentleman with not a care in the world. His long hands lay unmoving on his thighs, but his very stillness exuded an air of controlled strength.

Sir Penrith brought his hand down on the mantel with an exasperated smack. "But you've been in London for the Season for the last fifteen years! Surely you would not let a chit's capriciousness change your way of life."

"It has nothing to do with Miss Longmead," came the cold reply.

"Hogwash! It has everything to do with Miss Longmead. What is it that bothers you, Gareth? Perhaps seeing her paid court to by other men? Or that you will be talked about when it is obvious that she has refused you? Does that sting your pride? By God, I would have too much pride to let the world see that it had affected me in the least! If the last thing I wanted to do was go to London, you may be sure you would find me there."

"Well, going to London is not the last thing I wish to do, but it comes pretty far down just now. I have told you that I am interested in building a hunting-box. If I want it ready for next season, I will have to find the land and get started very soon."

Irritated that Rushton would not rise to the bait, Sir Penrith narrowed his eyes and tapped impatient fingers on the mantel. "This is surely folly, Rushton. If you stay away from town, there is certain to be talk. No one need ever know that you even offered for her if you go and let it be seen that your interest has waned. You made no mention to anyone else that you'd gone to her home, I'll be bound. Just go to town as though nothing had happened and no one will be the wiser."

"I think I *will* ride over to Barton," Mr. Rushton commented as he unfolded himself from the chair. "You need not come if you would prefer to stay here talking to yourself."

Muttering darkly of "stubborn addlepates," Sir Penrith agreed to accompany his guest. "Just give me a moment to see if my mother or Cassandra wants anything from the shops."

"I await your pleasure," Mr. Rushton replied, his eyes once more full of amusement.

Their way lay over snow-covered roads, but there was no hard freeze to make the beauty of the scene fraught with danger. Mr. Rushton managed to keep the talk of hunting, though his disgruntled friend more than once glanced in his direction with the clear intent of reopening the subject of Miss Longmead and London. The frown he drew discouraged him each time, and difficult as it was for him to remain silent, he said no more of the matter. Let them speak of the Quorn, Sir Penrith raged inwardly. If one cannot give some friendly advice to a man one has known for fifteen years, then they might as well talk of Meynell and Osbaldeston, Lord Kintore and Valentine Maher. What were friends for, indeed? It was with a certain amount of satisfaction that Sir Penrith received the news from Mr. Dodge that the farm he remembered had been sold and that there was no land available in the neighborhood at the moment.

With mock sympathy he consoled Mr. Rushton. "Such a shame. Here you were with high hopes of diverting yourself, building a little nest in our humble county, and all is dashed. You know, Gareth, you'd do better to rent a box for next season if you don't want to stay at Oak Park. There is no need to go to the expense of building a whole damn house just to have a spot to retire to when London or Farnside becomes fatiguing. Lord, man, you could rent a place at Brighton or one of the watering holes in the summer and something here in the winter. Assure you it is by far the wisest course."

"You are full of wisdom today, Pen," his companion retorted as he swung himself onto his horse. He pointed to a road going south out of the town and asked, "Where does that lead?"

"Nowhere in particular. Winds around until it joins up with our road again, or goes to Ashfordby. Passes a few country places and farms." Sir Penrith eyed his friend suspiciously. "If there were land available there, Mr. Dodge would know of it."

"Hmm. No doubt. Let's take it."

"You know, Gareth, I am beginning to believe that you are purposely trying to annoy me. What have I done?"

"Nothing, I assure you. Do you mind taking the long way about? If you are in a hurry to return to the Park, I can ride over the south road by myself. You need only say so."

Sir Penrith surveyed Rushton's enigmatic face with exasperation. "Oh, very well, but I don't see what good it will do."

"Good? Well, for one thing it will give us a longer ride, but I personally am looking for nothing but variety in my route."

A snort escaped Sir Penrith as he put his heels to his black stallion. Being a very easygoing person himself, he generally had no difficulty in getting along with his acquaintances, but the perversity Rushton was showing this afternoon was another matter entirely. In fact, for the entire two weeks he had been a guest at Oak Park, he had not been himself. Oh, he was as pleasant as ever in company, but when the two of them were alone, he withdrew into himself. Brooding, that's what he's doing, Sir Penrith decided, totally unfamiliar himself with that state of mind. The sun always shone on Sir Penrith, or so one would assume from his perpetually optimistic outlook on life. Short in comparison to his friend, and tending to be stocky, yet his cheerful countenance and masses of flaming auburn hair met with approval everywhere. He did not perhaps inspire the ardor of so many young ladies as his friend, but he was welcomed everywhere for his good nature and courteous manners.

Penrith had a good mind to tell Gareth that if Miss Longmead would not have him, there were plenty of others who would. And better ones, in Penrith's humble opinion. For he was secretly pleased that Miss Longmead had refused his friend. Certainly she was possessed of a rather astonishing elegance, but he could not feel that there was any warmth of heart to back it up, and for all his own polish and address Rushton was a surprisingly sensitive man with strong loyalties. Yes, that was the thing to do, Penrith decided. Point out to him that there were any number of ladies who would welcome his attentions. No matter that Rushton would ignore him; the seed once planted would surely blossom into the fruit Penrith most desired—that his friend would appear in London for the Season, and in a more cheerful frame of mind.

Before Penrith could speak, Rushton turned to him abruptly, his face transformed from moodiness to sharp interest. "That parcel of land there. The one set off by the hedgerows in the vale. Who owns it?"

Bewildered, Penrith followed the line of Rushton's pointing finger. "Must be Lord Benedict's land; all of it is on this side of the road. No, hold a moment. I remember that vale, caused quite a stir years ago. The present viscount's father lost it on a wager to Mr. Easterly-Cummings. Some sort of row over a document Easterly-Cummings found which showed it deeded to his father. The old viscount wouldn't credit it, so they settled the matter with the turn of a card. It's surrounded on all sides by Benedict land, but I hear on good authority that the deed was valid."

"So a Mr. Easterly-Cummings owns it now?"

"Well, no, he had his notice to quit years ago. Must belong to his daughter, unless the present viscount bought it from her. Wouldn't think so, though, the way it's still set off from everything around it."

"That's the piece of land I want," Rushton said firmly.

"But, good Lord, man, it ain't for sale. Miss Easterly-Cummings don't need the money; her old man left her pots of it. That whole valley over there," he waved impressively to the other side of the road, "belongs to her."

"She isn't doing anything with the vale. I see no reason why she shouldn't sell."

Penrith laughed. "I'd love to be there when you tell her so."

Suspicious, Rushton asked, "Why? What's she like?"

It would have been a little difficult for Penrith to give an accurate idea of Miss Easterly-Cummings, and suddenly he was far from desiring to do so. His feelings were hurt that Rushton would not listen to or confide in him, and it seemed a vastly amusing plan to mislead his friend ever so slightly. "She's the source of all good works in the neighborhood."

Rushton sighed. "One of those? An old tartar who upholds God and country for all the lesser folks of the countryside, dispensing elixirs with moral platitudes?"

Such a description could hardly have been further from the truth, but Penrith, his eyes dancing, vowed, "I won't say another word."

Detaching his gaze from his friend's merry face,

Rushton once again surveyed the charming vale. "I want that piece of land quite enough to beard the lioness in her den. Where does she live?"

"You wouldn't call on her at this time of day, surely! It's almost dinner time."

"No, I shall call tomorrow."

"Shalbrook is over that rise about half a mile. The entrance gates are a ways down the road." Penrith had the most amusing vision of the two strong personalities meeting. To insure the success of his plan he said, "Really, Gareth, you have no idea what you're doing."

"What harm can there be? The old lady can only refuse, and who knows? I can be very persuasive when I want."

"No doubt."

TWO

Shalbrook was a medieval manor house, complete with towers and battlements, but with no observable fortifications where it stood on its slight eminence overlooking the valley. As Mr. Rushton swept around the curve of the gravel drive in his curricle he noted the truly magnificent proportions of the building, and wondered how it had come into the possession of such an obscure family as the Easterly-Cummings must be. It had the presence of a peer's seat and a well-kept look which, in such a large structure, denoted the expenditure of vast sums of money in maintenance. No doubt the old lady kept half the neighborhood in her service, Rushton thought grimly as he reined in his chestnuts. Well, all the better, for even if she had inherited "pots of money" from her father, it was no small undertaking to manage such an estate.

What the devil had gotten into Penrith to refuse to accompany him when he knew the old lady? She was sure to be a high stickler, and the proper introduction might mean a great deal in the transaction Rushton hoped to promote. He handed the reins to a liveried groom who appeared as the horses clattered to a halt, and traversed the innumerable stairs and terraces to the grotesquely out-size oak door.

All the snow had been cleared from the walkways, an enormous task at this time of year and undoubtedly useless, he thought with amusement, as the skies were once again leaden and promised a new fall before the next morning. A formidable-looking butler appeared

17

in answer to his rap upon the door, a sound which seemed to echo hollowly throughout the interior. Handing the butler his card, Rushton said politely, "I wonder if it might be possible to have a word with Miss Easterly-Cummings. I am a guest of Sir Penrith Southwood at Oak Park, and he has mentioned her to me."

"If you will step this way, sir, I will enquire if Miss Easterly-Cummings is available." The butler led Rushton into an antechamber which was dimly lit by the wintry light outside creeping past the monstrously thick walls to make its way through the narrow twin arches of the window. The chairs were comfortable enough, Rushton decided when the butler had excused himself, and the view over the valley was delightful, but the damp penetrated the outer walls, which were devoid of any ornamentation—no paintings, no knick-knacks—and the room was chilly. During the wait Rushton considered the best possible way in which to put his request to the old lady, but decided that he would have to wait before meeting her to see where her weak points were.

Not more than five minutes had passed when the door opened and a young lady entered. Obviously this was Miss Easterly-Cummings' companion, and Rushton immediately rose and smiled. "I am Gareth Rushton, ma'am, and I wondered if your mistress might spare me a few moments of her time to discuss a matter of business."

"Perhaps if you were to give me some idea of the nature of the business. . . ."

"If you will excuse me, I would prefer to discuss it only with Miss Easterly-Cummings."

"I see." The young lady stood calmly before him, frankly appraising his features and clothing without the slightest shred of discomfort. "You are a friend of Sir Penrith's?"

"Yes, indeed. We have known each other for the past fifteen years, I dare say. I have frequently stayed at Oak Park but have never had the opportunity to call on Miss Easterly-Cummings."

"And how is it that Sir Penrith did not accompany

you?" Her puzzled frown caused her brown eyes to narrow somewhat, which put Rushton on his guard.

"As to that, he had pressing matters this morning, and I was too eager to see Miss Easterly-Cummings to wait until this afternoon." One really could not say that Pen had refused to call on a neighbor. "And besides, he knew that it was a matter of business which I had in mind."

"Very well. If you will follow me, please." She turned abruptly and led him through the medieval hall and down a corridor as cold as it was dark before opening a door and preceding him into a spacious chamber with a roaring fire blazing on the hearth. There were the same arched windows on two sides of this room, and the sofas and chairs were gaily upholstered in gold satin which matched the carpet, the whole giving an effect of warmth and comfort. "Please be seated, Mr. Rushton. I am, as you appear not to be aware, Selina Easterly-Cummings."

"*The* Miss Easterly-Cummings?" he asked incredulously.

"Yes, Mr. Rushton. The only Miss Easterly-Cummings. Did Penrith lead you to believe that I would be other than I am?"

Rushton's eyes betrayed his astonishment and he silently cursed Pen for playing such a prank on him. Now that he had made such a stupid error, there was little chance of convincing this young lady with her cool brown eyes and calm air of assurance to listen to his proposal to buy the land in the vale. But, dear God, it was no wonder that he had mistaken her for a companion. Although Miss Easterly-Cummings' dark brown hair curled quite naturally, and her brows automatically arched over those distressingly frank brown eyes, and her nose was undoubtedly straight and patrician as that of an Easterly-Cummings should be, there was something to the set of her lips and the pointing of her chin which was decidedly provocative. It may have been this circumstance which led to her adoption of the most bizarre costume Rushton had ever seen on a young lady of position. Miss Easterly-Cummings of Shalbrook dressed routinely in high-necked muslin gowns of an inordinately depressing shade of muddy brown (varied only occasionally by a similarly deplorable yellowish-green creation of her own fashioning) and complemented this with the sturdiest of walking shoes.

One would have thought that she spent her days hiking about the countryside, from the very substantial nature of these shoes, and so she often did, but she was wont to receive those morning callers who dared to invade her sanctum in the same fashion. The dowdy brown (or green) gown could not disguise her equally provocative figure, and she had recently adopted a scarlet shawl which was swathed about her as inelegantly as possible. Combined with the shawl, the gown and the shoes, it was perhaps unnecessary to go to a step further, but she had done so, nonetheless.

The linen drapers in Barton were provided with a wide assortment of fetching chip hats and wide-brimmed bonnets which the young ladies of the neighborhood sighed over for hours before determining which they would have. There were also, for the more elderly of the female population of the area, lacy caps to be had at a reasonable price. Even Mrs. Carstairs, now in her eighty-first year, had not the least difficulty in searching amongst the frilled pieces of linen to find a cap which was suitable for her age and dignity. Not so Miss Easterly-Cummings.

The frivolity of such items was abhorrent to her very soul, it would seem, and she chose instead to effect a rather unnerving head-covering of muddy-brown fustian, trimmed with a white band, which for all the world gave her the appearance of a nun. And though this was not what she had had in mind originally, she was rather pleased with the effect, and made herself a matching cap from the remains of the yellowish-green fabric out of which she had made her gown.

The total effect was of the height of eccentricity. Rushton could not believe that a rich young lady of obvious beauty could so distort her image. For a moment he was tempted to think that Penrith had somehow arranged with this woman to play a part which would throw him into utter confusion, and he regarded her searchingly. There was no wavering of the eyes, no flush of embarrassment, just that calm self-possession that surely proclaimed that she was indeed Miss Easterly-Cummings. "I fear Penrith allowed me to picture a much older lady," he said at last.

"Well, that was naughty of him, no doubt, but the matter is clarified now. You say you wish to discuss business with me, Mr. Rushton? I am at a loss to understand how that can be."

Mr. Rushton was never daunted for long. He had not been on the town for fifteen years without developing a great deal of polish in his manners, and, when added to his natural forcefulness, this produced a formidable personality. With a charming smile, he said, "Yesterday Sir Penrith and I were riding about the area in search of some land on which I might build a hunting-box. I have hunted the Pytchley, the Cottesmore and the Belvoir, but I have seldom had such sport as with the Quorn. My own home is in an area of Suffolk which is indifferent for the hunt, you understand, and I desire a location where I may indulge my pastime."

On Miss Easterly-Cummings' face there was a lack of interest so profound that Mr. Rushton felt a momentary spark of anger, which he carefully suppressed. It behooved him, he decided, to get to the point without further delay. "I saw a piece of land in the vale which would be the ideal location for my hunting box, and it is apparently not in use. Sir Penrith informed me, in fact, that the land belonged to you, though it is surrounded by Lord Benedict's lands. My purpose in coming to you is to ask if you would consider selling it to me." Once again Mr. Rushton allowed his charming smile to spread over his features.

"No."

Long experience with women had suggested to Rushton that they were inveterate talkers. For a moment he waited to hear what explanation she would make, what qualifying statement she would attach to her simple negative. Once a woman started to make excuses, there was always the chance of poking holes in her reasoning and eventually accomplishing one's purpose. And if she did not essay into muddled explanations and excuses, she invariably fidgeted with her hands and

21

shifted in her seat under his scrutiny. Miss Easterly-Cummings did neither.

At length he commented, "I would be willing to pay handsomely for the land."

"I have no interest in selling, Mr. Rushton." She rose gracefully to her feet and offered him her hand. "I appreciate your calling and hope you will give my best to Penrith, Lady Southwood and Cassandra. I believe Cassandra is the only one still living at Oak Park with her mother, is she not?"

"Yes," he agreed as he shook her hand before watching her tug the bellrope.

"No doubt she too will marry one day and move away," Miss Easterly-Cummings suggested by way of conversation, as she eyed him speculatively.

Between Sir Penrith and his youngest sister there were three other daughters, each one of whom, as she had arrived on the London scene, Mr. Rushton had, for his friend's sake, assisted to entertain. There had never been any question of his marrying any of them; they were not in his style, though certainly very agreeable young ladies who had the same sunny disposition as their only brother. Somehow Mr. Rushton received the impression that Miss Easterly-Cummings thought him a suitor of Miss Cassandra's, and found him wanting. He had in mind to set her straight, but the butler arrived to show him out before he could think of a way in which to deny such a ludicrous notion. His irritation with Miss Easterly-Cummings perceptibly grew.

"Good day, ma'am. I appreciate your taking the time to see me," he murmured with a note of sarcasm as he bowed to her.

She returned no response but watched indifferently as he stalked from the room. When he was gone, however, a grin stretched her generous mouth and a gurgle of laughter escaped her. Stuffy sort of fellow, she thought, and it surprised her that Pen should have such a friend of no recent acquaintance. Although Sir Penrith was ten years her elder, she had known him well some years ago, being the same age as his sister Maria. Dropping onto one of the gold satin chairs, she sighed. Five years ago she had known most of the gentry in the neighborhood well.

The door opened quietly and a teenage boy stepped into the room. "Is something the matter, Selina?" There was the merest trace of a limp as he crossed the colorful carpet to seat himself beside her.

"Heavens, no, Henry." Her rich laughter escaped once again. "I have had a call from a guest of Sir Penrith's. A very stiff sort of person named Rushton. First he mistook me for my own companion, and then he was miffed that I would not sell the land in the vale to him. I suppose he is a suitor of Cassandra's, though she seems a bit young for him. He must be all of Pen's age, and what he would do with a merry little soul like Cassandra is beyond me. I can see them now at the breakfast table."

Her eyes sparkled with mischief as she enacted the scene. "Cassandra would be dressed in a round dress of jaconet muslin over a pale peach-colored sarsnet slip, made high with a triple fall of lace at the throat. A pure vision of the shepherdess with a leghorn hat (with a wide brim, of course) swinging in her hand. She would say, 'Oh, Mr. Rushton, it is the loveliest day! We must certainly walk in the park, for every bird on the estate is singing the sweetest song.' And he would grunt at her, 'My dear Mrs. Rushton, can you not see that the day is fine for shooting? Birds! Yes, of course, there are birds. I shall bag any number of them in two or three hours.'"

"You are absurd, Selina," the boy chuckled. "Did Sir Penrith tell him you would consider selling the land?"

"No, I don't think so. Actually, I think it was rather a joke of Pen's. Mr. Rushton arrived obviously believing that Miss Easterly-Cummings was an aged lady."

"And so you are, my dear cousin," he retorted, flipping the cap off her head. "Who would believe you were three and twenty when you insist on wearing that hideous item. You know, Selina, you cannot hide your light under *that* bushel. You are an extremely handsome girl," he remarked gallantly.

"Silly child!" she returned as she reached down to retrieve the ugly cap. "What does a sixteen-year-old know of feminine beauty? You can hardly brush your own hair!"

"Now that's doing it a bit too brown, Selina." He grimaced as she carefully restored the cap to her brown curls. "Do you have any special reason for not selling the land?"

A flicker of caution passed over her eyes but he did not notice. "I have no need to sell it, and it's rather a charming spot, don't you think? Where else would we go for our picnics?"

"Dozens of places, I dare say, but it *is* nice. Did this fellow wish to build a house there?"

"A hunting-box. He's been riding with the Quorn, I take it, and thought to provide himself with a small residence in the area. That may all have been a diddle, of course. Perhaps he simply wishes to offer Cassandra a house not so far away from Oak Park. He mentioned that his home was in Suffolk." She glanced at the case-clock in the corner and lifted a brow inquisitively. "Have you finished the Homer already?"

"Well, no. The thing is, I feel a little restless this morning, Selina. Thought I might ride out for a bit. Would you like to come?"

"The snow . . ." she began hesitantly and then smiled at him. "Yes, Henry, of all things, I would like a ride."

Mr. Rushton left Shalbrook in rather a dudgeon. Of course, the young lady had every right not to sell her land if she did not want to, but she could at least have been pleasant about it. Perhaps explained why she wished to retain it, or at least excused her abruptness. Instead of following the road straight around to Oak Park, Rushton turned at the gates so that he could once more pass the vale. He halted the curricle and sat for some time gazing into the small valley between its two rounded hills. Right there in the clearing would be the ideal spot for his retreat. Surely that was a stream meandering through the property, partially covered with snow-covered bushes as it now was. He could perfectly envision how the land would look in spring, the bare branches disappearing under the new growth of luscious green leaves, the meadows beyond as richly

24

colored. But even now, under its cloak of snow, it was one of the most delightful spots he had laid eyes on. Drat the girl! What use had she for it, with all of her land on the other side of the road?

In summer the heat would shimmer around the hills on either side and flowers would decorate the borders of the woods. And surely in fall the maples would be aglow with color from that special sharpness in the air. Damn! It was all too real to picture a house in such a setting. He dropped his hands and allowed the chestnuts to move forward at a brisk pace. There must be some way to convince Miss Easterly-Cummings to sell the land.

Before searching out Sir Penrith, Rushton politely conveyed Miss Easterly-Cummings' greetings to Lady Southwood and her daughter. The ladies were seated in the winter parlor, companionably chatting while they worked lace on large pillows.

Lady Southwood sighed. "Such a dear girl. A pity she does not go out in Society anymore, but there, I fear she has become a trifle...unusual in her dress. She and Maria were the greatest of friends many years ago, and certainly Selina showed no sign of such eccentricity then. Two hoydens they were, though," she chuckled. "Forever following Penrith about when he had become far too conscious of his dignity to bear it. Many were the times when he would come stomping in to say, 'Really, Mother, it is too much! Can you not keep better track of Maria and her friend? I was driving Miss Sotherby about the lanes near her home, and what should I find but the two of them up an apple tree giggling at us.'" Lady Southworth seemed to recall herself abruptly. "But that was years ago, Mr. Rushton, and I have no doubt my reminiscences are the greatest bore to you."

"No, no, not at all," he swiftly replied. "How old were the girls then?"

"Oh, I should think eight or ten, but it was years before they behaved properly," she admitted with a rueful shake of her head. "And to think of Maria with two children of her own now."

Cassandra turned her merry blue eyes from her

25

mother to Mr. Rushton. "Does she wear that awful brown dress at home? And the religious-type cap?"

He laughed. "Yes, indeed, with a scarlet shawl and the sturdiest walking shoes I have laid eyes on, I promise you."

"Well, that is going a bit far," Cassandra said cryptically. "One would think that at least in her own home she might dress as she pleased."

Her mother turned startled eyes to her. "Whatever do you mean, Cassandra?"

Confused, Miss Southwood waved an airy hand. "Not a thing, Mama. It is rather chilly weather for a muslin dress, though, is it not?"

"I dare say she has them in wool, too," her mother replied shortly with a reproachful look at her youngest.

When no more information on Miss Easterly-Cummings appeared to be forthcoming, Mr. Rushton excused himself to find the master of the house. He had a few choice words to say to Sir Penrith.

THREE

"I did not find it at all amusing to look such an idiot, my dear Pen," Rushton explained to his friend, who was regarding him with innocent eyes. "At first I took Miss Easterly-Cummings for some sort of companion. After all, who would dream that an excessively wealthy young woman would dress as she does?"

"Did you think a companion would dress like that?"

"Frankly, I have not the least idea how companions dress, and I have no desire to learn. She was dowdy, Pen; no, more than that—she was absurd."

"Well, I did hint that she was unusual, did I not?"

"You allowed me to think she was an old dragon," Rushton said grimly. "What chance was I to have of buying her land after such a *faux pas?*"

"You had no chance from the start, Gareth," Sir Penrith told him patiently. "I tried to warn you. Benedict has been after the land for years to tie it in with his estates, and Selina will have none of it."

"You did not precisely tell me that."

"Well, perhaps not, but I told you it wasn't for sale, didn't I? You were not in a mood to listen to me yesterday, if I recall correctly."

A wide grin eased the gloom of Mr. Rushton's face. "So that is what you were paying me back for. I wondered about it most of the way home." His face became serious as he stretched out his legs. "You must not think that I do not value your advice, my friend. I do. But in this matter I shall have to take my own counsel. Can you bear with me?"

"Why, of course. You know I have only your best interests at heart. We won't discuss the matter again."

"Thank you." Rushton draped one leg over the other and stared thoughtfully at the grate. "What I *would* like your advice on is how to convince the eccentric Miss Easterly-Cummings to sell me that piece of land."

"Devil take you, Gareth! I thought we had just established that she did not wish to sell the land."

"True. She does not wish to sell it and she has no need to sell it. Now we have to decide how to convince her to sell it, all the same."

"You know, I think your mind has snapped!"

"Not at all. I am set on having that piece of property. Tell me about Miss Easterly-Cummings. What does she do? Who lives in the house with her? Is she a recluse? Yesterday you called her the source of all good works in the neighborhood. What did you mean?"

Sir Penrith paced up and down the room for a while before speaking. "I won't have you harass her, old fellow. She's a family friend—m' sister Maria's boon companion, a few years back. And though Selina is an oddity these days, you should have seen her when she was younger. Sparkling with vitality, full of fun, dressed to the nines. Outshone anyone else in the area. A bit after her father died, all that changed. She stopped attending parties, very seldom came to call, stayed mostly at Shalbrook. But she is not inactive. Her interests simply seemed to alter. In many ways your assumption yesterday was correct. Oh, not that she lords it over the lesser folk and dispenses moral platitudes. Her father was active in the community—first to employ new methods of farming, supported the local charity school, saw that the indigent were employed on his estate, whether he really had work for them or not. Selina has taken over those responsibilities, and more."

"I don't suppose there was ever any question of her marrying, considering the way she dresses," Rushton mused.

"Well, there you are wrong. Before her father died, she and young Benedict were thought to be planning a match of it. But Benedict had joined up and was off

28

in the Peninsula. When he returned, nothing came of it, and that was a few years ago. Lord, she was the belle of all the assemblies when she was eighteen. If her father hadn't died, she would probably have had a London Season, and I don't doubt it would have been very successful. As to that, my mother offered to bring her out when the mourning period was past, but Selina refused."

"And she lives alone in that mausoleum?"

"No, she has a young cousin living with her. A boy of fifteen or sixteen, I should think. No companion any longer, but an army of servants. She's as good as her father was about seeing that there's no one on the poor roles, and supplying aid to the needy and sick. I won't have you harass her," he repeated.

"I don't harass girls," Rushton said bitterly.

"I say," Sir Penrith protested, "I didn't mean that you would purposely do so. It's just . . . well, Selina is not a neighborhood joke, or anything of that nature. She's respected, you see, in spite of her . . . oddities. Everyone sort of looks out for her. No, that is not precisely what I mean, because she's perfectly capable of managing for herself."

"She's the good fairy hereabouts," Rushton suggested.

"Oh, it's more than that. She's our own special . . . achievement . . . no. . . . Well, dash it, we're all fond of her."

"Like the village idiot."

Sir Penrith turned blazing eyes on his friend. "There is absolutely nothing wrong with Selina's intellect. And I for one do not believe the theory that she was emotionally disturbed by her father's death. Or that of her other relations. A whole pile of them were killed in a coaching accident on their way here to Mr. Easterly-Cummings' funeral. Very shocking, bound to be! But Selina has all her wits about her. And she didn't stay in mourning longer than usual. Well, as to that, it's a little hard to say, because after then she began to dress like she does now. But there was none of that hair-tearing, weepy-eyed grief about her. Didn't throw

29

herself in the grave, or bring flowers to the tombstone every day. You know the kind of thing I mean."

"Yes."

"What I mean to say is . . . Well, she's just like everybody else, really."

Reviewing his interview with the young lady, Rushton could not agree, but he said nothing as he rubbed a hand thoughtfully across his chin. There was, perhaps, the grain of an idea in what Sir Penrith had told him. "Is there much unemployment hereabouts?"

"Not if Selina can help it, but a lot of folks won't go to her when they know she doesn't really need any extra workers. Oh, she'd take them on all right, but there are those who consider that charity. We're like every other county in England, Gareth. The enclosures have displaced a lot of people. Some go to the towns, but others try to eke out an existence here as best they can. Sometimes it's pathetic."

"I imagine your new stables gave some much-needed employment."

Sir Penrith flushed. "Yes, well, the old ones really had seen better days."

"No doubt." Rushton smiled as he rose. "Building an entire house, with a modest stable, would surely provide even more employment."

An appreciative gleam lit Sir Penrith's eyes. "You know, you might just have something there."

"Will you come with me this time? She may not let me in again without reinforcements." When his friend hesitated, he murmured, "And you could see for yourself that I did not harass her."

"Oh, very well. But not today. I want to have a look at that hunter Prester has for sale."

Henry Forrester absently gazed out the window of the study over a new fall of snow. Although his translation of Homer was going well, he could not keep his mind on it. Not an hour past he had watched the Quorn pass, the hounds in full cry, the scarlet coats of the gentlemen blazing against the sparkling white of the hills and valleys. To be out there with them! The study suddenly seemed cramped and over warm. Nothing would do but to be out of doors, and yet the vicar was expected within the hour to go over his work with him, and lay out his course of study for the next week. Selina would be disappointed if her cousin failed to meet the old man's exacting requirements. Not that she would say anything; she never did, except for praise. Still, it was a burden to Henry, one which he gladly assumed in exchange for her perpetual good nature and unfailing care of him. The trouble was that she took too great care of him!

"Daydreaming, Henry?" Selina asked, amusement making her eyes sparkle.

He started up from his chair. "I didn't hear you come in. Do you think the vicar will make it with all this snow?"

"Oh, undoubtedly. It has never deterred him before. A more persistent man I have never met." Selina studied his averted face. "Henry, if you wish me to ask him to ease the pressure on you, I will gladly do so. You know how it is with Dr. Davenport. Once he realized your capabilities, he determined to push them to the limit. But, really, there is no reason for you to spend all your time working. I dare say you will be far better prepared for Cambridge than any of the boys from Eton or Harrow at the rate you're going. Dr. Davenport is using you, in a way."

"How so?" he asked curiously.

"He will be able to point to you as his prize pupil. That is very flattering to a man of his age and dignity, I think. Can you not hear him at his dinner table, sipping at his port with his friends from the next parishes? 'My dear fellows, I taught that young man everything he knows. He has a brilliant future! Brilliant!' And then he will quote how many lines you have translated this week, and how perfectly you did them. And *voilà*, his prestige is greatly enhanced—as you and I know that none of the others have such a rising star." She smiled and linked her arm with his, and they walked over to the window. "When he leaves today, I have a surprise for you."

In spite of Henry's belief that he had long since outgrown childhood, that he was indeed as she had referred to him—a young man—his eyes lit with enthusiasm. "Do you mean to tell me now what it is?" he demanded.

"Hmm. I have not decided. Now I wonder, would you be more attentive to Dr. Davenport if you knew beforehand, or if you had to wait to find out?"

"Well, it stands to reason, Selina, that now you have told me there is a surprise, you must also tell me what it is. Otherwise, I shall fidget throughout the entire lesson trying to guess. On the other hand, if I know, I shall do my best to please Dr. Davenport, because he always leaves sooner if I am well prepared."

"Do you think so? No, I cannot believe it would be wise. If you know the surprise, you will be eager to be done with the lesson and will probably rush through it. And you know how Dr. Davenport detests undue haste." She eyed her cousin mischievously.

"If you don't tell me, you wretched girl, I shall toss your beloved cap on the fire," Henry proclaimed sternly as he whisked the offensive item off her brown curls and held it out of her reach.

Selina sighed with mock gravity. "Very well, you undisciplined boy. Return my cap and I shall tell you."

"Oh no. Tell me and *then* I shall return your atrocious cap."

"Don't you trust me? Despicable child! What have I done to deserve such ingratitude?" she asked dramatically, a tear forming in her eye.

"You know, Selina, you really should go on the stage. Your talent is wasted on me. Tell me this instant or your cap becomes a cinder." He made as if to toss it on the blazing logs, and she squealed, unable to wrest it from his grasp.

"I have had an old sledge repaired for us! Now give me my cap!"

"A sledge!" Henry unconsciously retained his grip on the cap, staring at his cousin with wonder. "One pulled by horses?"

"Yes, of course. I thought you would enjoy trying your hand at just such a new game." Selina pried his fingers from the crumpled cap and attempted to smooth it out. "Now look what you've done! I shall look a fright in it."

"You always do, anyway," he retorted. "Let me buy you a real bonnet, Selina. One with ostrich plumes that you can tilt at an angle. It would do wonders for your appearance." At her glare, he laughed. "Never mind. I can hardly wait to try the sledge. Will you be ready the minute Dr. Davenport leaves?"

"I shall invite him for a cup of tea before he meets with you. That way you will have longer to prepare, and we can be away as soon as you've finished," she promised.

"You're a love, Selina. I give you my word I'll not botch the lesson. And thank you." With an affectionate tug at her curls, he determinedly pushed her toward the door, his restlessness forgotten in the excitement of the new sport.

Selina sighed when the door closed behind her. For the moment he would be satisfied with the sledge; it would be a unique demand on his driving skills and would no doubt prove diverting. Were all sixteen-year-olds so eager to throw themselves into every kind of amusement, she wondered, as she paced about the drawing room. For five years Henry had been content, more or less, to attend to his studies, interspersed with picnics and rides, walks and shooting. Now it seemed that every day he grew more restless and less content to lead the quiet life she had worked so hard to achieve for him. Selina agonized over what was best for the boy, and yet there was really no one to turn to with her problems. Dr. Davenport would merely counsel more studies, she felt sure, and Lord Leyburn would as soon swoop down and pluck her cousin from her household as discuss the matter with her. No, it was something she would have to handle from day to day, and pray fervently that Henry did nothing in his youthful exuberance which would come to his guardian's ever-receptive ears.

An interview with Dr. Davenport was not Selina's idea of the supreme pleasure of the week. He entered the drawing room with his grave smile, the white hair standing out from his head after the removal of his voluminous scarf. Try as she might, Selina could never remain in conversation with him long without finding her eyes drawn irresistibly to the snowy tufts of hair which sprouted from his enormous pink ears. As much as she might joke with her cousin about the people they met, she had never revealed her acute fascination with this aspect of the divine's appearance. Somehow it seemed sacrilegious to poke fun at any element of the worthy old gentleman, deserving of it as he might often be with his pompous attitude.

"It has been a long winter, Dr. Davenport," Selina at last commented, "and I fear Henry is a bit bored with being house-bound. I do not blame him! I myself cannot like spending so much time indoors as we have been forced to do for the last few months. Perhaps, too, he is working too hard at his studies. I am aware," she hastened to add, forestalling his protest, "that you have made incredible progress with him and mapped out a commendable course of study from which he will benefit all his life, and most certainly when he goes to university. I fear, however, that he is feeling the pressure somewhat, and wondered if you might ease your requirements for a few weeks—just until he is feeling more . . . amenable, you understand."

Dr. Davenport regarded her with a sad smile. "My dear Miss Easterly-Cummings, you are as aware as I of Lord Leyburn's instructions. He wishes his ward to be ready for university within the next eighteen months. That is no small undertaking! Lord Leyburn himself has agreed to my course of study, I must tell you, for I sent him a prospectus and he returned it with his approval." The vicar did not mention that his lordship's comment had been a boldly scrawled "Very well, get on with it!"

"Yes, yes, I fully understand," Selina said somewhat impatiently; any talk of Lord Leyburn made her impatient. "But Henry has not had a break in his studies since our holiday last summer. Surely you must agree that a child's mind needs a rest from such matters occasionally. Why, if he were at school right now he would enjoy several weeks vacation from time to time.

Dr. Davenport, the poor boy was translating Ovid on Christmas!"

"Very well, Miss Easterly-Cummings. For the next two weeks I will give him only half of the usual allotment of work, but, mind you, it is against my better judgment." His face set rather grimly. "I would not wish to incur Lord Leyburn's displeasure over this matter. If you wish for a longer respite for your cousin, you must write to Lord Leyburn yourself and suggest it. I doubt he would agree."

Selina doubted it, too, but she smiled graciously. "Thank you, Dr. Davenport. I am sure Henry will benefit from the change, and probably will attack his studies with renewed vigor for the relaxed interval."

"Let us hope so."

When the vicar had completed his lessons with Henry, and the front door had snapped shut behind his retreating back, Selina found herself caught up in a bear-hug by her cousin. "Dear Selina, lovely Selina, you have worked a miracle! The old goat has given me only a half load for this next week!"

"Henry Forrester, I did not go to all this trouble to have you acting like a spoiled brat. 'Old goat' indeed! I have half a mind to call him back this minute and see that he doubles your usual work."

"No, no, please don't. My most profuse apologies. Didn't mean a word of it," her cousin gasped, appalled. "I am just so very grateful, and he *is* overbearing, Selina, you know he is. Am I forgiven?" He bowed his head in mock contrition, but watched her impudently the while.

"Oh, Henry, what am I to do with you?" she asked in a despairing voice, wringing her hands.

"There you go again. We should have a large house party and put on a play so that you could exhibit your talents. I won't call him an old goat again, I promise."

"No," she murmured, "next time it will probably be worse."

"I have no doubt you call him worse in your mind," he retorted. "Selina, may we try the sledge now?"

"Yes, you unconscionable puppy, anything to get me away from the house." She shook her head at his delighted grin. "I want you to know, Henry, that Dr. Davenport agreed to reduce your studies for only two weeks. After that you're on your own again, I fear."

"Two weeks seem like a lifetime right now, Cousin. And with the sledge, why, who knows? We shall have any number of larks."

FOUR

Selina was destined to share a "lark" with him in no
less than an hour's time. Muffled up to her eyes with
scarves against the bitter wind which had started to
blow across the fields, she was in no position to restrain
her cousin's enthusiasm with this new mode of trans-
portation. While no one would ever have labelled
Henry a cautious driver, he was no daredevil, either,
as a rule. Perhaps the freedom of being able to drive
the sledge over the fields, rather than keeping to the
snow-covered lanes, went to his head. Or maybe it was
simply the sense of release from the crushing burden
his studies usually presented that made him oblivious
to any dangers hidden beneath the cushiony-looking
white mounds. In any case, he was inspired by the sight
of two riders on the road to set up a race. With a jaunty
wave of his hand, he challenged them. Far too distant
to call out his intention, it was yet perfectly clear to
the riders.

While Mr. Rushton murmured, "Devil a bit!," Sir
Penrith joyously took up the gauntlet and dug his heels
into his stallion. The beast leaped forward with the
alacrity of one used to the chase, and they could hear
the faint cry of "Tally-ho!" from the sledge's driver.
Although he had visions of a second disastrous interview with Miss Easterly-Cummings, for he had no
doubt she was a passenger in the sledge, Rushton had
no intention of being left behind. The riders galloped
down the lane keeping pace with the gliding vehicle
in the fields.

Horrified by her cousin's foolhardiness, Selina none-theless remained mute. This was no time to distract his attention from his driving. Besides, the pace he had set caused the icy wind to nearly take her breath away, and she found it difficult to keep her eyes open. How dare those fools accept Henry's challenge? It was all very well for them on the road, another matter entirely gliding over hidden precipices. At a reasonable pace the horses could be expected to manage any ordinary difficulty, but at this speed it would be upon them be-fore they had a chance to adjust.

As the riders approached the entrance gates to Shal-brook, and Henry faced the walls lining the drive, Se-lina experienced a moment of panic. But Henry merely waved his whip gleefully toward the manor house and expertly turned the horses' heads in that direction. After a moment he glanced back to see whether the riders had taken his meaning and, reassured, urged his team to even greater efforts. Selina clung to the side of the sledge, her booted feet braced to support her in the event of an accident. This had no appreciable effect when they did in fact suffer the inevitable.

One of the sledge runners encountered a rock hidden beneath the drifts and the sledge swung crazily out of control, smacking against the wall and dislodging its occupants. The horses shuddered to a halt a short dis-tance away, and Selina picked herself up unharmed but covered from head to foot with snow. Her anxious gaze quickly swung around to where her cousin lay.

"Henry! Oh, dear God." In an instant she was at his side and attempting to turn him over when he quite calmly stood up, brushing the snow from his driving coat. "Are you all right?"

"Never better, my love," he responded cheerfully.

Selina's eyes flared with anger. "How dare you do such a stupid thing? Don't you know you could have killed us? Have you no regard for my horses?"

Shocked by her fury, Henry could only open his mouth to protest, "Now, Selina . . ."

"No, not a word! There is nothing you can possibly say to excuse yourself. You are to go to your room instantly and stay there until I come to speak with you."

"But the horses," he began.

"*Now* you would think of the horses," she rasped. "*I* will take care of the horses; *you* may sit in your room and consider your folly. Be off with you."

Henry had never before seen his cousin anything but mildly irritated, and he had no idea that her current violent emotions were occasioned by profound relief at his safety. When he looked up to see that Sir Penrith had been an auditor to this humiliating scene, he flushed to the roots of his lank brown hair, bowed stiffly to his cousin, and trudged off toward the house, his limp more pronounced than usual. For a moment Selina felt choked with remorse, and anxiety that he was indeed hurt, as the exaggerated limp would seem to indicate, but she would not call him back. She had not, after all, said anything that was not true, and this might be a lesson to him. Her throat ached with the struggle to suppress kinder words, and she turned to Sir Penrith flushed with anger.

"And you and your friend are no better, Sir Penrith! If you haven't a care for yourselves, could you not have some mercy on your horses?"

"But, Selina . . . Miss Easterly-Cummings, the hunters are used to such a run. Trained for it, you know," he murmured.

"Well, my pair is not trained for a run over snow-covered fields. You should not have accepted Henry's challenge. Why is it that men can never resist such an invitation? Have you no sense of responsibility? To encourage a child in such folly . . ."

"Your horses are unharmed," Mr. Rushton informed her calmly as he came up to join them.

"No thanks to any of you," came the bitter reply. She stretched her hand out toward the wall to steady herself, suddenly spent by the emotions she had sped through in the last few minutes. Her knees felt curiously weak, and she was grateful for the strong hand which grasped her arm.

"Take the sledge around to the stables, will you, Pen? I'll see Miss Easterly-Cummings to the house."

Mr. Rushton considered the possibility of carrying her, but decided that she would not care for such cavalier treatment, even in her present condition. Instead he encircled her waist and guided her uncertain footsteps toward the building. "Have you taken some hurt from your fall, Miss Easterly-Cummings?"

"No, none." Although Selina would have liked to disclaim the need for his support, her legs would not obey her orders to carry her as they usually did. She was very aware of his arm about her, of his closeness and his strength and most especially of the blue eyes studying her face. The thick black brows were lowered, and not in concern but, as it seemed to her, disapproval. The distance to the house was not far, though she felt it an eternity before they reached it.

Rushton said nothing further until the butler responded to his knock and then he ordered, "Send for Miss Easterly-Cummings' maid. Your mistress will need to lie down for a while."

With a surprised glance at Selina, McDonough did as he was bid while Rushton methodically divested her of the soaking scarves, cloak and gloves she wore. Selina stood unprotesting as he chafed her hands, but she would not meet his eyes. As the alarmed maid hastened across the hall toward them she abruptly withdrew her hands and turned. "Alice, we have taken a tumble from the sledge. If you would come with me, please..." Expressionlessly she faced Rushton again. "I must thank you for your assistance, sir. If you will excuse me..."

"Of course." When he had watched her ascend the stone staircase without any assistance from her maid, he retrieved his beaver hat from the table where he had flung it and allowed McDonough to hold the door for him. Outside he found Sir Penrith just ascending the stairs. "I think she will be all right, but she's in no condition to talk about the vale. After this, I doubt I shall make any headway about purchasing the land at all. Lord, but she's a termagant!"

"Nonsense," Penrith snorted. "She'd just been given a nasty spill. What did you expect?"

"I hardly expected her to rake the young cub over

the coals that way. She would have done justice to my father, and he was an expert at ringing a rare peal over one's head. Doesn't she like the boy?"

"Didn't your father like you? Of course she likes the boy! You'd understand better if you'd watched your mother raise a parcel of younger children, like I did. Pity you're an only child, Gareth." Penrith stomped his boots on the lowest stair to rid them of the clinging snow.

"I have not the slightest idea what you're talking about."

"No, I don't suppose you do." Penrith studied his friend's scowling face for a moment and shrugged his shoulders. "I remember a time when Cassandra was a child, maybe six or seven. She had found a half-crown near the flower border and in her excitement to show it to m' mother she dashed across the drive without looking, and right in the path of my horse. Very nearly snuffed her, I did—might have, if I hadn't been on Trooper—and my mother's face went white with horror. Thing is, as soon as Mother saw there was no harm done, she lost her temper. With Cassandra, with me, though God knows it wasn't my fault. It was just a way of venting her emotions. Loves us, you know, and it scared the devil out of her to see such a near thing. Parents are like that."

"Miss Easterly-Cummings is not the boy's mother."

Penrith regarded him disgustedly. "Oh, never mind. If you don't want to understand, I can't make you."

After a warm bath, Selina felt much better physically, though her emotions were still tumultuous. A trace of fear remained, and even some anger, but uppermost was embarrassment. She was not accustomed to making scenes, or hurting people's feelings, or misdirecting blame. As she towelled her hair dry, she mentally composed a note to Sir Penrith apologizing for her hasty words. There was no reason he should take responsibility for her cousin's actions. Really, only Henry was to blame for the whole episode. But no, she could not excuse herself so lightly. The boy had been in her care for five years and surely it was her duty to instill in him some sense of caution, some care for his own neck and for those of others.

But she *had* done so, she thought desperately as she tossed the scarlet shawl about her shoulders. Ordinarily Henry was a reasonable, thoughtful young man, polite and good-humored, accommodating to the utmost. Studious and gentle, yet high-spirited as well, she was inordinately fond of him and thought of him as her brother. There must be some dividing line between indulging in riotous spirits and doing something downright dangerous. How was she to teach him that, if he didn't know it instinctively?

Her tap at his door was hesitantly answered, and she entered to find him seated by the window. He rose but did not come to her, his face a polite mask. That in itself was unusual, for he was too unaccustomed to hiding his feelings to have much experience at it. Selina silently seated herself on the sofa and gestured for him to join her there, which he did with a formality foreign to their relationship.

"First, Henry, I should like to apologize for scolding you in front of Sir Penrith. I had forgotten his presence, in the heat of the moment, or I might have put a curb on my tongue. As to the rest...I feel no differently now than I did then. I can understand your desire to race the horses, but not the foolhardiness of the way you went about it. We could have checked out a course for obstacles, and then gone about it properly. You had no way of knowing what the drifts of snow covered—rocks, holes, bushes, any number of things which might have caused an accident. The horses are unharmed, but not through any care of yours. How would you have felt had one broken a leg? They are dumb beasts, Henry, and cannot complain of our treatment of them. You are not generally so careless about such matters."

His face still unreadable, he kept his eyes firmly locked on the mantel when he replied. "I am quite familiar with that field. I could remember no hazards."

"I was not aware of any, either, Henry, and yet we encountered one, as I felt sure we must. Can't you see how different it is riding about when everything is open to your view, and riding like a maniac over snow-ob-

42

scured ground? What you could easily skirt on horseback in the light of summer, you can't even know exists in such conditions." Selina felt she was pleading with him to understand her, and yet there was no softening of the frozen face.

"I am sorry if I drove recklessly," he replied stiffly, "and I had no intention of endangering you or your horses."

"Ah, I see," Selina murmured as she possessed herself of his hand. "Look at me, please, Henry."

He reluctantly lowered his eyes to her face and she squeezed his hand. "Nothing is more precious to me than you, Henry. I can't say that I do not care about being killed myself, or having my horses ruined, but they pale in comparison with your own safety. When I saw you there in the snow, unmoving . . ." She bit her lip and tried to control the quaver in her voice. "Well, I could not bear it if anything happened to you."

"You did not seem so very concerned. All you talked of was your precious horses."

"But not until you had assured me that you were all right! I cannot bear the thought of your taking such chances with yourself."

"And that is why you don't want me to ride with the Quorn? So that you won't be inconvenienced if I should injure myself?"

"Inconvenienced!" Selina jumped to her feet and stamped a foot on the floor. "You put me out of all patience, Henry. I am telling you that it would break my heart if anything happened to you, and all you can understand is that I am a cautious old fuddy who stands in your way to having fun."

"Well, that's really what it amounts to, isn't it, Selina?" he asked stubbornly. "If I break my neck, *I* certainly am not going to be the one to suffer. I shall be dead."

"How can you talk that way? What has gotten into you these last weeks?" Her face was white and she drew a shaking hand across her eyes.

"I am no longer a child, Selina. I am tired of studying Lucian and Virgil, of composing Latin verses, of memorizing Greek grammar. Even geography is a great trial when it is only the dull facts one studies. Personally, I can see no relevance to any of it! What do you want of me? Are you preparing me to study law, or to take orders? Perhaps to sit for Parliament? Am I to have no say in what I do with my life?"

Bewildered, Selina could only stare at him for a moment. "But, Henry, your studies are to prepare you for university. Your guardian is desirous that you go there. I have no say in the matter."

"Lord Leyburn has never consulted my wishes. How does he know that I even want to go to university? And what does he care? You are all smothering me with your own good intentions, but no one ever asks me what I want to do." He began to pace up and down the room, his hands clenched at his sides. "It is five years until I come into my inheritance. My God, five years, Selina! For the next five years am I to do what everyone else wants me to do? Am I to be given a pittance of an allowance and kept on leading-strings? Am I to meekly say, 'Yes, sir, if you wish me to study law, I shall do so.' Do you realize that I cannot even remember Lord Leyburn, Selina? How many years is it since he has even bothered to come and see me? Three, four? All he wants is for me to kick up no fuss, put him to no bother. Why should I allow my life to be directed by such a man?"

"He is your guardian. He stands in place of your father," she whispered.

"No one stands in place of my father, and certainly not Lord Leyburn. Once a quarter I get a note from him, written in the language one might use for a twelve-year-old, instructing me to use my allowance with care and to study diligently. Damnation! I won't stand for it!"

Selina dropped onto a chair and followed his restless pacing with her concerned eyes. "What is it you want, Henry?" she asked softly.

"I don't know," he wailed. "But I know what I don't want. I don't want to be hedged about on every side, to be forced to follow the dictates of his lordship when he cannot even be bothered to come and see me once a year. Is that asking too much?"

"I don't know," she said honestly. "Legally you are in his power until you come of age. But he cannot force you to go to university if you don't want to, or to study some particular subject. Where it is a matter of money, well, that is easily outmaneuvered. You know that I am more than willing to give you any sums you may need. I have no call for half the income Shalbrook brings. Would you like me to set up an account for you?"

"I can't take your money," he protested.

"If I were purse-pinched, it would be another matter, Henry. You are my only relation, and there is no reason why you should not share in my good fortune."

"Some day you may need the money."

"If I do, some day you will be in a position to repay me."

"Would you let me earn the money, Selina?"

"Earn it? How would you earn it?"

"I should like to learn about farming. You know, about planting barley and wheat and oats and such, and about raising sheep and pigs and cattle. I could assist Mr. Sands; he's getting on in years, you know, and could use a hand." When his cousin looked skeptical, he continued eagerly, "I shall have a small estate of my own to manage one day, and I want to know how to go about it. What do you say, Selina?"

"It would cut into your study time drastically."

He frowned. "It would be a more practical course of study."

"Perhaps it would. Do you think you could convince Mr. Sands that you are serious?"

For the first time during their interview, he grinned. "Within a week! He's a great sort, Selina, always ready to answer your questions."

"I have a mind to give it a try," she mused, "though we may hear repercussions from Lord Leyburn. Would you like to write him explaining the situation?"

"Could we not just try it for a while? No, I suppose not. Davenport would be sure to set up a row. Very well, I will write him."

"Good." Selina rose and walked over to her cousin, placing her hand on his arm. "I had no idea you chafed

45

so under your restrictions, Henry. I wish you had told me sooner, for I would do anything in my power to make you happy."

"I...I know you would, Selina." His face suffused with color. "I didn't mean to rant and rave at you. God knows I owe you so much! I must seem the most ungrateful beast in nature. Can you forgive me?"

"Silly fellow," she laughed, rumpling his hair. "We were used to sharing our problems, Henry. I hope you have not grown so old that you can do so no longer."

"I didn't know if you would understand, Selina. And I *am* sorry about the sledge. That was stupid of me."

"We won't mention it again," she assured him as she slipped out the door.

Selina was not at all sure that she understood, or if she wanted to. He was growing up, and away from her. From the time he was eleven she had cared for him, sympathized with him, laughed with him. Dear God, he was only sixteen! Surely that was too young for him to be trying to stretch his wings. Too young to have the maturity to make important decisions, ones which could effect his entire life. But to thwart him would doubtless lead to an estrangement between them which she could not bear. If only Lord Leyburn were a *concerned* guardian ... She found that her mind had wandered to Mr. Rushton's disapproving face and she shook herself with annoyance. It did not matter in the least what he thought of her, but she must write that note to Penrith.

FIVE

"You see?" Sir Penrith declared triumphantly as he waved a folded sheet under his friend's nose. "I have had a note from Miss Easterly-Cummings in which she apologizes for her 'rash and ridiculous' words to me. I am not held to blame for anything, and she regrets that she should have caused a scene, and can only excuse herself on the grounds of her shock and fright. And," he added with a mischievous smile, "she has invited the lot of us to tea this afternoon."

"Has she now? I imagine that is very unusual," Rushton commented sardonically.

"Well, it is. I cannot remember the last time I was invited there, and I dare say it is not much more recent an occurrence for my mother and Cassandra."

"It is her way of apologizing, no doubt. Just as bizarre as the costume she wears."

"Does that put you off? The way she dresses? Lord, Gareth, you'd have to be blind not to see that she's beautiful, even under those dowdy drapings."

"I had not missed her essential loveliness," he retorted dryly. "All the more odd of her to dress so peculiarly. It would be a real treat to see her in London dressed that way."

"Perhaps she'll dress more conventionally for this occasion," Penrith suggested hopefully.

And there was some lessening to the strangeness of her costume, he noted as he followed his mother and sister and friend into the green drawing room at Shalbrook. Selina had honored the tea party with her yellowish-green gown, to be sure, but she had attached a fall of lace at the high neck and discarded the walking shoes. The scarlet shawl was replaced by one of brown and she sported an uninspiring cap, but it bore no resemblance to her nun-like ones. Sir Penrith could not know that Henry was responsible for this change in his cousin's costume. The boy had adamantly refused to attend this social gathering unless Selina made some effort to observe it with dignity. "For how on earth am I to face Sir Penrith after the trimming you gave me yesterday? I shall have quite enough discomfort without blushing for your appearance, my dear cousin."

Lady Southwood curiously surveyed the room into which she had been shown with its fourteenth century wainscot and painted ceiling. It was not a chamber she was unfamiliar with, though it was many years since she had been in it. "Your mama used to entertain here, my dear," she said, turning to smile at Selina. "It was done in green then, too, but I can see that you have recently refurbished it. And your taste is quite as exquisite as hers. Who would have thought the plank chest would fit perfectly under that ancient tapestry? And you have brought the set of globes from the gallery, have you not? Delightful, absolutely delightful."

"Thank you, Lady Southwood. I was not aware that my mother used the room, for we have come to use the East Room extensively these last years." She turned to Cassandra, her eyes laughing. "I had no idea, from your demure appearance in church, what a dashing lady you had become, Cassandra. Are you to have a Season in London this year?"

"So Mama and Penrith promise me. And Maria is to be there, too."

"Yes, I have heard from her recently and she said they were going up to London. She sounds decidedly content with her life and family."

"Oh, yes, Franmore is the dearest man, and she has two adorable boys. Perhaps they will return with us for a while this summer so that you shall have an opportunity to see them."

"I hope so," Selina assured her. As the ladies seated themselves, she moved to Sir Penrith and Mr. Rushton, offering her hand to the former. "Am I forgiven, Sir Penrith?"

"You were used to call me Pen, Selina. And you have no need to apologize. Where is the young scamp?"

"He should be along in a moment. Punctuality is not well observed at Shalbrook, I fear. Would you be so very kind as to overlook my scolding him in front of you? It embarrassed him terribly, of course, and had I had my wits about me, I would not have done it for the world."

"He's a large responsibility for you," Penrith suggested.

"No, no, not at all. Henry is the only family I have and a delightful companion." With a nod she acknowledged Mr. Rushton. "I wanted to thank you for your . . . assistance yesterday, sir."

"You did so at the time, Miss Easterly-Cummings. I trust you took no harm from your spill." When she did not offer him her hand, he forced her to do so by extending his own.

Selina quickly withdrew her hand from his firm clasp. "None whatsoever. Here is Henry now. I don't believe you've met him."

After the introductions had been made and everyone was seated, Selina rang for the tea tray and guided the conversation to various topics of interest to the different members of the group. Henry's embarrassment at seeing Sir Penrith again rapidly disappeared under that gentleman's cheerful acceptance of him as one of the men of the group. Penrith's assumption that Henry was knowledgeable about horses and other sporting matters was flattering, if somewhat bewildering, to the young Forrester. Sheltered as he was at Shalbrook, he knew little of boxing and prizefights, even less of cockfighting or cricket. But he could hold his own on coursing, shooting, fishing and even horse-racing, as he managed to get hold of the *Turf Remembrancer* fairly regularly.

Mr. Rushton was not as oblivious to the gaps in the the boy's knowledge as Penrith appeared to be, and when Miss Easterly-Cummings was engrossed in a discussion of village matters with Lady Southwood and

Cassandra, he purposefully explored the matter. "I suppose there is no cricket team in the area?" he asked, directing his question at Henry rather than Penrith.

"Not that I know of," the boy replied, glancing questioningly at Sir Penrith.

"No, I haven't played since I came down from Oxford. Never was much good at it," Penrith confessed.

"I don't believe I've seen you with the Quorn, Mr. Forrester. Have you no interest in hunting?" Rushton probed.

Henry flushed. "I should like to hunt of all things. It's just . . . well, there have been my studies. . . ."

Mr. Rushton's eyes narrowed. "Perhaps your cousin has some objection to hunting?"

"Well, I . . . we . . ." Henry could not find a way to explain, and he fell silent under Rushton's intent gaze.

Penrith cast a disparaging glance at his friend and intervened. "I imagine Selina keeps no hunters at Shalbrook these days. No matter. I can mount you, Forrester. Why not join us tomorrow? Ride over to Oak Park and leave your hack there. We leave about nine."

"That's awfully good of you, sir. I mean, you have no idea whether I could manage one of your hunters, or anything. I don't know. . . ."

"Nonsense! Have the greatest confidence in you. Just be there by nine, and we'll have a great day's sport," Penrith assured him bluffly, not wanting the boy to think his cousin's scold of the previous day had given him any lack of faith in the lad's ability.

"I will then, thank you," Henry accepted with a worried glance at his cousin. He could tell by the slight tightening of her lips that she had overheard the conversation, but she made no sign to him, composedly continuing her discourse with the ladies. It was not so much out of rebellion that he accepted, but out of his strong desire to do so, and under the pressure of the two gentlemen expecting that he would. After all, he had just said that he wanted to hunt of all things, and what would they think if he refused when they had made it possible for him to do so? With relief he found the conversation turned to other matters, and the subject did not arise again until the Oak Park party was about to depart.

In taking leave of his hostess, Penrith remarked cheerfully, "I have offered to mount your cousin on one of my hunters tomorrow, Selina. Not to worry, you know. I shall keep an eye on him."

Biting back the retort she wished to make, Selina forced herself to say, "That is kind of you, Pen. He's never hunted before, but I doubt he will disgrace you."

"No, he's a spirited lad. I shall put him on Trafalgar—great strength there, but well behaved, don't you know?"

"Just see he doesn't override the hounds," she replied with a nervous laugh.

"Never fear. We'll coach him in hunting etiquette before ever we reach Ashby Pastures. Should be able to draw thereabouts! Do you never have an itch to join the field these days, Selina?"

"My hunting days are past, which is all to the good, as I do not believe Mr. Assheton Smith is fond of ladies joining the hunt."

"He tolerates them if they ride well and overlook his wayward tongue," Penrith laughed. "But few dare to join these days, all the same."

"Who can blame them?" Selina murmured as Mr. Rushton came to join them. She offered her hand, so that he could not fault her this time, but she found his touch disturbing, just as she did the faintly mocking light in his eyes, as though he were judging her, and not to her advantage.

"Who indeed?" Rushton rejoined to her rhetorical question. "Mr. Assheton Smith will never win any awards for his amiable disposition, but he is a worthy follower of Meynell's tradition in his mastery of a pack of fox-hounds and the sport he shows."

"My father rode with Mr. Meynell for many years. I hope the hunt will be enjoyable tomorrow." Selina ignored the mocking light in his eyes, and was relieved when her visitors had departed, though it left her to confront Henry with his unique decision.

When they had returned to the drawing room, Selina did not speak and Henry wandered about the room, twirling the globes and poking at the fire. A sideways glance assured him that his cousin was not watching him; she had picked up a copy of the *Ladies' Monthly Museum* and was perusing it with obvious interest.

"You know I have agreed to go with Sir Penrith on the hunt tomorrow," he blurted at last. "Are you not going to beg me to reconsider?"

"Did you want me to?" she asked pleasantly, looking up from the magazine. "I felt sure you were all eagerness to go."

"Well, I am, Selina. By God, it's some of the best hunting country in the land, and I've never been." He threw himself down on the sofa beside her. "Are you angry with me?"

"No." She forced herself to smile at him. "I have been protecting you like a mother hen, haven't I? Do forgive me. I rode with the Quorn several times when I was only a year or so older than you. When my father died I could not bear to part with his hunting coat, though I gave away his other clothing. Shall we see if it can be altered for you?"

"You would do that? Then you really are not angry with me?"

"How could I be? It is the most natural thing in the world to want to hunt when you've been raised on a horse and live in the Quorn country. Sir Penrith is the very one to teach you how to go on. It was kind of him to offer to mount such a stripling. Do not do anything to disgrace him," she commanded with mock severity.

"I shan't, you may be sure. I am all too conscious of his condescension. Could we look out the coat right now?" he asked eagerly.

"If we want it to be ready for the morning, we shall have to."

Refusing to give in to nervousness, Selina occupied herself with tasks about the house for the entire morning after Henry left. When her eyes tended to stray to the clock on the mantelpiece after luncheon, she assured herself that the pack had had a difficult time picking up a scent. As the hours crawled past, though, and the light began to fade from the sky, she could no longer keep still. It was possible that Henry had been invited to dine at Oak Park and had neglected to send her a message. Possible, but unlikely. Lady Southwood would not forget. Selina sent a message to the kitchen to put dinner back an hour. If Henry had not arrived by then, she would eat, if she could, but she would send a messenger to Oak Park to enquire, no matter how distressing it might be to her cousin to be checked on in such a way. She could not pay attention to her knitting for more than a few minutes at a time but jumped up frequently to gaze anxiously out the window.

It lacked but ten minutes to six when she heard the sounds of arrival in the drive. Tossing her handiwork carelessly on the spindle-legged table, she hastened from the room and out into the chilly hall, where no amount of fuel in the mammoth grate managed to alleviate the cold. McDonough, well aware of her anxiety (since he shared it), was already in the process of drawing back the heavy oak door. Up the stairs and across the terraces came Henry and Mr. Rushton, the former white-faced but grinning from ear to ear, the latter supporting his companion while they sang a sporting song incredibly off-key. Henry's arm was in a sling.

The boy gazed up and saw his cousin in the well-lit hall. "Ho, Selina! Sorry to be so late. Took a while for the doctor to come." He slurred his words as he spoke. "Famous day's hunting! They gave me the brush!" He dug with his good hand in the pocket of the red hunting jacket and withdrew his trophy, waving it about delightedly.

Exercising the utmost control over her tongue, Selina replied, "You must have done very well. Congratulations. What has happened to your arm?"

"Broke it. A clean break, the doctor said. Should heal in a trice." By now he stood before her, a trifle sheepish but defiantly proud as well. "Sir Penrith says I'm a bruising rider."

"I hope you did not injure his horse when you had your accident."

"Good God, no. Fact is, Selina, Sir Penrith said it was not in the least my fault. Practically everyone had trouble going in and out clever but Trafalgar was superb. Thing was, they must have been doing some draining on the other side, just where we landed, for there was a ling-filled trench under the snow. Trafalgar just sank right in and toppled over, but I got clear of him, all but my arm."

Mr. Rushton took up the narrative at this point. "Your cousin maintained the greatest presence of mind, Miss Easterly-Cummings. He held onto the reins and had the horse on his feet in no time. Then he mounted and rode off as though nothing had happened."

"You completed the run with a broken arm?" Selina asked faintly.

"Hardly hurt at all, my dear, and I had no need of my whip hand. Had no call to urge Trafalgar on. He's mad for the hunt. Sir Penrith says I may ride him again if I like." His speech had become more fuzzy as he stood talking and now he passed a hand over his face. "Had a bit of brandy before the doctor set my arm. I think I shall go lie down for a spell. If you will excuse me, Selina? Servant, Rushton." With some difficulty, he executed an awkward bow and wandered toward the stone stairs.

Selina answered McDonough's questioning look with a nod, and the butler moved forward to assist Henry in his dazed climb up the stairs. She did not say a word until they were out of sight, then she turned to Rushton. "I am in your debt for seeing him home, sir. Will you join me for dinner? Obviously Henry is in no condition to do so, and I don't doubt you have missed yours at Oak Park."

"It would be my pleasure, Miss Easterly-Cummings, but please do not speak of any obligation. Sir Penrith and I are distressed that your cousin should have met with an accident his first time out, but I must say it does not seem to have daunted the lad. He is all eagerness to have another go."

Rushton left unasked the question as to whether Henry's cousin would allow him to repeat his day's hunting, but Selina was uncomfortably aware of his curiosity. "I do hope he will wait until the arm is healed," she replied as casually as she could while she led him to the dining hall, where she absently instructed that dinner might now be served. Rushton seated her at the head of the long table and took the only other place set, immediately to her right.

"Henry and I see no reason for formality at meals, and I would not like to have to shout all the way to the other end of the table. Our other meals we take in the breakfast parlor, which is more comfortable, but it would seem somehow untraditional to dine there, or to have a shorter table brought in, for that matter. This one was fashioned from trees on the estate some two hundred years ago."

"Your family has lived here that long?" he asked, surprised.

"Oh, yes," she answered negligently as a footman ladled soup into her bowl. "The Easterly family goes back to the original building of the house. Somewhere along the line there was only a female heir, and her husband adopted her name as well as his own. In 1473, I believe, though I would have to check in the muniment room. I have never been as concerned with my ancestry as I might, I fear."

"And now there is only a female heir again."

"Yes," she sighed. "Father was very sad about that. I mean, even if I had married, one could hardly expect a man to take on Easterly-Cummings-Something-or-Other. I suppose Henry or his children will inherit Shalbrook one day, but it is hardly likely that they will live here. He has an estate of his own in Derbyshire, near Chesterfield, which, though smaller, is a much more comfortable place. I cannot see anyone choosing to live at Shalbrook when they don't have to endure damp walls, cold corridors and smoking chimneys, can you?"

"It's picturesque. Perhaps the family will produce a romantic," he suggested with a smile.

He had a charming smile, and Selina had rarely seen it before. For a moment she forgot what they had been discussing. "Well, we have no ghosts to offer, and a very uneventful history, but you may be right." He was studying with fascination the dish placed before him and Selina could not repress a chuckle. "Those are *bal-*

ons of legs of fowls. We have a very inventive cook, Mr. Rushton. You need not try anything that does not appeal to you. There will be a goose-pie larded with bacon and a leg of veal marinaded with endive sauce. Sometimes I feed the most unusual dishes to the dog, just so they won't go back untasted, you understand. But it's difficult to keep a good cook for just the two of us, and I feel it is only fair to allow him to experiment now and again to keep his hand in."

Selina laughed. "I have found it expedient to have the dog admitted only toward the end of the meal. Sometimes there is more than one dish which she would enjoy." The corners of his mouth twitched and they shared an understanding glance. The task of entertaining him with light conversation did not seem burdensome afterwards, and when she would have excused herself after the sweet wines, he asked her permission to withdraw with her.

"Certainly. I shall have McDonough bring whatever you wish to the drawing room. We have a fine old Manzanilla."

SIX

Established in the gold drawing room, Rushton was hesitant to bring up the subject of the vale. The former restraint between them had been broken down over their shared meal, and it was easier than he had thought to ignore the outlandish clothing she wore and merely enjoy her companionship. There was no artifice to her, no airs of any sort. She did not seem in the least perturbed to have dined along with him; in fact he felt sure that the thought of proper chaperonage had never occurred to her. Accustomed as she was to her life with her cousin, such matters undoubtedly did not arise very often.

Selina watched as he poured himself a glass of Manzanilla, the fine, long hands carelessly accomplishing the simple task while he spoke of his home and the wines his father had laid down. He had a way of meeting her eyes even across the room that was unnerving, as though he could tell what she was thinking or feeling. His black hair gleamed in the candlelight and his height seemed exaggerated as he approached and took a seat near hers. Selina had decided at tea the previous day that if there was an interest between Mr. Rushton and Cassandra, they hid it extrememy well. Though he was not perhaps as saturnine as she had originally imagined, she could not think them well suited, and curious as to his intentions in that direction she asked, "Will you be staying with Penrith long?"

"That depends on a number of things." It was the opening he needed, and reluctantly he took advantage of it. "As I mentioned the other day, I would like to purchase a piece of land in the area and build a hunting-box. I was disappointed to learn that you are not interested in selling the vale, for I had rather set my mind on it. There must be a need for employment in the area, especially for the building crafts, and such a project would probably be welcome."

"I'm sure it would, but there must be other parcels which would take your fancy."

"No, I've seen nothing else. Penrith and I asked in Barton and Mr. Dodge informed us that not a bit of land is currently to be had in the area."

"What a shame. As you say, there is a need for employment, especially in the building crafts. Sir Penrith's stables last summer were a real boon to the neighborhood."

"Yes, and I am sure the building of a house and stable would be even more welcome. I suspect that the hunting season provides miscellaneous jobs for any number of men, and they are thrown on the parish when the warmer weather comes. Has the vale some sentimental attachment for you?" His eyes, earnest and friendly, sought her own.

Selina looked away and shrugged. "Henry and I picnic there by the stream, but, no, there is no tradition attached to the land. It only recently came into the possession of the family, and is surrounded by Lord Benedict's land."

"So Penrith said. He also told me, after I had first talked to you, that Lord Benedict wished to purchase it, but you refused. Had he mentioned that when first I saw the vale I might not have allowed myself to become so enamored of it," Rushton admitted wryly.

"Oh, I doubt it," Selina retorted. "We always want what we cannot have, and when we get it we find it does not live up to expectation."

"I think you are mistaken in this instance, Miss Easterly-Cummings. The location is ideal, the land itself charming. I have envisioned it at each season of the year, and found nothing lacking. Would you not reconsider? New construction would be most beneficial to the neighborhood, and the permanent employment of a small staff would be an on-going reward."

She found herself not immune to his warm smile or his earnestness. Just so would Henry try to wheedle a treat from her. But this was not her cousin; this was a stranger when all was said and done. Still, Rushton was right about the need for employment in the area. Useful new jobs were hard to come by in the pastoral setting of Leicestershire, and no matter how many she attempted to invent, there were never enough. Too many families were forced to leave the countryside to earn their bread in the mills of Birmingham and Leicester. The new steam factories, brass foundries, iron works and mines sucked in the desolate and drained them of any hope for more than survival. No craft apprenticeship, but an endless, mindless labor. No cottage, but an accumulation of squatters' dwellings. Selina's heart ached when she journeyed through the industrial towns where the children were soot-covered and sullen, often hungry and almost always illiterate.

"I begin to think there is no possibility of stemming the tide," she replied, discouraged. "If there is work this year, there will probably be no work next year."

"But you can never tell, can you? There would have been no work last year if Penrith had not rebuilt the stables. It is not inconceivable that next year one of the landowners will have a project. One year at a time, Miss Easterly-Cummings, is all anyone can hope for." The intense blue eyes studied her gravely.

Selina nodded as she tugged the shawl closer about her shoulders. For the first time she became conscious that her being alone with a strange man might not be altogether proper. Not that she cared for such things, she scolded herself. After all, it was her own home and she might entertain whom she pleased. Well, not entertain, perhaps, but repay him for his kindness in restoring Henry to her. This was, as it were, an obligation. Selina stole a quick glance at her companion under the pretext of plumping up one of the pillows on the sofa where she sat. He rested casually in his chair, his eyes thoughtful and the black brows drawn into a slight frown, his fingers tapping lightly on his wine-glass.

At length she said hesitantly, "I have never wished to sell the vale to Lord Benedict. My father would not sell it to his father, though he risked the loss of it on the turn of a card to spare himself a fight in the courts. If I were to sell the land to you, I would have to be offered first refusal in the event you were to resell it for any reason."

Surprised, Rushton stared at her for a moment. "Of course I would offer you first refusal. Do you mean you will sell?"

"I suppose there is really no reason not to. Would you give me your word to employ men from the area, and not to import your own workers or craftsmen?"

"Wherever feasible, Miss Easterly-Cummings. You may not have all the necessary trades represented right here."

"Possibly, but I would expect you to do your utmost before going elsewhere."

"I have said I would." He watched her warily now, afraid any misstep would unbalance their negotiations. "Had you given any thought to what the land is worth?"

"Lord Benedict has offered me, at various times, seven, eight and nine hundred pounds. There are only thirty acres, and a fair amount of it is wooded."

"Would a thousand pounds be adequate?"

"You misunderstand me, Mr. Rushton. I thought Lord Benedict's offers were high for such a small piece of land."

"To me the land is worth a thousand pounds. I could spend more on a hunter, Miss Easterly-Cummings. Have we a bargain?" He watched her finger the shawl nervously, perplexed by her agitation. Was he harassing her, after all? She seemed unusually vulnerable. "There is no need to decide right now. I would be grateful if you would think over my offer."

"Yes, I . . . I should like to do that. I don't mean to be contrary; it is just that until this evening I had not really thought of selling it, and I should not like to make a hasty decision. May I send you word in a day or so?"

Selina was not in the habit of hesitating over business decisions. When she had all the facts at her fingertips, she saw no reason to mull over a decision interminably, for it did not make the problem appear any clearer, but often the reverse. There was no reason to withhold her agreement now, but she felt strongly affected by his presence and could not be sure that she would feel the same when he had left. No use pretending that when he fixed one with that compelling gaze it had no influence. Selina decided that he was used to getting his own way, and that rankled, for she would not let him twist her round his thumb, but she would not refuse to sell to him for that reason, either. It *was* a business matter, and her grasping at time to decide was an effort to keep any extraneous issues from coloring her decision.

Unaware that he had risen, Selina found him standing over her and started to her feet. "Forgive me, I have been lost in thought. How very rude of me."

Rushton found her delightful in her confusion, and smiled. "Think nothing of it, Miss Easterly-Cummings. I had just said that I will look forward to hearing from you, and that I thought it time I took my leave. Thank you for a delicious meal. I hope your dog has enjoyed those dishes we did not."

"Oh, Scamp will eat anything, the graceless pup. Henry even feeds her turnips. I appreciate your bringing him home, Mr. Rushton, and for keeping an eye on him today."

"I only wish we might have prevented the accident, but these things do happen."

Her face clouded and the brown eyes grew troubled once more. "Yes, of course." She gave a firm tug to the bellpull. "Did he have so much brandy that he will feel wretched tomorrow?"

"I doubt it, though if he is totally unfamiliar with such strong spirits..." He eyed her questioningly.

"No. No, he has had brandy any number of times before." Selina turned to McDonough as he entered. "If you would show Mr. Rushton out, please."

When Selina offered Mr. Rushton her hand, he had an unaccountable desire to lift it to his lips, but satisfied himself with pressing it gently before he reluctantly let it go, only to watch it flutter nervously to tug the shawl tightly about her.

Selina looked up from the breakfast table to survey her cousin. "How are you feeling this morning, Henry?"

He screwed his face into a grimace. "I've been better, but I'll live. My arm aches like the devil." A mischievous twinkle lit his eyes. "Do you think I could convince Dr. Davenport that I was unable to do my lessons because of it?"

"No, I don't. It's not even your writing hand."

"True, but I could tell him that the agony of it distracted me too much."

"Henry, he has already cut your lessons in half. Have you written to Lord Leyburn?"

"Not yet." When she frowned, he hastened to add, "I have not found the best way to phrase my wishes as yet. I've tossed a dozen sheets on the fire."

"Perhaps I could help you later." Her eyes wandered toward the window where a warm sun was at work melting the snow. "Do you think I should sell the vale to Mr. Rushton?"

Henry lifted his brows comically. "Never say you have reconsidered! I thought your word in business matters was law."

"Mr. Rushton pointed out that his construction project would provide numerous jobs for the men hereabouts. You know that has no little influence with me, Henry. I really have no use for the vale, except for walks and picnics, and as you said, there are other places for that. I have never wished to sell the vale to Lord Benedict because . . . I just never have," she said abruptly. "The case is different with Mr. Rushton. Lord Benedict would not build anything there, but would likely clear it and use it for grazing land as he does the areas around it."

"And Rushton would build a hunting-box? Lord, you should see him in the field, Selina. Even Sir Penrith can't top a flight of rails with such ease. And almost no one else even tried to jump the brook. I know I didn't. Perhaps when I have had more experience, but not now."

Delighted to learn that her cousin had shown some caution the preceding day, Selina smiled. "I'm pleased that you enjoyed yourself. If you take care of your arm, I imagine it won't be so very long before you'll be able to repeat the experience."

"And you won't mind? Even after what happened this time?" he asked incredulously, his toast suspended half way to his mouth.

"I will become accustomed, I feel sure," she returned ruefully. "About the land, Henry. You see no objection to my selling it?"

"No, how could I? It's a lovely spot, but entirely cut off from the rest of Shalbrook. Might as well let someone have the use of it, and if you don't want to sell it to Lord Benedict, why not Rushton? He's a good chap."

"Is he? I suppose so. He has made a generous offer for the land, and I have a mind to accept it. There are several projects which I had been contemplating, and I would not give a second thought to starting them with the additional funds. Some charities further from home than usual. I have a mind to drive over to have a look at the vale before I decide. Would you like to come?"

"In the sledge?"

"Yes, for the way the sun is shining, we won't have the use of it very long. Perhaps it would be too rough on your arm, though."

"A sight more comfortable than the phaeton in this weather, but the road is likely to be unfit for it."

"We'll drive across the fields and look at it from our side of the road."

After their easy-paced drive, however, Selina found she was not content to view the land from a distance. "Would you walk the horses a minute while I have a look?"

"Dash it, Selina, you can't go climbing over that fence. You'll break your neck."

"Now look who's being the mother hen!" she taunted and flounced out of the sledge. Her boots sunk into the mushy snow, and she squealed as the wetness assailed her legs.

"I told you so," Henry mocked.

"No, you didn't. You said I would break my neck

climbing over the fence." She stomped away from him to the whitethorn fence with its shallow ditch. The binding was done with brambles, and though the fence was now more than ten years old, it was not really fully grown, though it was very nearly cattle-proof. Some of the shoots of the bullfinch were eight or nine feet high, and they were protected by a rail on both sides. Having no wish to scratch herself needlessly, Selina pulled herself onto the rail before attempting to ease through the shoots, which were further apart at that height. When she could tentatively place a foot on the further rail, she ducked her head and made the plunge. Unfortunately, her cloak became hopelessly entangled in the brambles, and in attempting to free it, she tumbled off the further rail into the snowy road, the cloak hideously snagged.

"I see you have not changed, Selina," remarked the horseman who leaped down to assist her to her feet. "If I am not mistaken, Shalbrook is provided with a very wide gate through which most people gain the road."

There was no need to look up into the sardonic face; Selina would have known the voice anywhere. "Well, Frank, you know I am not like most people," she replied as she inspected the ruination of her cloak. "Though I would not have done it if I had thought to sustain such a catastrophe, you understand. This is the only really warm covering I own."

"I should think you would own a dozen just to sit around your medieval fortress," Lord Benedict rejoined. "Whatever were you trying to prove?"

At last she looked at him, noting the fair hair escaping from under his curly-brimmed beaver. "I had a desire to have a look at the vale before I sold it."

His hazel eyes sharpened with interest. "You have finally decided to accord me my fondest wish then?"

"No, Frank. I plan to sell it to a friend of Sir Penrith's."

An angry glitter shone in his eyes. "You are doing this to annoy me."

"Am I? I wonder. No. I cannot think so, for when the gentleman first asked, I did not agree. But you see, he intends to build a hunting-box which will provide some much-needed employment in the neighborhood."

Lord Benedict gripped her arm ungently. "You know I am willing to pay more for it than some crazy fox-hunter, Selina. That vale belongs with my land."

"We have been over this a dozen times, Frank," she said wearily, shaking off his hand. "I won't sell the land to you."

"You are a stubborn, capricious, self-willed woman!" he cried, slapping his whip against his leg. "Thank God you broke our engagement, or we might at this very moment be married."

"But then the vale would be yours," she said sweetly, as she stooped to retrieve her cap from the road.

"That would have been too great a price to pay," he returned coldly, his eyes raking her as she put the nun-like cap on her curls.

"I know. Do not let me detain you longer, Frank. I know you are a busy man." She offered her hand and a patently insincere smile.

He accepted neither, but stood scowling at her. "How much did he offer you? I will pay double the figure to save myself the bother of tearing his house down when he finally agrees to sell to me."

"Ah, but, Frank, a condition of the sale is that I have first refusal should he ever decide to sell."

"This is your idea of revenge, I suppose," he grated, the hazel eyes blazing. "Hell hath no fury . . ."

"Like a woman scorned."

"I did not scorn you. It was you who refused me."

"Do you still tell yourself that?" she asked softly. "It must be quite a salve to your conscience. Good day, Frank." Without a backward glance, she crossed the road and climbed the flight of rails into her property, where she stood with her rigid back to him until at last she heard the sound of his horse moving forward. Not until she was sure, from the quiet that descended on the scene, that he was gone did she turn to gaze in the direction taken. Dry-eyed but shaken, she wondered how she could still be so easily discomposed by him. It was years since they had parted. And was it true what he said: that she would sell the land to Rushton as a means to hurt her former fiancé? Thirty stupid acres of no great value were turning into a wretched strain on her emotions. Why had her peaceful life suddenly been turned into upheaval, first by Henry, and then Rushton and now Frank? The lesson to be learned from it, she thought bitterly, was that men were the very devil of a nuisance.

Her gaze wandered over the vale and she could hear the sound of the stream and the dripping from the trees as the snow melted. It was a lovely sight, and it entirely failed to soothe her. Remembering that poor Henry was walking the horses on the other side of the obscuring fence, she determinedly made her way back over the rails and across the road. The scramble through the briars did nothing to improve her temper; she got a nasty scratch across her chin, and she knew the moment she saw his face that Henry had heard every word of her conversation with Lord Benedict.

SEVEN

Henry extracted a large linen handkerchief from the depths of his greatcoat and patted at the cut on her chin, though his eyes never left hers. "Could you tell me what that was all about, Selina?"

"Lord Benedict has wanted to buy the vale for years, and I will not sell it to him. I fear he was very annoyed to learn that I am going to sell it to Mr. Rushton." Hard as she tried, she could not meet his gaze.

"There is apparently a great deal more to it than that," Henry suggested as he handed her into the sledge. "You know I am not one to pry, Selina, but you were very . . . harsh with him. Not that he was not the same! Still, it is so unlike you to carry a grudge. I don't remember much about your being engaged to him."

"It was a very long time ago, Henry, and best forgotten. There may be some truth in what he says. Certainly I would never have sold him the vale, though I honestly did not consider selling to Mr. Rushton with the thought of irritating Lord Benedict. Or, at least, I don't think so. I cannot recall that I thought much one way or the other about his lordship's reaction, though I should have. But when he pinched at me that way, I could not resist inserting the barb. How very intemperate of me! But I am always that way with him. A decided flaw in my character," she sighed with an attempt at lightness.

"He did something to hurt you," Henry suggested astutely.

Selina bit her lip as she gathered the reins. "Yes, he

did something to hurt me. I should have forgiven him by now, I suppose, though there has never seemed any reason to do so. He continues to bait me as though the whole episode were of my making, and that invariably annoys me. I would prefer not to discuss it further, Henry."

"Certainly, my dear."

They drove home in silence, the sledge gliding over the slippery surface without pause. As they left the stables, Selina commented, "I fear we may not have use for the sledge for a while now, but at least it will be ready for the next snowfall." She fingered the snagged cloak with chagrin. "I shall have to repair this, if I can, but it looks hopeless."

"That will teach you to climb through fences," Henry laughed. "And your cap is muddy. I sadly fear you will have to destroy it this time."

"Ho, you would like that, wouldn't you? Well, I have others, my dear Henry, so you needn't get your hopes up."

Henry felt relieved that she had recovered her spirits enough to tease him. Seldom in the years he had spent with her had he seen Selina in the sullens, and he realized suddenly that she must often suffer from loneliness with only his company. A spirited, attractive young lady such as she should be caught up in the whirl of country Society, attending dinners, balls, excursions. There should be a circle of young men in attendance on her and other young ladies with whom she shared her secrets and dreams. Without thinking what he was saying, he blurted, "It is because of me, isn't it?"

The alarm in her eyes could not be masked, though she forced herself to ask sternly, "Whatever are you talking about, Henry?"

"The reason you don't go out into Society. It is because of me, isn't it?" He was almost stunned by the enormity of the discovery he believed he had made.

Relief flooded her face and she smiled. "How absurd you are! It is rather the other way about, is it not? For your sake, I should mingle with the gentry so that you would be brought to their attention, instead of keeping you hidden away here at Shalbrook. I can tell Mr. Rushton thinks that. And very likely he is right. Shall we worm our way back into Society, ingratiate ourselves with our neighbors? Ah, I shall have to polish up my tea-time chitchat and quietly investigate whether half an hour is still proper for a morning call."

"You know I don't give a fig for all that nonsense, Selina," Henry protested. "There is no reason you should not go out a bit more, though. How long is it since you've danced or been to a musical evening?"

"Lord, I don't know," she replied airily. "You have no idea how dull some of those affairs can be. Fortunately I am far too busy to have to attend any longer. Now if you were to take an interest in such social dallying, I would most assuredly set aside my hesitation and bring you forward to the notice of every hostess I could dredge up. Is that what you want?" she quizzed him.

"No, of course not," he said disgustedly. Although he was swayed by her banter, the whisper of doubt remained lodged in his mind. He excused himself to his studies when they returned to the house, and with an effort, forced his worry to the back of his mind so that he could concentrate on construing his Greek verbs accurately. When he had accomplished enough work for the day, however, he slipped quietly out of the house and spent the long walk to the village thinking things through.

Selina thankfully settled on the sofa in the gold drawing room when Henry had left her. He was becoming far too clever, that lad. For a moment she had thought he had stumbled onto her most carefully guarded secret. Not that she could not have explained it to his satisfaction, but it would have been a trying interview. And seeing Frank was always unsettling. One of the decided advantages of keeping out of country Society was not meeting him frequently. She found her mind recalling the vision of him in the road, his hat tilted at a rakish angle over the shining blond hair, his hazel eyes glaring at her. Once she had thought those eyes could hold nothing but warmth for her, could promise nothing but happiness. Her throat ached when she remembered the first time he had kissed her and vowed, "We will marry directly I return from the Peninsula, my love. You will wait for me, won't you?"

And she had waited for him through what seemed an eternity, through her father's death and Henry's advent. It was the thought of him which had kept her going during those trying days, months, even years, because when he returned he would share her burdens, he would love her, he would take care of her. Selina gulped back a sob and remonstrated with herself. Bitter as it was to have ended in naught, probably without that dream she would not have managed. For that at least she should be grateful. There was no sense in going over these painful memories, but they insisted on thrusting themselves on her mind.

There was that early summer day when she had stood at the window in Henry's room—when Henry was an invalid—and looked out over the fields, lost in contemplation, Frank's last letter in her hand. His letters had changed almost imperceptibly. Although he still declared his affection for her, there was a growing absorption with himself that made her feel as though the letter were from a stranger. Carefully documenting each of his escapades and victories, he never asked of her own concerns or commented on the problems she poured out to him in her letters. As she narrowed her eyes against the sun, she had decided that her letters to him must seem as filled with her own concerns as his did to her. In the future she would try not to be so selfish. She had glanced over to find that Henry had at last fallen asleep when she heard the sound of hoofbeats in the drive. There could be no mistaking that glorious head of blond hair! The letter dropped from her nerveless hands and she stumbled in her haste toward the door.

Before Frank had reached the second terrace, she was outside the house and running toward him. Although his expression was one more of surprise than delight, he caught her in his arms and kissed her. She emerged from his embrace to breathlessly enquire, "Why didn't you tell me you were getting leave?"

"Not leave, my love. I've sold out," he said cheerfully.

"Sold out? But you never wrote..."

"A surprise, my dear. The old man's not getting any younger, you know. I could tell that Mother wanted me home...and I thought perhaps you did, too." He eyed her quizzingly.

"Oh, yes! I've dreamed of your coming home! But the fighting seems interminable, and I never thought you'd leave until the last enemy was routed."

"They're mismanaging the whole thing," he grumbled. "No one is willing to listen to how the war should be conducted."

"But you could tell them, couldn't you?" she asked playfully, taking his arm as they walked toward the house.

His body stiffened and he frowned down at her. "Damn right I could, Selina. Spare me your teasing. You know nothing of war, and never will."

Chastened, even hurt, Selina stammered, "I...I'm sorry, Frank. We are so far away from all that horror here. You'll have tea, won't you?"

Selina shifted uneasily in her chair as she remembered the days that had followed. Days of treading carefully, of watching her tongue as she was not used to do, of balancing the demands on her time from Henry and Frank. The returned "hero" had made it no less clear than Lord Leyburn that he did not share her affection for Henry. Selina had tried to rationalize that a soldier had seen too many mutilated bodies to be comfortable in Henry's presence, but she was daily torn by conflicting emotions. Cautiously she tried to explain to Frank her feelings of responsibility for Henry, her very real affection for the boy, her desire to keep him with her. Frank was noncommittal. He bruited their engagement about the neighborhood and took her to tea with his mother.

Most clearly Selina remembered the day they had ridden in the vale. It was unbearably hot, and her nerves were on edge because Henry was having a bad day. She had hesitated to leave him at all, but Frank had insisted. Their horses were tied to a tree and they walked past the stream and into the clearing where

71

the sun shone brightly and the murmur of the water could still be heard.

Frank made a sweeping gesture. "Once we're married, this will all be Old Hall land—not just the vale, but Shalbrook as well. Lord, what an estate I'll have when my father dies! I think we should live at Shalbrook until he has his notice to quit."

Tempted to protest at his cavalier treatment of his father and her own inheritance, Selina refrained in order to once again broach the touchy subject of Henry. "Would you like to do that, Frank? Then it would not be necessary to disrupt Henry's established routine. And I'm sure your parents would be more comfortable if we weren't in Old Hall."

"We shall need the privacy," Frank suggested as he drew her to him, pulling her to the ground and covering her lips with his. His hands began to wander about her body, as they frequently had since his return from the Peninsula. "You are the most desirable girl, Selina."

The freedom he took with her person alarmed Selina, but at the same time she could feel her body respond to his touch on her lightly covered breasts. Before he had left for the Peninsula he had done no more than kiss her. Now he seemed to demand more and more each time they were alone. She desperately needed the reassurance that his whispered words of love gave her as he held and caressed her. For so long she had depended on his love, used it as a shield against the difficult days of caring for Henry, and the desperate worry she suffered that her cousin would never walk again, that she was not strong enough to bear the burdens of an invalid cousin and an estate to run. She *wanted* to believe that Frank loved her and would care for her. There was nowhere else to turn.

His kisses deepened as he murmured, "Oh, my little love, my adorable beauty. We have all the privacy we need right now." He expertly slid the muslin dress down off her shoulders and breasts in such a way that her arms were restricted to her sides.

"Please, no, Frank. You mustn't." She felt trapped, panicked, embarrassed.

"But I must, my love." He touched the firm, white

breasts exposed to his view. "White as a lily. The Portuguese girls have a darker skin. You look so pure."

She caught at his wrists with her hands. "Don't, Frank. You shouldn't."

"Selina, Selina, where is the problem?" He pressed her hands to her sides and smiled down at her. "In a few weeks we'll be married and I don't think you'll be so missish then. You like to be touched, I can tell." Unaffected by her protest he continued to caress her. "You see, my love?"

"I...I...Yes, I...But, Frank..."

He released one of her hands so that he could lift her skirts. "Oh, my love, I want you."

"Not now. Not here. Ohh." Her free hand, with which she had been ineffectually trying to restore her skirts to their rightful place, stilled. The desire had risen in her as he continued to fondle her, until the cautioning voice within her seemed a mere whisper, too faint to recognize the message. Frank released her other hand and was quickly unbuttoning his pantaloons. Struggling for some reason in her chaotic mind and body, Selina clenched her fists and said firmly, "No, Frank. Not until we're married."

"Don't be simple, Selina. What difference can it make?" His brows quirked with annoyance, but he could see from the set of her chin that she was going to be stubborn. Frank was accustomed to having what he wanted, when he wanted it. He played his trump card. "Your cousin can live with us, Selina, if you'll just let me have you now. You know you want to."

The bile rose in her throat and her body shuddered. Ever since he had returned home she had been trying to tell herself that she still cared for him, that he was the same man she remembered. It was no longer possible to do so. He was a selfish, inconsiderate boor. Selina slapped him with all the pent-up emotion of the last two years. "Don't touch me, Frank."

Astonished, he very nearly struck her back, only managing to control himself by gritting through his teeth, "That's what you wanted, wasn't it, Selina? You've been whining at me about your cousin since I returned. Well, you may have a choice, my girl. It's me . . . or your cripple. After this, you shan't have both."

With shaking fingers, Selina pulled her muslin dress back over her bosom as she rose. "There isn't any choice, Frank. After this, I wouldn't have you for anything in the world. Good bye."

He had blustered and fumed, even half-heartedly apologized. After three years, Selina still could not look back on the scene with equanimity. What a fool she had been not to see him for what he was the moment he returned! How could she have allowed herself to be so deluded? Why had her body responded to his touch? She felt shamed every time the memory forced itself upon her. Never would she allow such a situation again.

Selina rose and went to the rosewood escritoire in the corner. Whether or not her decision was influenced by Lord Benedict, she had decided most definitely to sell the vale to Mr. Rushton.

"What does she say?" Penrith asked impatiently.

"She will sell it to me, on the terms we discussed." Rushton allowed a slow grin to spread over his face. "You are totally to be credited, you know, Pen. If it weren't for the weight you gave my arguments, I have not the least doubt she would have kept it. You should have heard how I harassed her: told her the whole neighborhood depended on her to sell the land to me, and that the poor folks dying of starvation would curse her name if she did not."

"If you had employed such tactics with her, you wouldn't have your acceptance, my friend. Benedict will be disappointed, of course, and you can't blame him. It would have rounded out his land. He's not a hunting man, himself. Don't know why. I would have expected him to have a go just so he could dash about in a scarlet coat; he was mighty proud of that uniform of his."

"I take it you are not overly fond of Lord Benedict."

"Don't know him very well. He's more than half a dozen years my junior. Bit of a loose screw, I've always thought. Oh, devilishly handsome and all that, but I was glad none of my sisters attracted his attention."

"I believe you mentioned that Miss Easterly-Cummings was engaged to him at one time."

"Yes, I rather thought so, even before he went to the Peninsula. Announced it when he returned, but it was called off. All for the better, in my opinion."

"I sometimes think you held a similar view of my own aspiration for Miss Longmead's hand."

Penrith flushed and ran a hand through his auburn locks. "Now, I've never said anything of the sort, have I?"

"You never had to, Pen. You are as transparent as glass."

"Well, well, perhaps it's just that I don't relish the thought of you marrying and depriving me of your company in the field," Penrith quibbled.

"I have never had the intention of giving up hunting when I marry. You know, Pen, you are not getting any younger yourself. Don't you think it time to settle down and get an heir for Oak Park?"

Exasperated, Penrith scowled at his friend. "Now don't you start on me. I have quite enough of that from my mother. I've told her I'll look about me in the next year or so. My father didn't marry until he was six and thirty. What would I do with a wife, for God's sake? I know all about living with a bunch of women, and it's no easy matter. They are forever coming to you for the silliest things." He mimicked, "'Oh, Pen, I have mislaid my needlework. Have you seen it? Oh, Pen, I am just the tiniest bit in debt from the card party at Mrs. Crompton's. Do you think I might have a little extra? Oh, Pen, would you just speak to the vicar about his sermons? They have become a dreadful bore. Oh, Pen....'"

"Spare me! This is an indictment indeed, when one is aware that you possess the most amiable of families. I can see that I have very narrowly squeaked out of an awful fate," Rushton laughed.

"I'm not saying that it wouldn't be comfortable to have a wife to come home to, you understand. I'd just like a breather after all my sisters. Once Cassandra is settled, well, then I shall think about it again."

"And you told me just the other day that it was a pity I was an only child."

"In some ways it is," Penrith said thoughtfully. "I have only to think of my sisters sitting alone on one of those gilded chairs at a ball to be quite agreeable to dancing with the most homely girl imaginable when she is presented to me. You choose purely on your own inclination. Nothing wrong with that, I suppose. You would say I allow people to impose on me, but there, I dare say I have had a greater variety of interesting companions than you have. Brains seldom follow extraordinary beauty, in my experience. Oh, I don't mean shrewdness; the diamonds have that by the ton. But wit and intelligence, sometimes you don't even find them unless you dig them out, and in the most unlikely places. Take my sisters. Not much amiss with their looks, but no one would ever proclaim them the gems of the Season. But they are good-hearted girls, clever and full of fun. And look how they've been snapped up! Not a one has spent more than one Season on the town! The beauties are intimidating, and more often than not grossly self-centered."

"Am I to take this as a comment on Miss Longmead?" Rushton asked coolly.

"Dear God, no! What do you take me for?" Penrith protested, once again running his hand through his hair. "I cannot even remember how I ... Oh, yes, we were speaking of only children. Look at Lady Eleanor. Diamond of the first water. It's been three years she's been on the town. Everyone acknowledges her a beauty. But is she married?"

"No, but that is not to say she hasn't received any offers. I personally know two gentlemen who have tried their luck."

"Ah, but that is my point. Only child, selfish, conceited, but also very shrewd. She can hold out for a marquess or a duke, and so she has. Watch her this Season, though. I'd be willing to bet you a pony she accepts the best that offers this time. You can see the lines developing in her mother's face. Probably the old lady has schemed herself right into a hole. This Season she'll push for getting the thing settled. So you might just give the word to your friends, if they're still interested."

"You forget that I do not intend to go to London this spring, but I will certainly write to my friends," Rushton offered with a suspicious sparkle in his eyes. "You are very philosophical today, Pen."

"Yes, well, I'm not a complete crackbrain, Gareth. I find the machinations of Society as amusing as you do, only I seldom speak of it. Probably wouldn't have now, except it seems to me you've lost your sense of humor recently. I'm not saying there aren't things that should be taken seriously, but you were not used to subscribe to such a pessimistic outlook."

Rushton regarded him with mock severity. "How can you say so when I have just been dancing for joy over this communication." He touched the note from Miss Easterly-Cummings with a careless finger. "I ask no more of life at this moment than to make a start on my hunting-box."

"I had hoped you would give Cassandra a send-off as you did the other girls," Penrith said reproachfully. "It did none of them any harm, you know."

"Nor any good, either, I dare say. Cassandra won't have the least trouble making her way in Society with your mother and sister to guide her."

"You could make it easier for her. The *ton* have a way of keeping their eye on which young ladies you pay attention to. Still, if you can't find it in you to do this one small thing for me..."

Casting his eyes heavenward, Rushton groaned. "Very well, Pen, I shall come to London for a few weeks, but not for the whole Season, mind you. I am serious about the hunting-box and have no wish to delay it. For her ball, then, and a week before and after. How would that be?"

Penrith grinned. "You're not such a bad fellow, Gareth, but I promise I won't tell anyone. Hate to spoil your image and all that. How about a brandy?"

Henry appeared in the drawing room late in the

afternoon mysteriously clutching an enormous box under his arm, a wide grin lighting his features. "I have something for you."

"For me? What is this, Henry? I had my birthday only two months ago." Selina regarded his mischievous face suspiciously.

"It is not a birthday present—though it could be. I seem to remember giving you only a few volumes of poetry and a bracelet. Yes, let us say it is a late birthday present." He pushed one package across the magazine-strewn table toward her. "Go on, open it."

Hesitantly, Selina set down her needlework and fingered the box. "I am almost afraid to."

"Your instincts are perfectly in order, Selina," he teased. "You shan't like it all, you know. None the less, I shall insist on your using it. Come, open it now."

She slid the string that bound it over the corners, and with one last questioning glance at her cousin, lifted the top from the box. Inside rested a crimson velvet mantelet luxuriantly trimmed with chinchilla. Henry whisked a hatbox from behind his back and removed the lid with a flourish. Too stunned to make a move, Selina merely gazed at the turban of crimson velvet with its two crimson ostrich feathers and a bandeau of chinchilla. Caught between a desire to laugh and cry, Selina shook her head wonderingly.

"If the crimson ostrich plumes are too much, I have brought you some white ones to replace them," Henry explained, digging through the paper at the bottom of the box. "Mrs. Baxter said the turban was all the crack, but I thought it a bit much, myself, with the colored feathers. See, these curly ones are much less flamboyant, and I do think with the brim that it is not really an older lady's hat, don't you?" he asked anxiously.

"I have never seen anything so delightful," Selina assured him truthfully. "I think you are right about the plumes, though. Oh, Henry, I love them both, but I don't understand why you have done this."

"You tore your cloak this morning and God help me, it isn't worth repairing, Selina. It's time you dressed more stylishly, you know. I have no doubt Lord Benedict would not have been so abrupt with you if you'd not looked like you were headed for an expedition to the Alps or something. He's used to fashionable ladies, spending so much of his time in London as he does. It was the greatest pity you should have been climbing through the fence when you met him; I imagine that is not considered quite the thing in his circles. But never mind. Will you try on the mantelet and the turban?"

As she lifted the mantelet from its box, Selina said, "It doesn't matter what Lord Benedict thinks of me, Henry. I hope you have not gone to this expense so that I may gain his good opinion. I could dress like Lady Caroline Lamb and not win his approbation."

"It's not just Lord Benedict, Selina. Would you shame me in front of Sir Penrith and Mr. Rushton? No, I will not allow you to put the turban over your stupid cap! You will find some perfectly acceptable lace caps in the box, too, and I expect you to wear them." Henry looked uncertain for a moment. "Am I asking too much, Selina?"

His cousin hugged the mantelet about her and turned to inspect herself in the glass. Her brown curls framed her face under the delightful confection, and she could not resist fingering the rich fabric. "No, of course not."

"You see, the other day when you were describing what Cassandra would be wearing at the breakfast table—you know, when you were pretending that she and Mr. Rushton were married—you described a most fashionable toilette and I thought...That is, you seemed to know what was the current mode, and you talked about it with a certain enthusiasm....Dash it, I just thought you might like to wear something pretty, Selina. And you do look pretty in it, you know. There is that portrait of you stuck off in the crimson bedchamber—it should be in the drawing room!—where you are wearing the most dashing crimson riding habit, so I knew that crimson would suit your coloring." He grinned at the enchanting picture she made. "Do you really like it?"

"Yes, I love it, Henry. It is a long time since I've

79

worn anything half so fine. You do not think I am perhaps a little old to wear..."

"Old!? My God, what are you thinking of? You are three and twenty, not forty."

"Perhaps you are right." Selina placed a salute on his cheek, which caused him to flush with embarrassment. "Thank you, Henry. I shall look quite the thing when I go out."

"You are more than welcome, my dear," he replied gruffly. "And you might think about getting rid of those brown dresses, too, Selina. And that grotesque green thing. I wouldn't get anything quite so frilly as Cassandra's was the other day, nor anything so sober as Lady Southwood's, but something that would suit you. *You* know the sort of thing."

"Yes, Henry. I know precisely what you mean," Selina laughed.

EIGHT

Rushton had been informed, in answer to a polite note to Miss Easterly-Cummings asking how quickly their transaction could be accomplished, that he might present himself at Shalbrook in a week's time, if he should be prepared to act so quickly. There was nothing to delay him, since he had deposited a substantial amount with a banker in Leicester on his way to Oak Park, so he arrived at Shalbrook at the appointed time, dressed for the milder weather in an elegant blue coat and buff pantaloons. Penrith had ceased to wonder how it was that Weston managed to turn out Rushton in such style when Penrith's own clothing, of precisely the same quality of material and workmanship, never seemed to carry the same visual impact. In order to have achieved the same effect, Penrith would doubtless have had to deny himself his apricot tarts and Chantilly cakes, which he was loath to do, and besides, somehow he doubted that he could achieve the naturally athletic figure of his friend, in any case. He consoled himself that his Hessians were every bit as well-polished and his beaver hats as jauntily worn as any Rushton could sport, but as his friend drove off in his curricle he decided once again that there was really no comparison between them.

The butler at Shalbrook led Rushton into a room he had not previously entered, the library. Seated at an enormous desk surrounded on all sides by a formidable collection of volumes was Miss Easterly-Cummings, a lace cap on her head and perfectly normally attired in a dove gray woolen dress with a high neck and long sleeves, a matching shawl about her shoulders. Rushton was not at first aware of the other party in the room, as he was seated in a high-backed chair facing away from him, but the man rose at his entry and bowed to him as Selina introduced them.

"Mr. Thomas, this is Mr. Rushton, the gentleman who is purchasing the vale. Mr. Rushton, Mr. Thomas is my banker from Leicester, who will witness the documents we shall be signing." Selina indicated a chair and continued, "In addition to the deed which I shall sign, I have had Mr. Thomas prepare a short document on which I will require your signature, Mr. Rushton. It contains nothing more than the terms we discussed previously, so it should present no problem."

Startled, Rushton took the paper she handed him and quickly read through the single paragraph, his brows drawing together in a frown. With an angry flick of the wrist, he tossed the paper from him. "Miss Easterly-Cummings, it is true that I have agreed to offer you first refusal on the property should I ever sell or dispose of it, and it is likewise true that I have endeavored to hire local artisans wherever feasible. I have given you my word as a gentleman that I will abide by those conditions, and I see no necessity for signing a superfluous document."

The gray-haired banker suggested soothingly, "And yet there is no reason not to, either, Mr. Rushton. It is merely a formality."

Rushton tapped the document with an impatient forefinger. "My word is as good as my signature, Mr. Thomas. I consider such a contract an insult."

"There is no insult intended, Mr. Rushton," Selina said calmly. "The purpose of the contract is to exclude any possibility of misunderstanding. This paper represents my interpretation of our agreement. You might have construed it otherwise."

"Well, I didn't, and I'll be ... I won't sign it."

"Very well, Mr. Rushton. There is no need for you to do so. However, if you don't, I will not sell you the land." Selina reached out a hand to draw the paper to her and found her wrist grasped firmly by Rushton.

"Why can you not accept my word?" he rasped.

"Mr. Rushton, this is a business undertaking. My father taught me to have everything put in writing so that there could be no subsequent confusion." Abruptly she withdrew her hand from his clasp.

"If there is any room for misinterpretation, Miss Easterly-Cummings, it still exists." He lifted the paper and read coldly, "'Mr. Rushton shall undertake to employ local craftsmen, artisans and laborers wherever feasible.' What if I am not satisfied with your local craftsmen, Miss Easterly-Cummings? How local is local? From Quorn, from Melton Mowbray, from Leicester? A ten-mile range, twenty? Who is to be the judge of these matters? Are you? Am I? Is Mr. Thomas? Shall I have the two of you breathing down my neck to see that the bricklayer does not come from as far afield as Ashby-de-la-Zouch?"

Selina remained untouched by his sarcasm. "I allowed the wording to stay precisely as you and I agreed, Mr. Rushton. This is not a matter over which I am likely to take you to court. I would be annoyed if you were to bring in a contingent of workmen from your own estate, and thereby deny the local workers an opportunity for employment. I am, after all, selling you the land so that some employment may be provided in the area. Of course, if you wish to be perverse, you can sign the document, buy the land and allow it to remain unimproved for the rest of your life. Certainly the contract, on that point, can be loosely interpreted. You fail to see, I think, that you gave your word only to me, and there are men who do not consider that their word to a woman carries a great deal of weight. A gentleman's honor is often reserved for gentlemen alone. Now, Mr. Rushton, you may sign the contract or not, as you wish. It is not a debatable matter. If you sign, you purchase the land. If you do not ..."

His eyes, sparking with indignation, raked her composed face, but he reached for the pen lying between them, dipped it in the standish and angrily scratched his signature on the document.

"If you would date it as well," Mr. Thomas suggested diffidently.

With a mumbled oath, Rushton did so. He found it difficult to maintain his seat, so great was his annoyance, and he withdrew the purchase price from his coat and thumped it down on the desk. Selina picked it up and handed it to Mr. Thomas, who calmly counted it while Rushton contemplated strangling the both of them.

"The sum is correct," Mr. Thomas murmured as he carefully wrapped the bills in a pouch he had extracted from his voluminous pocket. "You sign the deed just here, Miss Easterly-Cummings."

Selina signed where he had indicated and turned to smile at Rushton, in spite of his fierce frown. "The vale is now yours, Mr. Rushton. I hope you will enjoy it."

"I have every intention of enjoying it," he grumbled as he rose.

Selina hesitantly cast an appealing glance at Mr. Thomas. "I wonder if you would excuse us a moment, sir. There is a matter I wished to discuss with Mr. Rushton before he leaves."

"Certainly, my dear. I think our business is concluded in any case." The banker bowed to Rushton and took Selina's hand before making his departure.

Left alone, the two eyed one another warily and Selina motioned him to seat himself, saying, "If you would just give me a moment of your time."

With reluctant ill grace, Rushton acceded to her wishes. "What is it?"

"This is definitely not the time to broach the matter, I know, when you are feeling so out of sorts, but ... The fact of the matter is that I have brought someone here to be introduced to you, and now you will most certainly give him short shrift. And I didn't have him come because I in any way feel that you must use a local architect. That is not a part of the agreement at all! I thought you might be interested in meeting him because he has designed several hunting-boxes, and he did Sir Penrith's stables, and he has been invaluable to me at Shalbrook with a number of problems..." Selina allowed her voice to trail off under his malevolent glare.

"You had the temerity to invite an architect here to

meet me? Without asking my permission? Who the devil do you think you are, Miss Easterly-Cummings? I am not your cousin Henry to be ordered about and kept on leading-strings. Did you think I would be unable to find my own architect? Did you expect me to hire some obscure nobody to design a hunting-box for me? I suppose I must thank you for your thoughtfulness, though I had rather call it infernal meddling."

Selina bit her lip and did not dare to meet his gaze. "You are right, of course. I should never have done it, and I apologize. There is no need for you to meet him at all. You see, I thought you would be in an accommodating mood once you owned the land, and would agree out of benevolence to meet the young man. I had no way of knowing that you would be so astonishingly upset by the contract, when it was no more than we had agreed verbally."

"It was insulting."

"Yes, I am sure that if the situation were reversed, and I were buying the land from you, you would not have hesitated to accept my word," she retorted, an edge to her voice.

"The situations are not comparable."

"No, certainly not. Women have no honor. It is reserved exclusively for men, and naturally they are deserving of such a monopoly. Everyone knows that women are giddy things, incapable of managing business affairs, unable to sustain a thought long enough to write it down." Selina rose and faced him. "I shall not detain you longer, Mr. Rushton. I believe I have apologized for my absurd conduct, and no doubt you will take into consideration my frail hold on reality, being a female, when you judge me. Good day, sir." Her hands were clenched behind her back and in her agitation she did not notice the library door open.

Henry erupted into the room saying, "Selina, what is taking so long? Lord John Brindly is waiting in the gold drawing room. Servant, Rushton."

"Mr. Rushton has no need of Lord John's services, Henry, and has not the time to meet him today. If you will just tell him that I will be with him in a moment, we can discuss the estate cottages, as I had mentioned in my note."

While Rushton fixed her with a sharp gaze, Henry said cheerfully, "Right you are," and left the room as precipitately as he had entered.

"Cathford's younger brother?" Rushton asked abruptly.

"One of them. The Marquess of Ashbourne has four sons, I believe. Lord John is the third."

"You might have told me."

"I would have, had you been more amenable to my scheme. Lord John has built himself something of a reputation here in Leicestershire, though I doubt he is known in London for his architectural skills."

"His eldest brother is a friend of mine."

"How nice for you."

An overwhelming desire to shake her paralyzed Rushton for a moment. Obviously in spite of her more conventional attire, she was just as exasperating, just as eccentric as ever. He had had no clear idea of whom he intended to employ as an architect, though he had read Elsam's *Essay on Rural Architecture* some years previously, and had been fascinated by some of the ideas in the book. If he had realized that Cathford's younger brother had some experience, certainly he would have looked into the matter further, but to have this high-handed young woman force Lord John on his notice was too much to stomach. On the other hand, he could not very well ignore an introduction to one of his best friends' brothers, no matter how it came about. "I should like to meet Lord John," he said stiffly.

"As you wish, of course," Selina replied, making an attempt to disguise her amusement. "If you will follow me, Mr. Rushton."

After he held the door for her, he loosened his cravat in a vain attempt to ease his gall. He was not in the habit of being laughed at by ladies of his acquaintance, and he found the experience not in the least elevating. It made no difference, either, that she pressed her lips together that way, when he could easily see the laughter in her eyes. Miss Easterly-Cummings was deserving of a first class set-down, and Mr. Rushton intended, at the earliest convenient moment, to deliver one which she would not forget. Unfortunately, the present was not a particularly propitious time to do so.

A young man of medium height, with sandy-colored hair and an open countenance, rose on their entry, breaking off his dialogue with Henry. He came forward with his hand outstretched to Selina. "My dear Miss Easterly-Cummings, it is a pleasure to see you again! Cathford made promise to convey his regards when last he wrote, since he cannot be here for the hunting this year. You are looking splendid."

"Thank you, Lord John. I don't believe you know Mr. Rushton, though he tells me he is a friend of your brother's."

"I've heard him mention your name, sir. A pleasure. Are you at Oak Park, then? Cathford had intended to visit Sir Penrith, but found he could not tear himself away from Ashbourne Hall just now," he said, with a decided grin.

"Yes, I hear Miss Donningsby and her family are visiting. Penrith was disappointed but he seems to have adjusted very well. Hunts four days out of seven," Rushton informed him, "though it would probably be more if Cathford had come."

"A great trial for my brother, I assure you. Said he only gets out twice a week, if he's lucky. Miss Easterly-Cummings mentioned you were buying some land here to build a hunting-box. Did she tell you I have a finger in architecture these days? Not as acceptable to one's family as soldiering or divining, more's the pity, but I have always had the most pronounced interest, and my father don't mind, you know. Keeps me out of the gaming hells, he says, begging your pardon, Miss Easterly-Cummings. I should not like to impose on your friendship with my brother, but I have brought a few drawings of boxes I've done, if you should care to take a look at them. And perhaps you know that I did Sir Penrith's stables last year?"

Rushton studied the eager young man with rueful tolerance. Although Lord John bore a remarkable likeness to his older brother, there were distinct differences in their personalities. No one would have described

Cathford as outgoing; though he had charming manners and was extraordinarily well-bred, there was a definite reserve about him. The contrast with this easygoing, forthright young man was not to the latter's disadvantage, however. Rushton found himself liking Lord John at the outset. "Penrith had not mentioned who designed the stables, but I was impressed with how well they blended with the other buildings. I should like very much to see your drawings."

"Perhaps Henry and I should excuse ourselves, Lord John, so that you and Mr. Rushton may speak more freely," Selina suggested.

"No, no, that's not in the least necessary," the young man protested.

Henry exclaimed, "But, Selina, I have the greatest desire to see the drawings!"

"If it is agreeable with Lord John and Mr. Rushton, I have no objection." Selina could not doubt that Mr. Rushton would be relieved by her absence, and she walked to the door. "I hope you will take as long as you wish, Lord John. Perhaps you would wait on me in the library when you have finished."

There were always any number of matters to occupy Selina's time when she sat in the library, where she kept the record of estate expenditures and income, her own personal accounts and the household books. When her father had died, she had been left the ward of a distant relation, recently moved to Cornwall, who had no interest in overseeing the management of her inheritance, and she had been forced to assume the responsibility herself. The meek woman her guardian had insisted on thrusting on her had stayed, almost perpetually in her own room, until the day after Selina's twenty-first birthday, when she had precipitately departed, announcing that the manor was too damp for her comfort. Mrs. Morrow had been of no help in any of the matters which had occupied Selina's time; she had in fact been nicknamed "The Elusive Shadow" by the cousins long before her departure.

With several leather-bound ledgers resting in front of her, Selina attempted to concentrate her attention on bringing the books up to date, but her mind continually wandered. When she had erroneously entered a household expense under the Home Farm, she snapped the books shut and pushed them aside, allowing her gaze to fall on the bleak landscape outside. If she had not arranged to speak with Lord John about the estate cottages, she would have found some relief in a gallop across the fields.

Selina acknowledged to herself that Mr. Rushton had disconcerted her. Certainly he was handsome and had considerable address when he chose to use it, as he had the evening he had dined with her, but he had not the first idea how to cope with a woman in a business situation for all his social finesse. She had seen his type in Margate and Tunbridge Wells, and especially in Bath. Sophisticated men who dressed elegantly, flirted outrageously and kept a mistress on the side. Men who gambled recklessly and drove their carriages with the skill of a coachman. Men who rode to hounds and entered their prize race-horses at Newmarket. They could be surprisingly appealing men, as she well knew, but they were frivolous hedonists, when all was said and done. Of course, one might *superficially* describe Sir Penrith in the same way, but underneath Pen had a goodness which Selina respected. Pen would have understood about the contract, and not made such a fuss.

It was wrong of me, she thought restlessly as she drummed a pen on the desk, to presume on Mr. Rushton by bringing Lord John here without consulting him. But I do not think it was wrong, or even misguided, of me to have him sign the contract. And I was not stubborn about it, merely firm. He would have made me do the same were the situation reversed, and he knows it. An insult indeed! Well, he has what he wants now, and I shan't have to see him again, and it does not matter in the very least that he has misunderstood me.

When there was a summons at the door, Selina glared at it for a moment before calling, "Come in."

His face alight with glee, Lord John strode into the room. "Ah, you are an angel to have gone to this trouble for me, Miss Easterly-Cummings. Mr. Rushton says he will use me as his architect."

"Has he left?"

"Yes, Henry was showing him out."

"I see. Do sit down and tell me all about it, Lord John. I am so pleased for you."

NINE

In an effort to restore his disposition, Rushton drove from Shalbrook to the small piece of land he had just purchased. The sun was making an attempt to break through the heavy clouds, and a beam of light escaped to shine down on the clearing he envisioned as the site for the house. With an unusual disregard for his gleaming Hessians, and his pair of chestnuts, he tied them to the rails and vaulted over onto the muddy ground and began to pace about the property. The cut-and-laid fences appeared to be in good order, though it occurred to him that he did not know whether they belonged to Lord Benedict or himself. He would have to ask Miss Easterly-Cummings about that. No, devil take her, he had no intention of asking her for so much as the time of day. If necessary he would have a surveyor come and mark the boundaries out for him, should the deed itself not be specific enough. He returned to the curricle to extract the deed from the pocket where he had placed it. A careful study of the wording indicated that the south and west fences were his, while the east and north apparently belonged to Lord Benedict.

The sound of pounding hooves attracted his attention and he raised his head to watch the approach of a solitary horseman, who reined in as he came abreast of the curricle. There was something vaguely familiar about the younger man, but Rushton could not say for certain that he was acquainted with him. Probably he had seen the fellow in London; all the dandies had come to look the same to him. Even the fellow's riding coat was nipped in at the waist, and he wore it over bright yellow buckskins with matching yellow-topped black top boots.

"I say, you must be the gentleman Selina is selling the land to," Lord Benedict cried as he slid from his mount. "Wretched girl! I've tried to buy it from her these last three years but she's as stubborn as a mule! Said she intended to keep it herself, and then look what she does. Did she really retain the right of first refusal if you sell it?"

"Most decidedly," Rushton murmured.

"Hold on, I've seen you in London, ain't I? Selina didn't mention your name, just said you were a friend of Sir Penrith's."

"Gareth Rushton. And I assume you are Lord Benedict."

"Rushton! Of course! I've seen you around and about for years. We've never met." He offered his hand, which was accepted with some surprise by Rushton, who could not help but be startled by the glaringly yellow gloves Benedict wore. "I was on my way to speak with Selina. Not concluded the deal yet, have you?"

"Yes, I own the land now."

"I will pay you double what you paid her. You can see that the vale belongs with my land. It was only her perversity which kept her from selling to me." Benedict eyed his companion speculatively. "You are a man of property yourself, Rushton. Must understand how it is to have one little chunk cut out of the whole. A constant irritation, like an itch you can't reach. Stand atop a rise and wave your hand about: All that is my land . . . except the little vale there which a stubborn chit owns and won't sell to me. I tell you what we could do! Selina said you wanted to build a hunting-box, and I have a very handy piece of land the other side of Barton, a little larger than this, don't you know? Perhaps fifty acres. We can exchange the two. Why not ride along with me and have a look at it? Repossessed it a year ago. Just an old farm. Easy enough to convert the farmhouse, or even tear it down. What do you say?"

"I am particularly attached to this piece of land, Lord

Benedict, and you are forgetting Miss Easterly-Cummings' right of first refusal."

"Pay no heed to that. Selina wouldn't go as high as I would for the land. Well, stands to rights she wouldn't pay more to get it back than she just got for selling it, now would she?"

Rushton regarded the young man coldly. "I have no intention of selling the vale. The location is ideal for a hunting-box, and I have already engaged an architect. I can understand your irritation at having a small piece cut out from the rest of your lands, but it has obviously been so for some years, and I would advise accustoming yourself to the state of affairs on a permanent basis."

"You might at least have a look at the farm," Benedict grumbled. "Nothing wrong with it for a hunting-box. We could say you were paying more for it than you did for the vale, and everything would be right and tight. Selina don't matter. We could make it an outrageous price that even she would hesitate to match for some long-past grudge. Serve her right for selling it under my nose. You'd get more land with the farm, and it could be productive during part of the year," he suggested persuasively.

"Thank you, no, Lord Benedict."

"Oh, very well," the young man snapped as he swung himself onto his horse. "It's all her fault, anyway. When she does something obnoxious, you may change your mind, just to put her in her place. I shall be prepared to buy the land at any time, or exchange it for the farm, so you need only send me word." He gave an impatient nod, swung his horse about and galloped off, leaving Rushton with a very disagreeable taste in his mouth. Perhaps there had been some point to Miss Easterly-Cummings' insistence on the contract after all. Certainly Lord Benedict had no qualms about acting unscrupulously where she was concerned. Odd behavior, for a couple who had once been engaged. No, perhaps not, when one considered that they had not in the end allied themselves with one another. It would be fascinating, Rushton thought, to know the history of that romance.

Since his pair was prancing impatiently, Rushton returned the deed to the leather pocket in the curricle, and released the reins from the rails. Penrith would probably have returned from hunting by this time, and there were a number of matters Rushton intended to discuss with him. He could not stay on at Oak Park indefinitely, in spite of Pen's generous hospitality, and the Southwoods would be leaving for London in a few weeks, in any case. The best solution was to check out the accommodation at the local inn to see if he would be reasonably comfortable in a suite of rooms there for several months. The hunting season being near its conclusion, there would likely be rooms available, and decent stabling for his chestnuts and his hunters.

During the winter the village of Barton, serving the hunting community as it did, was prosperous. The Horse and Hound, set at the crossroads and opposite the green, was an ancient half-timbered hostelry which sprawled over a considerable area, its gables thrusting out in all directions, its leaded windows cheerfully distorting the view, and its chimney pots forever pouring billows of smoke into the gray afternoon sky. Rushton left his curricle and pair at the stables and entered through the old oak door with its brass fittings. Inside there was a buzz of activity, with laughter and voices issuing from the public rooms where welcome fires blazed on the hearths. The men grouped around were still in hunting coats, each with mug in hand trying to warm themselves while they recounted the day's runs.

"Did 'e wish to see the landlord?" asked a smiling serving girl.

"If I might," Rushton replied as he was accosted by an acquaintance who laughed, "You missed a spectacular day, Rushton. I had thought to see you in the field. Sir Penrith was there."

"A matter of business prevented me." Rushton wondered momentarily if Miss Easterly-Cummings could not have arranged for a time to conclude the sale that did not conflict with a day's hunting, but dismissed the thought as unworthy of himself. He was allowing the young lady to assume unnecessary proportions in his mind. If she had given a thought to the hour she appointed, it was probably only for Mr. Thomas' or Lord John's convenience.

"We had a run from Thorpe Trussels to Carr's Brigg, then to Scraptoft Spinneys, back over Life Hill and Adam's Gorse to Burrough Hill. Spanking pace the whole way; hardly lost sight of the fox the entire time. Never saw so many bullfinches and doubles, and, Lord, Assheton Smith took them all. Moreton's horse ran away with him, but he put a stop to that by covering the beast's eyes with his hands. Did the trick, I promise you. What a complete hand!"

Rushton smiled his approval, but changed the subject. "Are you staying here, Walters?"

"Yes, for another week at least."

"Find it comfortable, do you?"

"I've seldom stayed at a better inn in the country, but I thought you were at Oak Park."

"Oh, I am." Rushton watched as a ruddy-faced, middle-aged man steamed out of the kitchen area and down the passage toward him. "If you will excuse me, Walters, I would have a word with the landlord."

"Certainly. Perhaps you'll join us later for a round."

"Perhaps."

When Rushton had explained his requirements to Mr. Evans, the innkeeper suggested a suite of rooms at the far end of the building which would be available shortly. "Much quieter there, sir; more like a private house. Has its own parlor, bedroom and a room for your valet. And no skimping on the service, mind. The bell rings in the kitchen as they all do, and I won't tolerate any lagging on the way from my staff. Harder to keep the food warm, of course, but we've a right handy cart and everything covered. Or there are the private parlors off the hall here, if you should prefer. The rooms are empty right now. Would you like to see them?"

"Yes. You understand that I would require them for some time, while I oversee the construction of a house down the Ashfordby Road."

Mr. Evans' brow creased in a frown. "Had no idea there was any land down that way for sale. Mostly

Shalbrook land and Lord Benedict's. Pretty area, though."

"Yes."

"You'll be meeting Miss Easterly-Cummings," the innkeeper declared proudly, as though he were presenting the village treasure to Rushton. "Fine young lady. Made me a loan when we had a fire in this wing; no one else would, though I have no idea why not," he said indignantly. "Everyone knows the Horse and Hound is a flourishing hostelry. It was summertime, though, when business is not as brisk, but never mind. Miss Easterly-Cummings has a fine head for business and she knows that Joe Evans repays his debts. It's no small thanks to her that my children—all grown now, of course—have a village school for their own children. 'Tweren't a school at all when mine was little. Closest one was in Quorn, and times were harder then. Here's the suite—all fresh and modern, as you can see. Completely rebuilt after that fire I mentioned. Miss Easterly-Cummings suggested putting in the water closet, and I had my doubts at the time. After all, we have a perfectly good privvy in the yard, and it means I have to charge a little more for the rooms, you understand. But it's paid for itself a dozen times over, upon my word! You'd never credit what a demand there is for the conveniences."

Rushton, who would have taken the rooms sight unseen had he known they possessed such luxury, resented the fact that Miss Easterly-Cummings had her finger in this pie as well. Could she not mind her own business? There was a note of sarcasm in his voice as he eyed the purple draperies and murmured, "Perhaps she suggested the decoration of the rooms as well."

"Oh, no, sir, not on your life. Why, she's a lady, she is. Wouldn't interfere in the running of the Horse and Hound. My good wife is the one with the eye, I may tell you. Mrs. Evans said to me, 'Now with everything so spanking new, we should just see that the gentry has suitably rich draperies in that wing, Joe.' And you can see she's done herself proud. Everyone thinks of royalty, they think of purple, don't you see? Very clever of her, I thought, and the daughter is ever so handy with a needle that it was no sooner said than done. Well, what do you say?"

"I'll take the rooms," Rushton sighed, "in two weeks' time for a period of six months or so." He withdrew several bank notes from his pocket. "Will this suffice to hold them?"

Mr. Evans swallowed painfully as he accepted the money. "Ah, yes, that will be perfectly satisfactory, sir."

When Rushton entered the tap room at the Horse and Hound a few minutes later, he was immediately offered a mug of steaming punch and numerous accounts of the day's hunt. Thinking to at last escape any reference to the strange Miss Easterly-Cummings, he was brought up short as one of the gentlemen asked, "Do any of you know who that young lady we passed this morning was? The one in the scarlet mantelet trimmed with fur? Walters, you must remember her! You said at the time how striking she was. On the Ashfordby Road, in the phaeton. Had a lad with her, his arm in a sling. Didn't he ride with us a few days ago? I seem to recall . . ."

"Yes, Sir Penrith brought him; mounted him on Trafalgar. What was his name, Rushton?" Walters asked.

"Henry Forrester."

"Miss Forrester, then," the first man suggested. "Does she live around here, Rushton?"

"She's his cousin, not his sister."

As the others waited expectantly, Rushton stared meditatively at his mug.

Exasperated, Walters prodded him. "Well, what's her name? Does she live here? Is she married?"

"Her name is Easterly-Cummings and she owns a large estate on the Ashfordby Road. She is not married," Rushton murmured with a shudder.

"Ah, an heiress," Walters crowed. "Trust Rushton to meet an heiress. I tell you there is no justice in the world. It is Moreton or I who need an heiress, Rushton, not you. Besides, I thought you were all but leg-shackled to the Longmead beauty. Have a heart. Introduce us to Miss Easterly-Cummings."

"Sorry, gentlemen. I fear I am in no position to introduce you to her. You must apply to Sir Penrith. He's known her since she was in leading-strings, by all accounts." Rushton set down his empty mug and rose. Having no desire to discuss either Miss Longmead or Miss Easterly-Cummings, he excused himself.

JOURNAL. February 26, 1813. Purchased land on Ashfordby Road today from Miss E-C for one thousand pounds. Met Lord John Brindly, Cathford's brother, and agreed to use him as architect on hunting-box. He is to come to Oak Park on Friday to discuss the plans. An agreeable young man.

The saloon at Oak Park bore all the signs of a very successful gathering. Knots of people gathered in various spots about the room, and the murmur of conversation was interspersed with laughter, while a plentiful supply of cakes and biscuits wafted their fragrance on the air. If the gentlemen present found the affair of afternoon tea insipid, they gave no indication of boredom, and the ladies, ever in their glory at such a function, sparkled under the attention they received by being well outnumbered.

Lady Southwood, on hearing that Lord John Brindly was to be visiting Oak Park, conceived the happy inspiration of inviting Miss Easterly-Cummings and her cousin, as well as several of the neighborhood families, to tea, and suggested to her son that he enlarge the gathering by including some of his hunting cronies. "For it is certain to be a good experience for Cassandra, Pen, before dumping her on London Society, to have met some of your friends. Just an informal gathering, you know, but Cassandra will benefit from the advantage of being on her home ground. You must realize that it is hard for her, being the last, and both of her sisters having been so successful. She's a dear child and sure to be quite as well received as Maria and Jennifer, but you may be sure she has her doubts, and is alarmed at trying to live up to the model they've set her."

Although Penrith had been dubious as to the success of this venture, he studied the scene before him with satisfaction. His sister, as Lady Southwood had predicted, was not in the least shy, but appeared to be enjoying herself enormously, surrounded by Lord John Brindly, Mr. Walters and two of her neighborhood friends. Not for the first time, Penrith regretted the dearth of young men in the area. Aside from Lord Benedict, who had not been invited, Henry Forrester was the only lad within any reasonable distance of Oak Park, and Henry was no more than sixteen. Still, Cassandra seemed comfortable in the gathering, with no sign of intimidation to daunt her lively conversation.

In yet another group, Henry Forrester listened avidly to Mr. Moreton describe his stroke of genius in handling his runaway horse. The tale was obviously directed to his cousin in hopes of stirring her admiration for the young man's intrepid horsemanship, and Miss Easterly-Cummings appeared duly impressed. Since Rushton had not informed his host of Selina's more conventional dress at the time of the signing of the deed, Penrith had been delighted to see her enter the room in a dove gray dress which, if not the height of fashion, became her. She was the object of considerable curiosity amongst his hunting friends, who found it difficult to believe that she was content to remain sedately settled in the country, unmarried, rich and attractive.

About Lady Southwood were gathered the other matrons and several of Penrith's friends. Rushton and Penrith moved between the groups, and once again Penrith admired his friend's ease in mingling with the diverse elements in the room. Without a pause he could discuss hunting, Lord Byron's latest cantos, Wellington's retreat to Portugal, or any household matter the older ladies happened to be mulling over. In fact, the only difficulty Penrith could see at all was Rushton's stiffness with Selina. Only the necessary greetings were exchanged between the two, and those with a constraint which surprised Penrith. He was given no time to consider this circumstance, however, as a late arrival was announced.

"Ah, Geoffrey. I thought we were going to be denied your company," Penrith remarked cheerfully as he escorted the gentleman to his mother, and then introduced him to the others. When he presented Selina to Mr. Haslett, he experienced his second surprise of the afternoon.

"Miss Easterly-Cummings and I are acquainted," Haslett announced as he raised her hand to his lips.

"Yes," Selina murmured.

"It has been some years, however. In Bath, in '09 or '10, I believe," the young man continued relentlessly.

"In '10, I am sure," Selina replied, her eyes calmly taking in his exquisitely tailored blue coat and gray pantaloons. "We did not go to Bath in '09."

"I didn't, either, come to think of it," Mr. Haslett said with a grin. "But I've been back every year since. You had a young cousin, and a mouse of a companion, as I recall."

"Your memory is exceptional. I doubt that Henry's is as accurate, Mr. Haslett. My cousin, Henry Forrester." As Selina watched them shake hands, aware that Henry had not the slightest recollection of the man, she caught a look of astonishment on Mr. Rushton's face, and she had to suppress a desire to laugh. She knew that Mr. Rushton could not imagine how the dowdy Miss Easterly-Cummings should ever have come into contact with the dapper Mr. Haslett, but she could tell also, from the look on the newcomer's face, that he was about to tell his assembled audience. In an effort to forestall him, Selina offered her most charming smile and said, "Are you in the neighborhood for the hunting, sir?"

"I've been riding mostly with the Cottesmore, but Penrith suggested I stay at Oak Park for a few days and have a taste of the Quorn. I hope you will allow me to call on you."

Selina knew a moment's hesitation, but answered smoothly enough. "Certainly. Sir Penrith can direct you."

"Tomorrow afternoon?" Haslett pursued with twinkling eyes.

"Unfortunately I can recall no prior engagement," Selina retorted.

"Now I have found you, I have no intention of letting you disappear again."

"I never disappear from Shalbrook, Mr. Haslett."

"Good. I shall look forward to reminiscing with you."

As the conversation became more general, Selina allowed her attention to be captured once more by Mr. Moreton, but she was aware of Mr. Haslett's teasing, and Mr. Rushton's mystified gazes upon her. Perhaps they were not, after all, as like as she had thought. Oh, they were both good-looking, with strongly defined features and a decided air of authority, but there the resemblance ended. While Mr. Haslett was light and airy, almost to frivolity, Mr. Rushton was heavy and grave, almost to sternness. But Selina had little doubt that they both led useless lives, after their own fashion. Certainly neither of them could compare with Sir Penrith's good humor and open-heartedness, nor with his humane outlook or candidness. It was a great pity, she thought ruefully, that she was not in the least attracted to Sir Penrith. There must be innate rewards in holding a worthy man in high regard, whether or not he returned your affection. Obviously I have a defective emotional temperament, she mused as she donned the scarlet mantelet to depart; first there was Lord Benedict, then Mr. Haslett, and now...

JOURNAL. February 28. Gave Lord John a list of my requirements for the hunting-box, together with my ideas for its design. He is to get back to me in about a week with some preliminary sketches. Haslett has arrived.

TEN

Henry watched impatiently as Mr. Haslett lifted his cousin's hand to his lips. It was a wonder to him that ladies tolerated that sort of thing, especially when Haslett had already made a most handsome leg to Selina. What more could one ask than such an elegant gesture? Not that Selina had asked Haslett to kiss her hand, of course. As a matter of fact, she had withdrawn it as quickly as possible without positive rudeness. Henry determined on the spot that *he* would never subject a lady to such silly treatment.

"Servant, Forrester," Haslett said, turning to him. "I wouldn't have recognized you from when we met in Bath. You've shot up like a weed."

"Yes, sir," mumbled Henry with a flush of embarrassment.

"And it seems that Bath has done wonders for you. I remember ..."

Selina interposed to say, "Won't you sit down, Mr. Haslett?"

Haslett smiled down at her. "I had hoped to convince you to come driving with me, Miss Easterly-Cummings. We are having our first taste of spring weather, and it would be the greatest pity to miss it."

The relief in Henry's eyes did not escape his cousin, and though she would have preferred not to have a tête-à-tête with Mr. Haslett, she immediately agreed. "I won't be above an hour, Henry."

"How can you be sure?" Haslett quizzed her.

"We were only acquainted for a few weeks, sir. I

shouldn't think we would have more than an hour's worth of conversation between us," she laughed.

"Thirty-five days, to be exact, and I can squeeze well over an hour out of that, to say nothing of the years in between. Don't be alarmed if we're a little longer, Forrester."

Selina regarded him skeptically. "If I remember your driving correctly, Henry had best send out a search party if we're gone very long."

"My driving has improved with age, as you have," Haslett responded smilingly. "Come, Miss Easterly-Cummings, we are wasting precious minutes . . . and my horses will be very cross with me if you don't honor them with your presence."

Such foolishness, ever mingled with flirtatiousness, was precisely how Selina remembered him. Probably it was why he had been so appealing when she met him, a delightful change from the cares which weighed her down at the time. Nothing was of any importance or seriousness to him; life was a meal to be tasted to the full—the delicacies enjoyed and the pits discarded. "I'll just get my wrap."

Selina could see no marked improvement in his driving, and the bays were not particularly well matched, but the day was indeed unseasonably fine and she had spent the morning over her books, so she leaned back against the padded seat to enjoy herself.

"You must direct me," Haslett said as he approached the gates. "I am not yet familiar with your neighborhood, though I intend to become so."

"Take your right, then."

"Will we pass the land you sold to Rushton?"

"No, that is in the other direction."

"I should like to see it."

"As you wish. The road leads only to the village, however."

When they arrived at the vale, Haslett drew in the horses and sat contemplating the land for a moment. "Yes, very nice. Too bad I didn't see it first. The hunting was excellent this morning, and I wouldn't mind having a box in this area." He gave her a speaking glance, which she attempted to ignore as he inexpertly turned the horses to retrace their path. After he had them trotting easily on the straightaway, he asked abruptly, "Why did you leave Bath without letting me know? And why did you give me the impression that you lived in Hampshire?"

"I never said I lived in Hampshire."

"Oh, I know you didn't, but you made every attempt to have me think you did. I thought we got on very well together. Was I wrong?"

Selina studied her hands before answering. "It was a most enjoyable time for me, Mr. Haslett. Without your company, I doubt that I could have convinced Mrs. Morrow to attend so many lectures, and concerts, and plays."

"Nor the Assembly Rooms; don't forget those. Pity we didn't waltz in those days. I should like to waltz with you."

"I don't know how."

"Don't tell me they still frown on it in the countryside! It's all the rage in London. Even the old fogies are wearing down, what with dancing parties in the mornings to learn it. You'd be very good, you know."

"Thank you."

"Miss Easterly-Cummings, did I . . . do something to upset you in Bath? Say something which you took amiss?" He glanced at her, his frown half real, half mocking.

"I don't know how to answer that, Mr. Haslett. It seemed wisest to end our acquaintance when our holiday was ended." Selina did not meet his eyes.

"I tried to find you, you know. Stopped in to see my friend Wetherby in Hampshire and asked if he knew any family named Easterly-Cummings. I never thought to ask Penrith. Well, it stands to reason I didn't expect you to be in Leicestershire when you only spoke of Alton and Winchester." Drawing in the horses to a walk, he eyed her reproachfully. "Have you ever been to Alton or Winchester?"

"No, but I had a friend in Bath who lived near Four Marks." Selina made a nervous gesture with her hands. "I'm still not quite sure why I did that, Mr. Haslett. There were personal reasons; I never meant to deceive you, just to obscure my identity. Being in Bath, well, I could be anonymous for a change. No one knew me, you see. Sometimes it is very trying living in a small community such as this where everyone knows your business. I hope you won't hold it against me."

"Not if you will allow me to take up where we left off," he replied, coaxingly.

"You don't mean that, Mr. Haslett. That was years ago, and people change, times change. That summer in Bath is a very pleasant memory, and should stay that way."

He regarded her thoughtfully, and then laughed. "I shall never forget poor Henry in his Bath chair coming rolling down the hill at me with you in hot pursuit, and your mousy companion having hysterics. It was a sight one sees only once in a lifetime!"

After she had shared in his laughter, Selina remarked, "I'm glad you didn't relate it at Sir Penrith's, though. Henry has never seen it in quite the same light as you and I, as you might expect. Nor would I if any harm had come to him. You were very quick-witted."

"I had to be to avoid being run down," he protested, still laughing. "By far the most stupendous introduction I have ever had to a lady. Your cousin walks very well now, I noticed."

"Yes, there is only the merest trace of a limp. He is very fortunate."

"Your companion is not with you any longer?"

"No, she left several years ago, but she joins Henry and me when we go on holiday most years."

"Where do you go now that you have abandoned Bath?"

"Oh, to Tunbridge Wells, or Margate, or one of the other watering holes."

"And you never come to London?"

"I haven't been there since I was a child." Selina watched a tiny yellow-hammer winging through the branches of a barren tree, its flash of color enlivening the scene. "Perhaps one day I shall go again."

"You should, you know. Bath is nothing compared to London. Every night during the Season there are two or three balls or routs to attend, and the theater and concerts are infinitely better. Lady Southwood or Penrith could procure you vouchers for Almack's, and though it is a little dull, you meet absolutely everyone from the *ton,* sooner or later. I understand Miss Southwood is to have her come-out this Season, so you would know someone."

"No, no, Mr. Haslett. I said I might one day go there. I have not the least intention of going this spring!"

"But why not?" he asked, astounded. "It is the perfect time for you to go, can't you see? Your friends will be in London, and I shall be there to escort you about." He took her hand and pressed it. "There is no need to take up where we left off, my dear ma'am. We shall begin all over again."

Selina shook her head. "No, Mr. Haslett. I am not going to London this spring. There is more than enough for me to do here, and I have no desire to leave Shalbrook."

"Then I suppose I shall have to take lodgings in Leicester or Barton so that I may see you," he said mournfully. "And I had so hoped to enjoy London after a very dull winter."

"You are absurd, sir! I would not for the world keep you from London and I feel sure you have no intention of denying yourself your pleasures there. Am I to be like the trout that got away? You have exaggerated my importance from the very fact of having misplaced me. Take your hunting instincts to the fields, Mr. Haslett, for they are misguided in being aimed at me."

"Ah, you think this is just sport, do you, Miss Easterly-Cummings?" he asked sternly. "I'll have you know I had every intention of offering for you in Bath."

"I know."

Her voice came so softly that he dropped his hands in surprise and the horses took off at a spanking pace. Several minutes elapsed before he had them under control once more, and his decision to bring them to a halt was perhaps wise in view of the following discussion.

"You mean, you thought from my behavior that my intentions were serious?"

Selina shook her head and forced herself to meet his eyes. "I heard you tell someone."

"But I didn't . . ." Haslett broke off in confusion, the dawning of enlightenment in his eyes.

Once again studying her hands, Selina explained, "I was often restless during those days in Bath. Henry's progress was so erratic; Mrs. Morrow was nagging at me to stay on indefinitely; I had sustained a decided disappointment but a few months previously. Even the household was topsy-turvy, with the footman coming down with a stomach disorder and the housemaid called home to her sick mother. And you were indeed acting as though your intentions were serious."

Selina shifted her gaze to the stream that ran along the side of the road, gently lapping around the rocks and gurgling against the banks. "I took to walking in the mornings. There was no need to be accompanied; no one was about at that hour. I have always thought best when I walked, and I had so many things to decide. Would it indeed be beneficial to Henry to stay there? Was Shalbrook too damp for Mrs. Morrow? If you were to ask me to marry you, did I want to accept? Oh, any number of things. One morning I wandered as far afield as Charles Street."

When Selina looked at him he shrugged his shoulders helplessly. "You were leaving a small house there. As I entered the street I saw you kiss a pretty, cheerful-looking girl and heard you tell her that you would be back. I was embarrassed; I didn't want you to see me, so I slipped into a doorway. The rest of your conversation I could not avoid overhearing, and certainly it was most instructive."

Haslett was casting his mind back frantically to the day she spoke of, trying to remember exactly what he had said. It was too long ago, too many mistresses past. "It wouldn't have mattered to you and me," he protested.

Selina almost laughed. "That is exactly what you told *her*. You were reassuring her that, although you were off to ask me to marry you, it need make no difference to your understanding with her."

"Well, that's quite true, Miss Easterly-Cummings. I mean, they are very separate things, a wife and a mistress, and needn't interfere with one another in any way."

He was so sincerely adamant in his argument that Selina felt more like crying than laughing now. With an effort she stilled the agitated movement of her hands. "So I am given to understand. Foolish of me, but I cannot see it quite that way, Mr. Haslett. And, being of such an eccentric turn of mind, I found it easier to disappear than to face you. Obviously we were not suited, after all."

"Well, I ... Of course, one's wife doesn't usually know about one's mistresses, I suppose. Still ..." He dangled the whip against the traces, drawing it back and forth while he thought. As though it clinched his argument, he finally blurted, "But everyone does it."

"Do they? How very interesting. Why?"

"Because ..." Haslett looked at her sharply to see if she was roasting him, but could find no trace of merriment in the frank brown eyes. "It's probably not a matter I should discuss with you."

"No, but I really am curious, Mr. Haslett."

Her companion was not in his element. By nature he was light-hearted and enjoyed nothing more than teasing and flirting, and the present situation did not allow of either. He could not believe that he owed her an explanation of his own conduct, but then, she had not requested one. All she asked was to understand why a man needed both a wife and a mistress. Something about her eyes held him as it had in those days in Bath. Alongside the strength and openness, there was a vulnerability which somehow placed an obligation on him. He would answer this one question, and then he wouldn't see her again. He wasn't that great a fool!

"Gently-bred ladies are too ... fragile to be ... imposed on all the time. Most wives are willing to do their duty, but they don't want to be constantly ... bothered." Oh, hell, obviously he was a fool to have tried to explain this. "Ladies just want to run a house and be social and all. Oh, and they don't want to be increasing all the time, either."

"And mistresses do?"

"Do what?"

"Want to be increasing all the time and constantly bothered."

"Well, dammit, Miss Easterly-Cummings, they are paid for it! That's to say..."

Selina could not resist laughing at his dismayed expression. "No, never mind, Mr. Haslett. I believe I understand what you are saying, though I find it difficult to believe you are entirely correct. We won't discuss the matter further."

Gratefully, he set his horses in motion once more, taking the first opportunity to head them back in the direction of Shalbrook, convinced that he should have listened to his first instinct and not tried to explain anything to her. It all came from heeding those distressing eyes, but he would not be caught in that trap again. There were any number of flirtatious ladies in London who could not cajole him, or trick him, or whatever it was, into doing one whit that he did not wish to do. He had had a very lucky escape in Bath, he told himself, and he was not going to make the mistake of staying in Miss Easterly-Cummings' vicinity one moment longer than necessary.

"Have you known Sir Penrith long?" Selina asked to break the silence.

"Several years. I see him in London frequently, at White's or Manton's shooting gallery, though he don't go in much for the Fancy. Boxing, you know. Rushton now, he's often at Jackson's, sparring with someone or other. Has a very powerful right, too. But he says he's not going to London for the Season."

"Why not?"

"Because of the hunting-box, he says, but I think from the way Penrith keeps avoiding the subject of Miss Longmead, that she's shown him the door."

"Shown who the door?" Selina asked, confused.

"Rushton."

"Was she his mistress?" Selina asked, with a brave attempt at appearing sophisticated.

"Lord, no! Whatever gave you that idea?" he asked, astonished. "Oh, I see. You don't know her, of course. Quality," he provided succinctly.

"Then you think she has refused his offer of marriage?"

"I can't be sure he offered for her at all, but the bets were on that he would and that she'd accept. Now he's not going to London. What do you make of that?"

"I haven't the slightest idea, and I am sure it does not concern me," she answered faintly.

"No, well, you don't even know her, so of course it wouldn't. Beautiful girl, but no dowry to speak of, I hear. Still, that needn't matter to Rushton. She's from an excellent family, though I don't care in the least for her mother, or her father, for that matter. Forever putting on airs, and only the junior branch of an earl's family. The way they act you'd think they were royalty itself." He offered her a sheepish grin. "So far today I have annoyed, distressed and embarrassed you, and now I seem intent on boring you, too. Do forgive me. I shall tell you instead of the most unusual dinner party I attended a week ago, for it cannot fail to amuse you."

Selina settled back to allow his light chatter to wash over her. There was no denying that he could be diverting when he chose, which he usually did, and there would be time enough when she returned home to consider the information he had imparted. Considering her own standing with Mr. Rushton, it should not make the least difference, in any case. Unfortunately, it did.

ELEVEN

"I don't understand what is happening here," Rushton said as he drew his finger in a circle over an area of the sketch Lord John had laid before him.

"Let me come to that in a moment if I may, Mr. Rushton. I have sited the house so that these three rooms will have the southern exposure, and get light for the majority of each day. Perhaps I should tell you that I have been greatly influenced by Mr. Nash in some respects, like his Cronkhill villa, where he attempts to catch the morning light to great advantage. Your entry would be a gallery to the central hall with a fireplace and stairs to the first floor. The two major rooms—dining and drawing—are octagonal in shape, providing an excellent basis for massive beams. Between the two would be a library/gun room with entry from each, and a shared fireplace with the dining room. Beyond, running along this corridor are the kitchens and servant quarters. I think stone walls at the corners, where they are necessary, but with stucco between to simplify the building. Otherwise, it will look like a ridiculously small fortress."

"You haven't explained this area," Rushton protested, tapping the spot he had indicated previously.

Lord John grinned engagingly. "That is something rather unique, I think, though I have done it once before, and most effectively. But first, let me explain about the first floor. The master bedchamber is just here above the dining room, with the dressing room over the library. There are two further bedchambers over the drawing room, with lesser guest chambers along the corridor above the kitchens and so forth. The sharp slope of the roof over these areas will make the bedchambers considerably smaller than their lower counterparts, but more than adequate, I think. Now," he said dramatically, "I shall explain about the verandah."

"Verandah? Surely you are jesting. I intend to use the hunting-box almost exclusively in the winter."

"Precisely. That is why I have enclosed it entirely in glass, with the roof providing a balcony above. Have you a greenhouse or succession houses at Farnside, Mr. Rushton?"

"Yes."

"Then you understand the principle on which I am working. The room will have the feel of being out-of-doors, and yet will be heated by the morning sun and through most of the day, sited as it is. With such an expanse of glass your library and both major rooms will not be blocked from any view, but will have glass doors opening onto it. From here stairs lead down to a terrace when the weather is finer."

"But surely it will look very strange!"

"Not at all. I think perhaps Miss Easterly-Cummings thought so at first, too, but she is delighted with the results."

"Where in God's name did she put such a thing at Shalbrook?"

"Oh, not in the manor house. When we built a house for Mr. Sands, her estate manager, we used the idea. The Sands children were grown and they no longer needed the size dwelling they had inhabited, but another family did, so Miss Easterly-Cummings commissioned me to design him a new residence. In talking with Mr. Sands I found he has an interest in rare plants, and the idea of incorporating a greenhouse occurred to me. His house is not so large as yours will be, but I see no reason, with your requirements, that a larger space would not accept of the same solution. Not that you will use it as a nursery for plants! But when it was finished, it made a most remarkable portion of the house, and he tells me that it is his favorite room, even aside from his pineapples and such."

"But what would I use the room for?"

"Almost anything. A sitting room with a distinct difference, an outdoor spot enclosed from the weather, a conservatory, a reading room. It will serve the additional purpose of an entry from the grounds where it won't matter if you track snow and mud—not a light consideration at this time of year." Lord John watched his companion with eager anticipation.

"Hmm. I don't know. The house is sufficient without it, as far as I am concerned. I like the design very well, and these elevations would look equally promising without the 'verandah.'"

"But you would lose the balcony above," Lord John suggested. "Although the clearing is on a slight rise, the ground floor offers no view over the trees, which the balcony would."

"So would the windows in the bedchambers," Rushton reminded him. Lord John looked crestfallen, and Rushton shook his head ruefully. "Is it so important to you, then?"

"Not to say important, sir, but I think you would regret a decision to omit it. Could I suggest something? Have a look at Mr. Sands' house and see what you think. If you are still against the idea after that, well, there is no reason to pursue it."

His eagerness and the hopeful light in his eyes caused Rushton to agree, albeit reluctantly. Seeing Mr. Sands' house would necessitate an interview with Miss Easterly-Cummings, he felt sure, a circumstance which he did not view with pleasure. "Very well, Lord John, I shall have a look at the house and send you word of my decision. Now, about the plumbing and some kind of heating system ..."

Selina set down the note from Mr. Rushton and stared vacantly at the portrait of her father on the opposite wall. There was no reason she need see him; he could as easily have Mrs. Sands show him about her own house. Yes, that would be best. She rose and went in search of Mr. Sands, who assured her that his wife would be more than happy to show Mr. Rushton about the house that afternoon. He would just tell her when he went home for his mid-day meal.

Back in the drawing room, Selina drew a sheet of writing paper toward her but hesitated before she dipped the pen in the standish. If Lord John had suggested that Rushton see the house, possibly he counted on Selina's enthusiasm to persuade his client. If he did, he was wrong, Selina decided with a frown. More likely Mr. Rushton would choose to do precisely the opposite of what she suggested, simply because he was annoyed with her. She let out a long breath and began to pen her reply to his note.

Attempting to put any thought of him out of her mind, she set herself the task of sorting through the old papers in four boxes in the library, deciding whether they were old enough that they might be clearly marked and removed to the attics. From the housekeeper she borrowed a smock which easily enveloped her twice over, and began working her way through the piles of paper, dusty with age and boring beyond description. As she finished each stack, she relegated it to its proper place, and brushed back the tendrils of brown hair which clung to her forehead, leaving smudges on her forehead and cheeks.

"You look a proper sight," Henry remarked as he entered the room and spied her seated amidst the stacks of papers on the floor. "I was just coming in from a ride when I saw Mr. Rushton and persuaded him to have tea with us."

"Oh, Henry, how could you?" Selina moaned as she made a feeble effort to dust her hands on the smock. "You knew I was to be working on the papers this afternoon."

"All the more reason to give you a break," he said cheerfully.

Rushton, who had overheard the whole while he handed his hat and gloves to the footman, now appeared in the doorway to take in the scene. "Perhaps I should excuse myself, Miss Easterly-Cummings. You do not seem in any position to receive guests."

The obvious twitch at the corners of his lips made

Selina wish to box his ears and she said crossly, "Now you are here, you may as well sit down. I will have to change, of course." She attempted to struggle through the disorder to her feet, and Rushton with two lengthy strides reached her side and pulled her up by one dirty hand. "Thank you. If you will excuse me for a few minutes...."

"No, no, I won't stay. Forrester was a trifle rash in extending his invitation, I fear."

"This is Henry's home, too, Mr. Rushton, and he may invite whomever he chooses to tea. I needn't join you at all, and will just see that the tea tray is sent in," she remarked coldly as she retreated to the door.

"I say, Selina, no need to go off in a huff." Henry eyed his cousin warily but she had her back to him and did not answer. "We'll wait for you."

"Please don't bother. You might be more comfortable in the drawing room, however. Then I may get on with my work." Selina slipped out the door before anything further could be said.

Embarrassed, Henry turned to Mr. Rushton and shrugged. "Women. There's no understanding them. You mustn't take her amiss, though. She's just annoyed with me for bringing someone in when she wasn't looking her best. Though I don't see how she could mind," he mused, more to himself than his companion, "when it is only recently that she has put aside those ugly dresses and that ridiculous cap."

"I won't stay, Forrester, but let it be a lesson to you. It is never wise to bring home a guest without telling a woman first. I should have known better than to accept, come to that."

When Rushton made to leave the room, Henry said firmly, "No, I have invited you for tea and Selina didn't mean for you to go. I was hoping..."

"Yes?"

Henry shifted from one foot to the other. "I don't know anything about boxing," he blurted. "When you were here to tea before, you and Sir Penrith discussed a prizefight, and there was some mention of a sort of school in London where a fellow could learn to box."

"There is. A retired pugilist teaches those who are interested."

"Yes, well, do you think I could find someone to teach me? I know I have a limp, but it's not much, you see. I...I think I could... No, I suppose not. Some things you just have to be whole for," he said bitterly.

Rushton pursed his lips thoughtfully. "Can you dance?"

"Dance?"

"Are you nimble enough to do the steps of the cotillion and the contredanse?"

"Of course. Selina has taught me all the steps and says I do very well. Not the new one—the waltz. She has never learned it. But I have no trouble with the others. It's easier than walking, actually."

"Then I feel sure you could learn to box, Forrester, if you wanted to."

Henry's face lit with delight. "You do? Is it like dancing, then?"

"Not exactly," Rushton laughed, "but it's wise to move quickly on your feet if you don't want someone landing you a facer."

"I see. But do you think I could find someone to teach me?" he asked eagerly.

"I can teach you."

"Would you? No, I could not impose on you that way. Selina would have my head! But if you knew of someone in the neighborhood... Or perhaps Sir Penrith would know someone."

"Nonsense. It would help keep me in practice. How is your arm healing?" Rushton asked, noticing for the first time that the sling had disappeared.

"Famously. In another week I shall be riding, I feel sure. It's not my writing arm," he offered with a grimace, "so Selina has kept me at my lessons. Couldn't even get some benefit from it."

"A regular martinet, your cousin," Rushton suggested.

Henry flushed. "No, no, she's a great gun. Just a little out of sorts these days, what with one thing and another."

"Hmm, yes. Here, let me show you the proper stance.

We won't put any strain on your arm. I'll just show you how to hold your hands and where to put your feet."

Returning to continue her sorting of the papers, Selina found her cousin and Mr. Rushton posed as though in combat, and she stopped on the threshold, dumbfounded. Engrossed in their lesson, the two men did not notice her advent and were startled when she exclaimed, "For God's sake, Mr. Rushton, he's only a boy!"

Henry immediately swung around to face her, his countenance comical in its anguish. "Good Lord, Selina, he isn't fighting with me! He's just showing me how to box."

"Well, of course he is," she retorted with heavy sarcasm. "Any sensible man would naturally teach a lad with a broken arm how to box. What better time could there possibly be for such instruction? Perhaps he also teaches his dogs tricks while they are suffering from some ailment. It is a novel prescription, I must admit, and I will certainly suggest it to Morris the very next time I am in the stables. Your tea is in the drawing room." In the astonished silence which followed her outburst the slamming of the library door sounded infinitely louder than it might at any other time. At the end of her patience with everyone and everything, Selina fled to her room.

Although his jaw tightened almost imperceptibly, Rushton gave no other sign of discomposure, while Henry struck his good fist on a table and muttered, "Damn! Now I've gone and upset her again."

"Shall we have our tea? I don't think your cousin intends to join us."

When there was a hesitant tap on her door an hour later, Selina did not respond. Henry called to her and she forced herself to tell him as calmly as she could that she was resting and would see him at dinner. Her throat ached as she heard his uneven footsteps retreat slowly down the hall. Analyzing her upset did nothing to relieve it. To be sure, she had been distressed to have a guest when she was so disheveled. And it had added to her turmoil that she had read the amusement in Rushton's eyes. Then to misinterpret the scene she had come on in the library was embarrassing, but she could think of no excuse for that gentleman's behavior. Was he so annoyed with her that he would purposely risk injuring Henry to get even with her? Selina had judged him a careless hedonist, perhaps, but not a deliberately cruel man. Where there were no illusions to shatter, he still managed to shake her to her very core. Exhausted by the continual emotional upheavals, she finally slept, to be awakened by her maid only in time to dress for dinner.

Henry was pacing restlessly about the drawing room when she entered, but stopped abruptly and came over to take her hands. "Are you feeling all right, Selina? I have never known you to rest in the afternoon before."

"I feel better now."

"You mustn't be angry with Mr. Rushton, Selina," he said urgently as he released her hands and watched her seat herself. "I was asking him about boxing and whether I could learn, and he offered to teach me. Of course I said that wouldn't do, but he said it would keep him in practice. We weren't really doing anything strenuous, I promise you. He was just showing me how to stand and what to do with my hands."

"I cannot see why you shouldn't wait until your arm is healed."

"Certainly I will, but he offered to start now. It didn't hurt my arm in the least."

"Is boxing something you have taken an interest in, Henry?"

"Oh, yes. All the sporting fellows have a hand at it these days, and Rushton said my limp needn't handicap me. He said if I could dance, I could box."

"Did he? I fail to see the relationship between the two."

"It's a matter of being agile enough on your feet, don't you see? You have always said that I dance well enough, and I have never doubted you. Between us, we have always been honest about my limp, and I trusted you spoke no more than the truth." He regarded her anxiously.

"You dance as well as anyone without a limp, Henry," she replied firmly. "And better than most, I dare say, but surely there is a difference in the movement of a dance and the jumping about you must do in boxing."

"Rushton thought not. And it's not jumping, Selina! If I find I can't do it, then I shall just forget the whole thing." A frown creased his forehead. "You won't forbid me to learn, will you?"

"No, of course not. You may do as you wish, but I cannot think Mr. Rushton will have the time to see to your instruction properly. Perhaps we could find someone else in the neighborhood."

"He was quite sincere, Selina, and I never asked him if he would. He simply offered. I don't think there *is* anyone else in the neighborhood who could teach me."

"We'll ask around," she suggested with an attempt at casualness. "It can't do any harm. Once Mr. Rushton is started on his hunting-box, his days will be heavily occupied, my dear."

"If you wish, but I like him, Selina. He treats me as an equal, just as Sir Penrith does."

"I should hope so," she murmured as McDonough arrived to announce dinner.

TWELVE

Selina gave specific instructions the next morning that if Mr. Rushton came to call, she was to be denied. "If he asks for Mr. Henry, then you will have to check with him, but I am not at home to Mr. Rushton." The surprised look she received from McDonough she ignored and proceeded to the library to finish her task there. She was debating the importance of an old receipt when Henry entered, and she smiled up at him. "Do you suppose I will need to refer to this bill for the range? We have never had the least trouble with it and it is entered in the books, but I can never seem to remember the shopowner's name when I try."

"Why did you have yourself denied to Mr. Rushton, Selina?"

"I have no wish to see him, Henry, and I am very busy. Has he called?"

"Yes, he wished to speak to you, but McDonough told him you were not receiving, so he asked for me. Rushton would be willing to wait if you have to change or anything, but he's anxious to see you."

"I am not anxious to see him, Henry."

"He said he wished to discuss a facet of Lord John's design with you."

"Pooh. Mr. Rushton doesn't give a farthing for my opinion. He has seen the Sands' house, and there is an end to it. I won't see him, Henry."

"What the devil has gotten into you, Selina? I thought you were interested in promoting Lord John's career."

"And I tell you I can do no more than I have. If you will excuse me, I really must finish with these papers."

"I have never known you to be so stubborn. What harm can it do to see him?" Henry drew a hand distractedly through his hair, a pained expression on his face.

"Have you perhaps told Mr. Rushton that you would get me to see him?"

"Well, yes, I rather did."

"You must stop putting me in these positions, Henry. It is all very well to be generous with your own time, but you have no right to dispense with mine as you see fit. I have a great deal to do, and am not willing to waste time on every Tom, Dick and Harry who comes along."

"It's not as though you didn't know Mr. Rushton," he grumbled. "I can see your denying yourself to Mr. Walters or Mr. Moreton, for you've only met them at Sir Penrith's. But you introduced Rushton to Lord John, and you sold him the land, and he has been very kind to me."

"To *you,* Henry. Not to me. If you can think of a way which does not involve me, to repay him for his kindnesses, by all means indulge yourself in doing so. You may tell him I highly recommend that he incorporate the glassed-in room in his hunting-box. Unfortunately, that will only make him reject the idea, but it will be his loss." Selina purposefully turned back to her papers. "I shall see you at luncheon, Henry."

Defeated, her cousin turned on his heels and stalked out of the room. He had not previously been aware of the animosity between Selina and Rushton, but now that he looked back he could see that they had not hit it off from the start. Reproaching himself for being thoughtless, Henry still felt a bit annoyed with Selina for her implacable stand. What difference would it make to her to answer a few questions from Rushton? Selina was, after all, very enthusiastic about Lord John's designs.

On entering his study, where he found Rushton patiently waiting by the window, Henry moved awkwardly, as he always did when he was embarrassed.

"I . . . I'm afraid Selina is busy, Mr. Rushton, and cannot see you. She did tell me that she highly recommended the glassed-in room."

His visitor's face remained expressionless. "I see. My thanks for approaching her for me, Forrester. I shall take my leave. No, no, there's no need to see me out. I know my way. When your arm is fully healed, we'll have another lesson."

Henry nodded mutely and watched as the door closed behind his visitor. Now he would probably never learn to box, he thought mutinously, and all because of Selina. Rushton might pretend to overlook her rudeness, but Henry felt sure such a slight would weigh with a proud man. It was a very small thing he had asked of his cousin, and surely she knew that it was important to him if he had asked her. Perhaps he would not take luncheon with her, after all.

In the hall Rushton did not turn toward the entry as might have been expected. Instead he walked toward the rear of the house where the library was located, and tapped on the door. There was the possibility that Miss Easterly-Cummings was elsewhere in the house, but he thought not. Those stacks of paper yesterday would likely require a great deal of time to sort. Her impatient voice called, "Yes?"

Since he had no intention of waiting to be bid to enter, sure that he would receive no such invitation, he opened the door, stepped into the room and closed the door behind himself. She glanced up, an annoyed frown on her brow, and stared at him speechlessly.

"I realize you are busy, Miss Easterly-Cummings, but I really feel that I must have a word with you." He strolled over to where she sat on the floor and offered her his hand to draw her to her feet.

"I will not see you, Mr. Rushton. Kindly leave my house immediately." As her hands gripped firmly in her lap, she fixed him with a cold glare.

"There are several things which need to be said, and I will not let your stubbornness deter me from saying them." Since she apparently had no intention of rising, he carelessly seated himself on the floor across from her. "If you are angry that I was showing Henry the

122

proper boxing stance yesterday, let me assure you that I was not taxing his broken arm. Surely he told you so himself."

Selina continued to ignore him, ostentatiously lifting another paper from the box to peruse its contents.

"Do you object to your cousin learning to box, Miss Easterly-Cummings?"

There was no reply as Selina discarded the paper and withdrew another.

"There is nothing more reprehensible than watching a woman crush the spirit out of a lad Henry's age," Rushton said provocatively.

Startled eyes met his for a moment and the color rose in Selina's face, but she made no reply.

"It is obvious that your cousin spends most of his time studying. At his age he should be exploring more than just books, Miss Easterly-Cummings. He has never played cricket, or seen a prizefight, or been to the races. I dare say you would faint if you found he had visited a cockpit. He is mad for hunting, and yet his recent experience was the first time he had ever joined the field. And I have no doubt you will point to his broken arm the next time he indicates a desire to go again, and beg him to remember how dangerous a sport it is."

Goaded at last, Selina said coldly, "You know nothing of the matter, Mr. Rushton. I find it absurd that you should take such an interest in Henry when you have just met him. He has lived here for five years and has had the run of Shalbrook. He shoots and rides, takes an interest in the farming, drives a phaeton, any number of things. To be sure it is a pity there are no young men of his age in the neighborhood, but we make an annual visit to one of the watering places where he quickly forms friendships with his contemporaries. I do not unduly restrict his movements, and in fact did not protest his decision to go hunting. He's only sixteen, for God's sake. There is plenty of time for him to do the exploring of which you speak. Just leave us in peace."

"You would like that, wouldn't you? To continue to hold sway over him? To keep him like a lapdog for your

123

entertainment? I have seen it happen before, Miss Easterly-Cummings. I watched powerlessly as my aunt stifled all the spirit in my cousin. As a boy he was full of life, forever up to a lark, but after his father died she tied him to her apron-strings and never let him go. Even now she is dead, he does not break loose. The habits of a lifetime are too well ingrained. He is a pathetic case, and I should not like to see your cousin follow in his footsteps."

"Your reasoning is ludicrous, Mr. Rushton," she snapped. "I have no intention of stifling Henry's exuberance, nor keeping him around to amuse myself. He has been preparing for university, where he will no doubt learn all the wonderful masculine sports—drinking, gambling, women. His life will be so truly enriched," she said scornfully. "Do you know what Henry wants to do? He wants to learn about farming. We have just reached an agreement where he will drop his studies for a time to learn something of a practical nature. It is not I who chain him to a desk, but the wishes of his guardian that he be prepared for Oxford or Cambridge."

Rushton narrowed his eyes and said coldly, "I imagine you believe that, Miss Easterly-Cummings. You are deluding yourself. If you did not want to keep him here with you, he would probably be at school this very minute, as he should be."

"Yes, he should be!" she stormed. "He should have gone to school five years ago. Do you know why he didn't? No, of course you don't. And I dare say you don't care, either, so long as you can point a self-righteous finger at me. I am doing the best I can. There's no one else to do it for him."

"There should be a male hand guiding his upbringing," Rushton said more evenly. "You spoke of a guardian. Who is that?"

"An acquaintance of Henry's late father, chosen more for his proximity to the Forrester estate than for his wisdom, I fear."

"What is his name?" When she did not answer, he said, "Come, ma'am, I can easily find out. Penrith probably knows, or the boy himself would not hesitate to inform me."

Selina moistened her lips and asked, "Why do you want to know? What are you going to do?"

"If he is someone I know, I might have some influence in getting him to take more interest in the boy's welfare. You are not in a position to introduce your cousin to the masculine world of sports he longs to partake of. You are crippling him, Miss Easterly-Cummings, and I do not mean that slight limp he has. *That* will not interfere with his enjoyment, but your smothering him in cotton wool will."

Unhappily, Selina rose and walked to the window where she stood looking out. "Tell me, Mr. Rushton, is your interest in doing Henry good, or me harm? If it is the latter, you could certainly have chosen no better weapon than Henry. But do not think that I will allow you to ruin his life without a fight. I freely acknowledge that I am not always capable of providing him with all the guidance he should have, and that I am more protective of him than I should be. I continually struggle to overcome that failing. On the other hand, I cannot believe that his guardian would provide him with a more appropriate home. Here Henry has affection, a family connection, a home. His guardian is a cold man, with quite a large family, who has visited Henry only three times since he has been here. At first he intended to take Henry with him..." Unable to continue, Selina leaned her head against the windowpane and fought to control the tears which threatened.

Her distress was evident to Rushton, who had risen to his feet when she did, and now pulled a chair over to where she stood and gently pushed her into it. Not capable of facing him, Selina turned her head away and covered her face with her hands.

"Miss Easterly-Cummings, I assure you I have no wish to harm you. And I am not suggesting that Henry be taken away from you as though you were some unfit mother. But the boy needs a masculine influence in his life." He would not ask her again who Henry's guardian was; she was too precariously maintaining her composure as it was. "Why didn't he go to school?"

For a moment Selina did not answer, and then she began to speak in a low voice which Rushton had to come closer to hear. "When my father died, Henry's family journeyed here to attend the funeral. They were all in a coaching accident. His mother and father and sister were killed, and Henry was brought to Shalbrook more dead than alive. Dr. Turner didn't think he would live, and for some weeks... But he did live, the poor frightened little thing. He was only eleven then, and lost without his family. Lord Leyburn came then and tried to take him away, but Dr. Turner said the journey would surely kill him. So he stayed here with me, and I nursed him and cried with him and came to love him as my brother." Selina rubbed fiercely at her eyes. "He couldn't walk for two years."

"Two years!"

"Yes, but I worked with him every day, and we went to places with hot springs which sometimes seemed to help, and sometimes didn't. Even when he could walk, he had a great deal of trouble at first; the limp was almost grotesque then. We worked and worked together, and now it is hardly noticeable. That is why he didn't go to school, Mr. Rushton. And all those years of enforced inactivity... well, we studied together, then, and he is a very promising student. He has not chafed under his studies until recently. But now... He is growing up, and I don't quite know what to do with him. Please don't misunderstand me! I adore Henry and want only what is best for him, and am only too aware that I shouldn't hover about him like a mother hen. But all those years of broken bones! To watch him ride off to the hunt... He thinks nothing of it, of course, and I should be happy that he can forget all his past experiences so readily. It is not as simple for me."

Rushton said softly, "Penrith told me none of this."

"I don't think he knew, really. None of them did outside Shalbrook. Oh, they heard that the boy was unwell, but you don't expect to see an eleven-year-old out in Society, so they didn't think much of it. I was far too busy to continue in Society myself, so we became rather isolated here." Selina looked at him and spoke hesitantly. "I should not have bored you with all this,

126

Mr. Rushton, but I want you to understand that you are only partially right. My fondest wish is not to keep Henry with me, but for him to grow into a gentleman of honesty, courage and kindness who will enjoy the world about him, and benefit it as well for his presence. Right now he is confused. He feels restricted, and yet he is not sure exactly what he wants to do. Perhaps after all it would have been best to send him to school this last year, but his tutor advised Lord Leyburn against it."

"Why?"

"Dr. Davenport, his tutor, is inordinately proud of Henry's progress under him, and thought he could better prepare him for university." Selina bit her lip and looked away. "I admit that I did not protest his decision. I thought it might be difficult for Henry at his age to suddenly find himself amidst boys who all knew each other and had been to school for some years." Not knowing why she did it, she asked, "Was that wrong of me?"

"You were protecting him again," he replied, but not with anger. "I think you would have found that he adjusted very easily. Why have you not asked Lord Leyburn's assistance?"

"I don't like him," Selina replied frankly. "How could anyone be so heartless as to suggest that Henry be taken away when he was obviously unfit? Lord Leyburn came back a year later . . ."

"And?"

"Henry was still unable to walk, of course. I could see the disgust in the man's eyes when he looked at Henry, and he spoke of his six healthy children at home as though Henry were some kind of freak. Can you imagine what would have happened if he had taken Henry?" Selina shuddered in remembrance.

"How did it come about that Henry stayed?"

"There were some difficult interviews." Agitated, Selina rose and began to pace the room. "Lord Leyburn said I was far too young to have charge of a boy his age. I told him that I had done very well so far and felt confident that I could continue to do so. He was not impressed, but he really did not want Henry in his home. In order to convince him, I . . . told him I expected to be married, and could thus provide a more usual home for Henry. He accepted that for the time being."

"And were you to be married?" Rushton asked curiously.

"I thought so at the time."

"I see. When you didn't marry, what happened?"

"Oh, Leyburn came again a year or so later, all puffed up with his concern and self-righteous indignation that I had lied to him. It was the time when Henry was beginning to walk, but very ... awkwardly. Undoubtedly, Lord Leyburn had intended to take Henry away with him that time, but he really could not bear the sight of a cripple. Never once did he try to talk to Henry, or find out what he was like. I had the happy inspiration of suggesting that Lord Leyburn provide a tutor for Henry here, so that he need not leave. The solution recommended itself to him."

"And he has not come again?"

"No. He writes a note with Henry's quarterly allowance, and has regular reports from Dr. Davenport. We seldom hear from him otherwise. I have suggested that Henry write and tell him he wishes to learn something of farming and ease off his studies for a while, though I fear that may provoke him into coming here."

"He would not be disgusted by Henry now."

"No."

"You are afraid he would take your cousin away from you?"

Selina gazed abstractedly at the piles of paper on the floor as she fingered a volume lying open on the table. "Yes."

"Has his guardian boys of Henry's age?"

"One five years older and one much younger. The rest are girls."

"I can see no value in his going to them, then. And you are probably wrong that Lord Leyburn would want the responsibility of another member in his household. It seems to me he is relieved that he doesn't have to give Henry any thought."

Her chin came up and she asked with only the slightest shake in her voice, "So you will not find it necessary to urge Lord Leyburn to involve himself in Henry's affairs?"

Rushton was struck by her vulnerability, and moved forward to possess himself of one of her hands. "I told you I had no wish to harm you, Miss Easterly-Cummings. Disabuse yourself of that idea, I beg you. My annoyance at your high-handedness and your questioning of my word, as it seemed to me, are not matters over which I would set out to destroy your happiness." He offered a wry grin. "I felt sure my ignoring you at Oak Park the other day was sufficient punishment for that."

"Did you?" Selina asked with an uncertain laugh, very aware that he retained her hand in his clasp. "I assure you I was crushed by your obvious displeasure with me."

"I must be losing my perceptiveness, for I didn't see that at all. You appeared totally impervious to my snub," he retorted as he reluctantly allowed her to withdraw her hand.

Serious eyes met his hesitantly. "I never meant to . . . irritate you, Mr. Rushton. Sometimes, from managing on my own for so long, I forget the social amenities and step on someone's toes. From organizing my own life and Henry's, I fear I unthinkingly take liberties which I should not. And I have just scolded Henry for doing the same," she said, wonderingly. "It is easier to see faults in others than in ourselves."

Rushton made no attempt to answer, fascinated by the way her brows contracted when she puzzled over her own behavior.

THIRTEEN

Suddenly Selina recalled how their interview had begun, and that he was not, after all, someone with whom she should speak so openly. "Now then, if you would have a seat, Mr. Rushton, I believe you wished to discuss the Sands' glassed-in room."

Her abrupt change of manner, from confiding to businesslike, unaccountably disappointed him, though he had often said that emotional women were the very devil to deal with. During the entire interview, she had not, it was true, shed a single tear, though she had been on the verge several times, and only restrained by an obvious effort of will. As she seated herself, her dignity resumed in spite of the dusty smock and the disheveled hair, Rushton remained standing. "I was at fault to barge in on you as I did, Miss Easterly-Cummings, and impertinent to suggest that I best knew how your cousin should be reared. Do not let me detain you further from your work."

Selina smiled and said, "Let us leave off apologies now, Mr. Rushton. I am sure they could occupy the two of us for the rest of the day, and we would never discuss anything of importance. Did you like the Sands' glass room?"

"Very much," he admitted as he seated himself in a chair opposite her. "However, the one Lord John has designed for me would be a great deal larger, and more prominent, as it opens off both the drawing and dining rooms. And I have little interest in indoor horticulture."

"Could you draw me the layout, so that I would understand how the rooms are placed?"

"Certainly." He rose and walked to the desk. "There is paper in the top left-hand drawer."

In addition to a neatly arranged stack of paper, and a wooden tray with a number of pens, there was a delicate glass box with a red velvet floor on which rested two faded roses. From whom? Rushton wondered. And why hidden away in a desk drawer in the library rather than displayed on her vanity? He quickly drew forth a sheet of paper and chose a well-sharpened pen before carefully closing the drawer so as not to jar its contents. Without looking at Miss Easterly-Cummings, he dipped the pen in the standish and began to draw a rough sketch of Lord John's design for his hunting-box.

After a few minutes' concentration, his dark head bent over the sheet, he returned to her and explained, "I may have the proportions slightly wrong, but this is more or less the idea. Actually the library, also, gives onto the glass room. Don't you think perhaps the library should be larger, with a simple terrace off it?"

Selina studied the plan and exclaimed, "But this will be delightful, Mr. Rushton! How clever of Lord John. It is hardly the cottage I expected, however! The major rooms must be thirty feet across. How charming that they all open onto the verandah room."

"Charming, yes, but what use will I make of it?" he asked a trifle impatiently. "I don't wish to grow pineapples and orchids like your Mr. Sands, and if I wish to read, I may do so in the library."

"Pooh. It can serve any number of purposes. A breakfast room in conjuction with the dining room, a more spacious reading area than the library, an informal drawing room. There is very little you *can't* do with such a room, Mr. Rushton." His head was so close to hers over the drawing that she could feel his breath on her hair and she moved back on her chair. "A smoking room, a billiard room."

"A billiard room?" Rushton studied the plan more closely. "I believe you have something there, Miss Easterly-Cummings. Or a breakfast room. The dining hall is large for one person. I am mostly looking for comfort, and a lack of frills, though I shall entertain on a small scale occasionally, no doubt." He crumpled the drawing and accurately tossed it on the hearth. "I should thank you for recommending Lord John. His work so far has been impressive, and I fear I gave him little enough to go on."

"We have gradually been restoring and replacing the estate cottages, and I was struck by his ability to grasp the cottagers' way of life and build to suit it. Practical and yet innovative."

"Might I ask how you met him?"

"Through his brother, Lord Cathford. When Lord John first came here, Cathford brought him by to meet me."

Rushton raised a quizzical brow. "And how did you meet Cathford?"

Averting her eyes, Selina murmured, "When I was younger, I used to ride with the Quorn."

"You don't say," he drawled. "Now I would never have guessed that."

She flushed at the innuendo in his tone, and rushed hurriedly into speech. "My father sometimes forgot that I was not the son he would have liked. Not that he did not care for me! It was just that he prompted me to many activities which most females do not indulge in. But hunting *can* be dangerous! I have seen any number of appalling injuries. And I did not stop Henry going with you."

"No, but you would have liked to. What other intrepid activities did your father urge on you, Miss Easterly-Cummings?" Rushton asked with interest.

"You are making sport with me, and there is no reason I need answer your questions." She fixed him with a smoldering glare.

"Come, I am intrigued. Can you shoot?"

Selina nodded.

"Fence?"

"Some."

"Fish?"

"Of course."

"Row a boat?"

Another nod.

"I know you dance and ride, drive a phaeton and climb trees. Perhaps you could teach Henry to box." His eyes danced wickedly.

"I have never even *seen* anyone box," she said scornfully, "and I have no desire to do so."

"But you won't object if I teach Henry?"

Selina dropped her eyes from his demanding gaze. "No."

"Good, because I have every intention of teaching him when his arm is fully healed."

"I would rather he didn't impose on you, Mr. Rushton," she replied stiffly. "We may be able to find some retired pugilist in the neighborhood."

"I doubt it. You don't find them under every bush, dear ma'am."

He was laughing at her now, and the color rose in her face. "I am aware of that, sir, but your time will be consumed in directing the building of your house."

"Ah, now you are attempting to manage other people's lives again, Miss Easterly-Cummings. I really would enjoy teaching Henry, you know."

"And what of his limp? I could not bear it if he were humiliated by finding that it hindered him."

His voice was firm and his eyes stern. "You could bear it, and you would, Miss Easterly-Cummings. Remember your resolve to be less protective of him. If he cannot box, he will have to bear the disappointment. You cannot shield him from everything." His voice became more gentle. "I doubt the limp will hinder him much."

"You know, Mr. Rushton, before you came to this area, my life seemed infinitely less complicated. I look back on those days—only a few short weeks ago! — when I had no intention of selling the vale, had almost seen Henry through another hunting season without his joining the field, had never had to defend my rearing of my cousin—and I consider them golden days. Yes, cloudless, happy times," she sighed, poking a stray strand of hair under her lace cap. "People did not invade my library unless I asked them. No one yelled at me that I was smothering poor Henry with my good intentions. No one even knew I *had* good intentions, and no one cared. Fancy your caring," she said sweetly, her eyes mocking. "If anyone had asked me, I should have said, 'No, Mr. Rushton will not care how I raise Henry. Mr. Rushton is far too busy with his own concerns.' It just shows you how wrong you can be."

"Did you get your sharp tongue from your father, too, Miss Easterly-Cummings?"

"Probably. He didn't toad-eat *anyone,* Mr. Rushton."

"Toad-eat! Sometimes you are barely civil. I thought we had called a truce."

"Yes, but you started to pinch at me about Henry again," she remarked with asperity.

"No more than you deserved." He tapped his fingers on the arm of his chair and regarded her thoughtfully. "Did you know Cathford well?"

"Fairly. He was Pen's friend, and I Maria Southwood's. We often rode out, the four of us. The earl spoke of his family with genuine affection, and when Lord John settled near Leicester, Cathford made a visit to him, and they came round to call." Selina noted the puzzled quirk on his forehead and asked, "Do you find something strange in that, Mr. Rushton? I thought it unexceptional myself. Mrs. Morrow, my companion, was still with me in those days, you understand, so there was no impropriety, even though Henry was not much in evidence as yet."

"How long has Lord John lived here?"

"Oh, four years, I imagine. Is there some significance in all this, Mr. Rushton?"

He pulled himself out of his revery and smiled apologetically. "I was merely curious. Forgive me."

"We are back to apologies," she grumbled. "Did you have anything further to discuss, Mr. Rushton?"

"I think not," he replied languidly as he rose, his blue eyes trained on her face. "I will not apologize again for disturbing you, but I will thank you for your assistance about the glass room. Lord John will be instructed to include it in his design."

"I feel sure you won't regret it." Selina smiled and offered him her hand, and for just a moment she thought he intended to raise it to his lips, but the upward movement was changed into a hearty shake.

"I'll see myself out."

"Please see that you do this time. I should not like to run into you in the hall this afternoon."

"Am I not then welcome to call again?" he asked, only half teasing.

Selina adjusted the smock which covered her morning dress. "If you are to teach Henry to box, I imagine we will see you often enough at Shalbrook. Or shall he come to you at Oak Park?"

"I will be moving soon to the Horse and Hound. Pen and his family are off to London for Cassandra's Season in a few days. Mr. Evans at the inn spoke highly of you."

"He's an excellent innkeeper. Did you by chance take the rebuilt rooms?"

"Yes, Miss Easterly-Cummings, and heard of the hand you had in them."

"I made only one suggestion, Mr. Rushton."

"Ever involved," he murmured, and watched her eyes flash. "Mr. Evans himself assured me that you would not dream of interfering in the running of the Horse and Hound."

"Do leave before we have another quarrel," she begged. "I am quite spent from our discussion."

"Are you? For a moment I thought you looked ready to do battle again. No, no, I shall say no more. If it is agreeable with you, I will come here for Henry's boxing lessons. I don't feel Mr. Evans would appreciate our appropriating his yard for our sport."

"There is ample room at Shalbrook, Mr. Rushton. The least we can do, if you are to donate your time to Henry's instruction, is to provide a place for you to teach him. His arm, however..."

"Will be fit in another week or so. I shall call then," he said firmly.

Selina turned away from the intent blue eyes. "Very well. Good day, sir." After his murmured farewell, she heard his footsteps cross the room, and only looked in his direction in time to see him glance at her just as he was closing the door behind himself. No hint of triumph, or mockery, rested on his countenance, but rather almost a questioning look, as though he were concerned about her. Nonsense, she scolded herself, as she returned to the piles of paper. He might feel uneasy about upsetting her, as well he should, but concern for others was doubtless foreign to his nature. Well, not in Henry's case, perhaps, but certainly in hers.

When Henry did not present himself for luncheon, Selina sighed and went in search of him. He was not in the study, nor in his bedroom but she tracked him down at last in the stables, where he attempted to ignore her. Since there was no one else about she said softly, "Henry, if you wish to be treated as a man, you must learn not to sulk. I have seen Mr. Rushton, much against my wishes, and he persists in his claim that he will teach you to box. Are we agreed that I have a right to see whom I wish, and refuse anyone I don't?"

"Yes, Selina."

"Excellent. Then blame yourself for this morning's contretemps, Henry, as you should. It is a sign of immaturity to blame others for your own errors. Our household is run very informally, which we both enjoy, but it should not dim our awareness of each other's rights. I shall endeavor not to interfere with your pursuits except where I consider it my duty to do so. Mr. Rushton tells me I am too protective of you, and I know that it is true. You have been very patient with me, all things considered, and I promise you I am struggling very hard to reach a reasonable perspective. Please bear with me, dear Henry."

"Oh, Selina," he groaned as he hugged her. "You have been so good to me, I don't know how I can act so churlishly to you. I knew I was wrong this morning but . . . it meant so much to me, and I was sure Rushton would change his mind."

"I shouldn't think so," she said caustically. "He is unconscionably autocratic, but he prizes his word on a matter very highly."

"You are too hard on him, Selina," Henry protested. "It is extraordinarily kind of him to pay any attention at all to someone my age. From what I gathered when he and Sir Penrith talked, Rushton is a courted member of the *ton*. And I like him, Selina."

"Yes, I know you do, my dear. Well, he said he would come in a week or so for your first lesson, so the matter is settled. If he should change his mind . . ."

Henry grinned at her. "I won't sulk, I promise. Have I missed my meal?"

"No, scapegrace, it is a cold collation on the sideboard, and I haven't eaten yet, either."

JOURNAL. March 9. Have written to Lord John to proceed with the plans, including the glass room. The Southwoods leave for London in a week, when I will remove to the Horse and Hound. Could Cathford possibly have meant Miss E-C— the eccentric, incredible Miss E-C—when we spoke those many years ago? It does fit, in some ways, but I consider his notion preposterous. Of course, she was much younger then. . . .

The day before they were to leave for London, Sir Penrith and his sister Cassandra rode over to take leave of Selina and Henry. Lord John was there, discussing the Shalbrook cottages with Selina, while Henry sat listening as he contracted and released his injured arm in an effort to strengthen it. Determined to be ready when Rushton appeared, Henry daily extended the use of the arm, his cousin observing without comment, equally torn by amusement and chagrin.

"Are we interrupting?" Penrith asked as they were ushered into the drawing room.

Selina knew a moment's impatience with herself for being disappointed that Mr. Rushton had not accompanied them. "I for one am delighted to leave off talking of beams and plaster, Pen!" she exclaimed, greeting Cassandra with outstretched hands. "You look charming, my dear, and remind me most forcefully of Maria the day before she left for London."

As Cassandra murmured a polite reply, she glanced shyly past Selina to Lord John. "We didn't know you had company."

"Lord John is practically a member of the family," Henry interposed, leaving off his arm exercises to welcome the new arrivals.

Cassandra blanched at this information and looked helplessly at Selina, who immediately took pity on her and explained, "I fear we have imposed a great deal on Lord John this last week. There has been flooding in half a dozen of the old cottages, and he has practically had to live here in order to find some solution." She turned to Penrith to add, "Please explain to Mr. Rushton that our emergency has occupied a great deal of Lord John's time. It cannot help but have delayed his work on the hunting-box."

"Don't fret, Selina. Gareth will understand. Perhaps I can convince him to come to London for a stretch, after all. Haven't the faintest notion what he'll do with himself here until construction is under way." He turned to Lord John with enthusiasm. "Quite remarkable, your plans for his house! Dare say I wouldn't mind living in it myself. Heard anything from Cathford? He'll be in London for the Season, won't he?" Penrith asked with a touch of longing.

"Oh, yes. They're all to leave shortly, I understand," Lord John replied as he seated himself in the chair next to Cassandra's.

"You won't be coming to London this spring, Lord John?" Cassandra asked wistfully.

"No. That is, I'd like to, but with the hunting-box and all, I don't see how I shall have time to get away."

Penrith was watching the two of them with interest, as Selina was. Henry had returned to concentrating on his arm exercises. While the stables were under construction, Cassandra and Lord John had met frequently, of course, but Penrith had thought of her then as little more than a child, and had not noticed the interest developing between them. Certainly they had seemed to enjoy each other's company at the Oak Park tea party, but there had been far too many people that day for Penrith to notice them in particular. He glanced at Selina, who smiled and lifted her shoulders slightly, and then he cleared his throat. "Must have a holiday now and again to keep the mind fresh. Tell you what, Lord John, why not come to town for Cassandra's ball? Bound to be a grand affair with m' mother in charge, you know. Give you a chance to see your folks, too. The ball won't be for a while yet—probably the middle of April. Mother likes to get a feel for how the Season is going, but not wait so long that everyone's jaded. We'll send you a card when the date's set for certain."

"There's nothing I'd like more," Lord John assured him before he turned to Cassandra. "If I came, would you save a waltz for me?"

"Yes." She didn't flush or lower her eyelashes but regarded him steadily, a warm glow lighting her eyes.

"Then, if at all possible, I shall be there," he declared.

"I wonder, Pen," Selina suggested, "if you'd be interested in seeing our problem. Perhaps you've had trouble with flooding at Oak Park."

"Not this year, but several times in the past. Shall we walk over?"

"Yes, if you'd like. No, no, Lord John. Cassandra isn't dressed for walking. Won't you entertain her while we're gone? I think Henry has some studying to do."

"What?" Henry yelped. "I've composed a dozen lines already today!" He intercepted Selina's speaking glance and shrugged. "Oh, very well. Dr. Davenport will be here tomorrow, and I may as well finish my assignment this afternoon," he muttered darkly.

"You can exercise your arm while you study," Selina offered consolingly.

Outside in the brisk March air, Selina impulsively pressed Penrith's arm. "You know, Pen, you are one of the dearest people I've ever met, and I count myself lucky to have you for my friend."

Startled, he came to an abrupt halt. "Why, thank you, Selina. That is praise indeed coming from the most remarkable young lady of my acquaintance. Have I told you how pleased I am that you're going out a bit more in Society? And that you've discarded those distressing rags you were wearing? Cassandra has always hinted that she knew why you did that. Will you tell me?"

"Oh, because of Lord Leyburn, Pen. He's such a nodcock that he couldn't take me seriously as Henry's companion when I was young. When I was in mourning he didn't seem to notice my age, but later ... It seemed wisest to obscure my youth by dressing rather strangely. For some unfathomable reason, Lord Leyburn has the most profound respect for eccentrics. Henry used to tell me about an old woman in the neighborhood of Bromley Hall who juggled eggs and dressed as a cottager, but it turned out that she was the Dowager Lady Leyburn." Selina giggled. "Henry was too young for years to even notice how I dressed, and I never knew when Lord Leyburn would come here, for he likes to 'surprise' us, so I fell into the habit of dressing that way. Actually, I rather enjoyed it, but Henry has been nagging at me recently, so . . . And I am certainly old enough now that Lord Leyburn could not object to my having charge of Henry, could he?"

Penrith regarded her with amusement. "I'd change into your rags when you hear he's descended on Shalbrook, my dear. You don't look a day older than Cassandra when you wear that scarlet mantelet."

"Don't I? Perhaps that's why Mr. Rushton is so very cross with my being in charge of Henry," she mused.

His gaze sharpened. "Has Gareth upset you, Selina?"

A deep-throated laugh escaped her. "Every time I've met him. Oh, don't be alarmed, Pen. He has been so obliging as to offer to teach Henry to box, which apparently is Henry's fondest wish. I don't really understand boys, Pen."

"No one does, my dear. You are in good company. Henry is a credit to you, and never let anyone tell you differently."

That night Selina lay sleepless in bed for some time. There was no reason, of course, why Mr. Rushton should have come with Penrith, and even less reason that she should feel disappointed that he had not. The less she saw of him the better, she assured herself. There was no need for another disturbing influence in her life, and such a powerful one, with his searching blue eyes and his compelling personality. I will not give in to this attraction for him, she thought fiercely. But when she fell asleep at length she dreamed of a hot summer's day in the vale . . . but the man with her was not Frank, and she did not refuse him.

FOURTEEN

There were no visitors at Shalbrook for the next week. Henry began to look anxious, but never said a word, hopefully continuing the exercise of his arm, which grew steadily stronger. In an effort to distract his mind Selina suggested that they take advantage of a warm spring day to ride over the furthermost part of the estate.

"Could we ride cross-country, as though we were on a fox hunt?" he asked eagerly.

Selina rumpled his hair and said, "Certainly. You'll have to judge your jumps well, though, Henry, as you won't be on Sir Penrith's hunter this time."

"I've jumped on Catastrophe any number of times, and he's game as can be."

"We'll bring Scamp and see if she can raise a rabbit for us," Selina said with a grin.

"Hogwash! That dog wouldn't know a rabbit if it bit her," Henry returned scornfully.

"Tsk, tsk. Very unflattering, isn't he, Scamp?" Selina asked as she scratched the dog's head. Obligingly, the dog barked and offered a paw.

"You see," Henry declared triumphantly. "She's good for nothing but disposing of our unwanted food and doing tricks."

But Scamp surprised him. In the ecstasy of having a run with them, she accidentally stumbled on several rabbits in her mad dashes across the fields, and Selina sat laughing delightedly as Henry watched in astonishment while rabbits scattered in every direction. Her duty done, Scamp circled Selina's stationary horse, barking excitedly and waiting for a word of praise.

"Good dog, Scamp, but you are supposed to chase them," Selina instructed the furry mongrel. "How are we to have a run if you let them all get away?"

Scamp cocked her head questioningly.

"They're long gone," Henry said disgustedly.

"You wouldn't really expect Scamp to want to catch one, would you? After the delicacies she has from Cook?"

"Dogs are supposed to have a hunting instinct."

"Poor Scamp, she must have been left out. Don't be cross with her, Henry. She's so pleased with herself."

They rode on, with Scamp making wild forays into the underbrush and wriggling under fences which they jumped. When they had lost sight of the dog for a few minutes, Selina was startled by a piercing howl at her rear.

Henry, riding close by her, grimaced. "Now she probably *has been* bitten by a rabbit."

"Absurd creature," Selina scolded. "She's surely hurt herself."

Swinging down from the sidesaddle, Selina hastened to the brambles from which the howl emerged. In an attempt to investigate a suspicious burrow, Scamp had hopelessly tangled herself in the briars, only managing to more completely enmesh herself by her struggles. Her limpid eyes gazed pleadingly at her mistress, who surveyed the scene with exasperation. "Really, Scamp, how could you? Henry, have you a knife with you? Her hair is so snarled in the brambles I can't even reach most of her."

"Sorry, Selina. Shall I ride back and get one? Lord, what a mess!" he exclaimed as he came up to see the entrapped dog. "No wonder people only hunt with short-haired dogs. Selina, it's going to take hours to cut her out of there."

"Yes, I know." Selina soothed the moaning dog as best she could. "I'll stay with her if you'll go back, Henry. You'd best bring a scissors as well. Once we get her out, we'll have to cut off a lot of the hair to get out the brambles."

"Right-o. I'll be as quick as I can."

His cousin wanted to remind him to ride carefully, but bit her tongue. "Thank you, Henry."

Scamp watched dolefully as Henry rode off, and attempted to crawl closer to Selina's comforting presence, which caused the dog considerable pain and she howled mournfully. Selina was startled by a voice hailing her from the road, and she turned to see Mr. Rushton seated on a large bay some distance away.

"Trouble, Miss Easterly-Cummings? Is there something I can do?" he called.

"Have you a knife with you, Mr. Rushton?"

For answer, he set his horse at the fence and sailed over into the field where she sat by the dog. His eyes were troubled as he approached and swung down from his horse. "A knife?"

"Scamp is caught up in these brambles and I shall have to cut her out," Selina explained, moving so that he could see the dog. "Henry has gone for a knife and a scissors, but I could get started if you had a knife."

"I carry one on the saddle to remove stones from their hooves," he explained as he released the leather holder and returned to her. "No, let me do it. My gloves will provide more protection than yours."

"I don't think she will let you, Mr. Rushton. She's in pain and not disposed to be reasonable."

"She'll let me," he said calmly, as Selina reluctantly stood up and moved aside for him.

The frantic dog growled as Rushton stooped down in front of her, but he allowed her to sniff at his gloved hands before resting one reassuringly on her head. "Be still now. Good dog. We'll have you out in no time. Yes, it is bound to hurt you some. That can't be helped, and you have no one but yourself to blame."

Fascinated, Selina watched as he deftly cut away the brambles from the miserable dog, who made no attempt to snap at him even when he could not avoid causing her pain. Rushton continued his monologue throughout the rescue, occasionally referring to Scamp as a dustbin and a lapdog, expressions which he accompanied with a grin at Selina. Freed at last, Scamp leaped on Rushton, furiously licking his face while he warded her off, mumbling, "A totally undisciplined dog."

"Her gratitude is only exceeded by my own," Selina assured him, smiling as the dog bounded over to her. "Poor Scamp. We shall not take you rabbit-hunting again."

"Rabbit-hunting? Surely you're joking."

"Yes, it was a joke," Selina sighed. "But Scamp got caught up in the spirit, I fear."

"I take it she isn't much of an outdoor dog."

"I wouldn't say that precisely. She often goes for walks with me, for miles and miles sometimes. Her energy is limitless, and she enjoys being outside."

"She has some nasty cuts. I doubt she'll be up to running home just now, Miss Easterly-Cummings."

"No, I shall take her up with me after Henry has come with the scissors. Thank you for your help, Mr. Rushton. Are your hands scratched?"

"Nothing to speak of. I was on my way to Shalbrook." He watched for her reaction.

"Were you?" she asked easily, her face a polite mask.

"Yes. If Henry's arm is sufficiently recovered, I had thought to start his boxing lessons." He paused for a moment and then continued, "I waited some extra time to insure his full use of it."

"That was thoughtful of you. He has spent a great deal of his time exercising his arm, in hopes that you would come."

"I gave my word, Miss Easterly-Cummings," he said haughtily.

"I know. I told him you would keep it." She leaned down to fondle the dog at her feet and did not meet his eyes.

His face relaxed. "You are the most extraordinary girl! I never have the least idea what you will say or do next. Shall we bury our differences? I can see that it behooves me to stand in good stead with you."

"Dear me, and to think all this stems from my vouching for your word. I had no idea," Selina grumbled, "that it took so little to win your approval, Mr. Rushton." She met his gaze at last, and was disturbed by the mixture of amusement and warmth there. "Still,

144

I would like for us to be on good terms, especially for Henry's sake." Determinedly she extended her hand to him, unable to draw her eyes from his impelling gaze.

"For whatever reason," he said, firmly gripping her hand, "let us be friends. We are going to be neighbors, and it is always my policy to get along with my neighbors."

Self-consciously, she withdrew her hand. "Have you met your other neighbor? Lord Benedict?"

"Yes. He wanted to buy the vale from me."

She nodded. "He would, of course. I . . . would never sell it to him. That is why I insisted on first refusal on the land."

"He suggested a very clever scheme for circumventing that." The blue eyes studied her carefully.

"Frank is very clever about getting his own way. Often too clever."

Rushton laughed. "Yes, he only managed to give me a disgust of his principles."

"I have always thought I had very good reason not to sell to him, but he sees only what he wishes. It doesn't matter. You won't see him here often; he's usually in town."

The sound of hoofbeats growing nearer interrupted them, and they watched silently as Henry on Catastrophe easily took the fence from the next field. Scamp immediately trotted forward, barking vociferously in welcome.

"Servant, Rushton. I see you've freed the hairy baggage. You look a sight, Scamp," he scolded. "I brought the scissors, Selina. The ones from your workbox. They seemed most appropriate. Cutting a dog's hair must be very like cutting all those little threads of yours."

"Your appreciation of these finer nuances is remarkable, Henry," his cousin retorted, but her eyes danced. "Mr. Rushton was just coming to Shalbrook to give you a boxing lesson. You two go ahead and I'll be along when I have snipped out the worst of the brambles. She won't be able to ride with me with them digging into her."

"We can wait for you, Miss Easterly-Cummings,"

145

Rushton suggested. "You'll need assistance onto your horse."

"Thank you, no. I shall manage."

"Then I should like to stay around just to see how you accomplish it," he returned. "I can picture you managing for yourself, but what about the dog?"

"You are straining our new agreement already," Selina said with a flush. "Trust me. I can manage."

The corners of his mouth twitched with amusement, but he bowed formally and swung onto his horse. "As you wish, of course. May I look in on you before I leave?"

"To see if I have made it home?" Her chin lifted stubbornly.

"No, I long to see what poor Scamp will look like after her haircut."

"Do just as you please, Mr. Rushton."

It sounded very like he said, "I wouldn't dare," but Selina could not be sure, as their horses were moving off, and the thuds of hooves and the jingling of the harness obscured his softly spoken words. Without acknowledging their waves, she stooped to pet the dog. "He is the most infuriating man, Scamp! Hold still now and I will try not to pull too much. And he laughs at me all the time. How would he like it if I laughed at him that way? Oh, I'd like to box his ears. Scamp, you must be patient. This will not take long. If he *really* wanted to be my friend, he would not be so provoking. Lie still, Scamp! How could you let him cozzen you with a few soft words?" Although the last was directed to the shaggy mutt, Selina thought ruefully that it applied to herself as well. "He is only charming when he wishes to be, and that is not nearly often enough. Well, we shan't worry about him, shall we? There, that will do until I get you home."

Scamp shook herself thankfully, unaware of her decidedly unattractive appearance. Tufts of hair were missing in a random pattern all over her body, and Selina shook her head doubtfully. "McDonough will not approve of you, you know. I'll have to cut it all back to a decent length." Faced now with the problem of mounting her horse, Selina groaned. "Not for the world would I admit that he was right, so you had best co-

146

operate with me, Scamp. I will not arrive at the stables carrying you and leading Starlight."

The chestnut mare patiently allowed her mistress to lead her to a stump, and she did not move, other than a wild flickering of her ears, during the whole procedure which followed. First, Selina attempted to place Scamp on the saddle, but the frightened dog would not stay there, possibly could not stay there, but slid off to the ground. After trying this several times, Scamp became annoyed with her precipitate journeys and glared at Selina menacingly. "You could not have glowered in that manner at Mr. Rushton, could you?" she asked with asperity. "Oh, no, you had to fawn all over him. Very well, we'll try something else."

Her second maneuver was no more successful than her first. Although she managed to get herself on the sidesaddle, Scamp would not jump onto the stump so that Selina could reach her. No amount of cajolery had any effect. Selina was beginning to lose her temper.

Driven by the desire to prove she had not overestimated her resourcefulness, Selina once again returned to the ground and picked up the dog, tucking the ball of fluff under her arm. "You are not going to like this, Scamp, but if you bite me I promise I shall allow you to wander about the house just as scraggly as you are!" After two unsuccessful attempts to seat herself on the horse, she lost her temper and threw a stone with all her might against a hapless tree. The third time she was triumphant. Scamp did not in fact bite her, merely clawed her in a frantic effort to get away. Selina surveyed the ugly red welt on her wrist and decided, "It is better than proving Mr. Rushton right."

For the first time it occurred to her that she would have done better to mount her horse on the road side of the fence, and she almost cried with frustration when she thought of the fences she would have to jump with Scamp in her arms. Only one, really, she considered, if she jumped into the road instead of going across country. Surely she could manage one jump with the dog. "It's like flying," she assured Scamp as she set Starlight at the fence.

Whether or not Scamp agreed that it was like flying

was immaterial. She had never been on a horse before, of course, and did not like the experience at all. Selina had her hands full simply keeping the dog from scrambling out of her lap. When they touched ground in the road, Starlight continued her lengthy stride for the two-mile run home, while Selina occupied herself with calming the dog. The Shalbrook gates were open, but not the fence to the stable area. Tried beyond endurance, Selina could only think that she daren't get down to open the fence because of the dog; it never occurred to her that they were quite close enough that the dog could walk the rest of the way home, even in her tattered condition. So Selina put her heels to her mare and they jumped the fence, to the astonishment of the stable-hands, and the incredulous admiration of Mr. Rushton, who had moved to a window on hearing the hoofbeats approaching.

"My God, what a seat!" he exclaimed to Henry.

"Glorious, ain't it?" the young man replied proudly. "How I should have liked to see Selina hunt. A pity she has given it up."

"More than a pity, a crime. And with the damn dog in her arms, no less!"

"Poor Scamp. She ain't at all fond of horses at the best of times," Henry admitted.

"It doesn't seem to have done her any harm," Rushton commented laconically as he watched the frisking Scamp follow her mistress from the stable-yard. Selina's color was high, her hair blown unkempt by the ride and her eyes bright from the merciless wind. Rushton had never seen her look more enchanting. It is perhaps fortunate that Selina did not see him at the window, for in her present state of mind she would very likely have stuck her tongue out at him.

Selina took the dog to be bathed and her scratches attended to, then dried her in the library before the fire, after which she sat down and patiently attempted to even out the shaggy coat. Standing back to view her handiwork, hands on hips, she said, "You are undoubtedly the scruffiest thing I've ever seen. No more hunting for you, little one."

"She wasn't any good at it, anyhow," Henry an-

148

nounced cheerfully as he stuck his head around the door. "May we come in?"

"Just once I would like to be dressed properly when you bring me your guests," Selina complained in a voice that would have moved a stone to pity.

"She's being dramatic again," Henry explained to Rushton as the latter followed him into the room. "I've told her she is missing her chance for a fine career on the stage, but she pays me no mind."

"And why should I?" she asked, picking the dog's hairs from her dress. "A mere lad of sixteen who wouldn't know Shakespeare from Sheridan? And would probably find the latter more to his taste."

"Dr. Davenport has had me read half a dozen of Shakespeare's plays, and you know it," Henry retorted.

Selina sniffed. "Read them! Ha! That makes you an authority on the theater, I take it. Ask Mr. Rushton. Though he, too, is probably more familiar with Sheridan than Shakespeare. Not that I object to Sheridan. Far from it. I can laugh at the absurdities of life as well as the next," she proclaimed, eying Mr. Rushton balefully.

"So I perceive," he said evenly, though his shoulders shook suspiciously.

Pursuing her *grande dame* attitude, Selina waved them to seats, declaring imperiously, "I shall ring for tea."

"Not on my account, I beg you," Rushton protested. "I came only to see how Scamp has fared."

"I shall ring for tea!" Selina repeated, in a slightly louder voice.

"Well, for God's sake, do it, then," Henry advised her, saying aside to Rushton, "When she's in one of these moods, there's no gainsaying her."

"Do they come over her often?" he asked curiously.

"I think mostly when she's had a trying day. She often becomes exceedingly dramatic just after one of your visits," Henry said thoughtfully.

"I see. Usually she waits until I've left?"

"Yes, but perhaps today was especially trying for her."

"I don't doubt it."

Pointedly ignoring their dialogue, Selina swept over to the bellpull where she gave a violent tug. Returning with equal grace, she seated herself opposite Mr. Rushton and asked politely, "Have you had an enjoyable afternoon at your pugilistic activities?"

"Yes, the instruction went very well."

With a sweet smile, she turned next to Henry. "And you, my dear cousin, did you find boxing as much to your taste as you expected?"

"Dammit, Selina, we're not at a tea party. It was famous! I hadn't the least trouble with my limp. That's to say, only once or twice, and I shall easily overcome that."

His cousin nodded wisely. "There is nothing so rewarding as acquiring new skills. I note that you have survived this first session with no sign of damage to your person, Henry, and I congratulate you." She turned again to Rushton. "Now then, sir, I wonder if you think this fine weather will hold."

"My lack of knowledge of the spring climate in Leicestershire unfortunately prevents me from predicting with any certainty, Miss Easterly-Cummings, but it would certainly be a delightful prospect."

Henry said disgustedly, "If you *both* intend to carry on this way, I shan't stay for tea."

"What is that, dear? No tea?" Selina gasped. "You must keep up your strength, dear Henry. Think of the exertion you have just undergone! Think of how long it is until we dine! Think of the horror Lord Leyburn would experience should such a piece of information come to his ears! Think..."

Abruptly, Henry rose to his feet. "Stop it, Selina. You are embarrassing me." And then he stomped from the room.

The two who remained did not speak, or even look at one another. Rushton brushed an invisible speck of lint from his jacket. Selina gazed dumbfounded at the closed door for a moment, and then burst into tears.

"An especially trying day," Rushton murmured as he rose and went to Selina's side, thrusting a handkerchief into her hand. "Don't be upset on my account. I promise you I was thoroughly enjoying your performance." He waved away the footman who entered bearing the tea tray.

Too many times in the last few weeks Selina had repressed her tears. Too many emotionally charged events had overset her and yet gone unrewarded by the soothing balm of releasing those salty wet wonders. This time she made no effort to do so. It did not matter that Mr. Rushton was in the room with her; it would not have mattered if the whole village of Barton had been there. She cried until her body shook and Rushton pressed her head against his leg where he stood beside her, gently stroking her hair. She cried for a very long time, and when no more tears flowed she drew in gasping, hiccoughing breaths of air.

Scamp had awakened from the nap she was taking by the fire and came to thrust her muzzle between Selina's feet, looking sadly up at her mistress as though she sympathized, but Selina did not notice her. Once the storm had abated, Selina had become excruciatingly aware of Rushton's hand on her hair, and her head against his leg. There were tearstains on his buckskin breeches in spite of her use of his handkerchief. She could not force herself to sit back or get up; either way she would have to face him, and that she could not do.

As she had grown calmer, Rushton realized by the awkward angle of her head that she was no longer unaware of his presence. Placing both hands on her shoulders, he gently pushed her back on her chair and moved to stand behind it, his hands returning to her shoulders. "I had forgotten how difficult boys can be, Miss Easterly-Cummings. You have my sympathy. And yet I can remember that agonizing stage where my parents embarrassed me by almost everything they did when we were in company. I had my own ideas of how one should act. Everyone should act as I did! Boys outgrow it, and learn to accommodate a wide variety of acceptable behavior." He laughed. "You probably don't believe that even today I accept a wide variety of behavior, but I assure you I do. There is no one socially acceptable way to act. We would be a sorry society if there were. As I said before, I was thoroughly enjoying your acting. Stay here, and I will have your maid sent to you."

Unable to speak, Selina bowed her head and listened to his footsteps recede across the room and finally proceed down the hall.

FIFTEEN

McDonough, on hearing the footsteps in the hall, hurried down the passage on the other side of the stairs to intercept Mr. Rushton. "Will you be leaving, sir?"

"Not yet. Would you have Miss Easterly-Cummings' maid sent to her in the library?"

It seemed to McDonough that his mistress had recently had a great deal more need for her maid than she had in many years, but he merely said, "Certainly, sir."

"Do you know where Forrester is?"

"I believe he went up to his room."

"Have him sent for. I wish to see him in the study—immediately."

In spite of the fact that Rushton had not the least say at Shalbrook, which no one knew better than McDonough, the butler indicated no hesitancy. "Very good, sir."

"Thank you." With a nod, Rushton turned and strolled off to the study, the quiet murmur of voices behind reassuring him that his instructions were being carried out.

Quaking inwardly, Henry presented himself at the study door within five minutes. He had lived at Shalbrook for five years, and was not in the habit of knocking on doors, perhaps unfortunately, but he did not care to enter before doing so this time. He entered at Rushton's summons and attempted not to show his nervousness, but his cravat felt suddenly far too tight

153

and he was forced to ease it by tugging it away from his throat. "You sent for me, sir?"

No answer was forthcoming. Rushton merely raked him with his eyes until Henry flushed with embarrassment and something akin to despair. "I...I..." Henry wished desperately that Rushton would suggest that he seat himself, but no such relief was offered. "Did I upset Selina?"

"Naturally."

"Well, she was upsetting me," Henry managed with a touch of bravado.

"You don't say. She was not upsetting *me*."

"How can you say that?" Henry blurted. "There she was, acting as though she were on the stage at Drury Lane! In our library!"

"*Her* library, Forrester."

A wave of pain passed over Henry's face. "I know it's her house, but she chooses to have me treat it as my own. She has told me so any number of times."

Rushton pursed his lips grimly. "And you feel it necessary to take advantage of her goodness?"

"I don't! She's my cousin, and I love her dearly. You have no idea how much she's done for me."

"I think I do. More, perhaps, than a young gudgeon like you can comprehend, Forrester."

Henry shifted awkwardly from one leg to the other. "I didn't want her to make a fool of herself in front of you."

"What you need to learn, my boy, is that she has every right to make a fool of herself if she wishes to. And you have no right to set yourself up as her censor. If she puts you through agonies of embarrassment, you will sit and take it like a man, not snivel about your discomfort. You cannot truly believe that you added to the pleasure of our afternoon by the scene you created. The two major qualities of a gentleman are acting honorably and courteously. You did neither."

The stinging words lashed Henry as nothing else could have. His shoulders slumped dejectedly and he hung his head. "I'm sorry. I never thought..."

"The trouble with youngsters is that they never do think, beyond their own wishes. You are not alone,

Forrester, but that does not make your behavior any less reprehensible. In her concern for you, your cousin has allowed you more license than you should have. She has allowed your friendship to dull her authority over you. Her position is not enviable. Imposing the discipline which you should have would of necessity change your relationship, and she is far too young to realize that the benefits would outweigh the disadvantages...for you. And until recently it has not been necessary, I take it. Don't make it necessary in future, Forrester," Rushton said grimly, "or I shall have something to say about it."

"Yes, sir." Henry rubbed his temples and looked miserable. "I will apologize to Selina, of course. Honestly, I don't mean to hurt her, and sometimes I even know that she's right, but... Perhaps it *is* selfishness. But I'm not a child anymore, and I want to have some say in my life. Everyone is always telling me what I should do, and no one is asking me what I want to do. Selina tries to understand."

"Then see that you try to understand her. She has sacrificed a great deal to have the right to keep you with her, because she thought it would be best for you, and she was undoubtedly right. You may chafe under her protectiveness, and regret that she doesn't share your newly-discovered dream of independence, but she has devoted her life to raising you, and you cannot shrug aside the obligation that lays on you." Rushton crossed the short distance between them and laid his hand on Henry's drooping shoulders. "Don't think I don't sympathize with you, too. From sixteen to eighteen I was in a turmoil I shudder to remember. You can't make it an excuse for gauche conduct, though, as my father used to impress on me."

Rushton removed his hand and wandered thoughtfully to the window. "Do you resent my talking to you this way?"

Startled, Henry gulped, "No."

"You probably should," Rushton retorted smiling. "It is, after all, none of my concern. But I hope you will heed my advice; it is well-intentioned." He remembered Miss Easterly-Cummings' pungent remark on her good

155

intentions, and shrugged his broad shoulders. "I will be back in a few days for our next boxing lesson, if you wish."

"You will? But. . . . " Henry could not express the fear that he had so disgusted Rushton by his conduct that he would never see the man again.

"You and your cousin don't seem to understand my own supreme belief in my consequence," Rushton said querulously. "One word from me is supposed to so sufficiently dash your pretentions that it is not necessary for me to further annihilate you by word or deed. You do wish to continue boxing, don't you?"

"Yes, sir."

"Then I shall return in a few days."

Henry learned from Selina's maid that his cousin was in her room lying down. When she did not appear for dinner, he felt mortified and wretched with guilt. Rushton had not said how very upset Selina was, but Henry was beginning to draw an accurate conclusion. After his meal he sent a note up to her which said simply: *Please forgive me. May I see you?*

The slip of paper fell from Selina's hand after she read it. Of course she would have to see him, but she felt so exhausted, too spent to have another emotional scene. Tomorrow she would perhaps feel more like thinking about the problem, deciding whether she would do best to send him to his guardian. She flinched at the very thought, but considered it a real possibility. Where she had lost control over this burgeoning young man, Lord Leyburn, for all his coldness, might have more success. He was a man, and likely to better understand a boy of Henry's age than she. Such a solution appalled her, but tomorrow she might be able to look at the situation from Henry's point of view, or at least from what she considered to be best for Henry.

Selina took full responsibility for the afternoon's fiasco; it pointed out to her that she was really not the proper person to have charge of Henry. For years she had allowed herself an escape into drama when things became a bit much for her. She and Henry had found it a joke, and it was a way of relieving her pent-up emotions, and often of expressing her very real feelings on matters in a harmless way. Never before had she exhibited this penchant in front of anyone but Henry, and she could not blame him for being ashamed of her doing so in company.

Sadly she looked up at her maid from where she lay propped against the pillows. "Have Henry come up and join me, will you, Alice?"

The girl nodded and disappeared with the dinner tray, the food hardly touched, leaving the door open. In minutes Henry stood there, staring at Selina's pale face, uncertain of his reception and unwilling to enter the room until she noticed his arrival. He cleared his throat.

The dark eyes seemed enormous in her face. "Come in, Henry, and bring a chair by the bed. I wasn't up to coming down for dinner. Did you eat the calves' ears, or give them to Scamp?"

"Scamp is in hiding because McDonough laughed at her haircut. I'll see she gets something to eat later." The chair he was carrying knocked against the bed. He grimaced and sat down on it heavily. "Selina, I ... I know my behavior this afternoon was inexcusable. I was only thinking of myself and I made a scene. You see, I wanted you and Mr. Rushton to like each other. Well, he's being awfully good to come and teach me to box, and he helped with Scamp today.... I know you don't get on very well, but if he is to come around every so often, it would seem strange for you to avoid him all the time. You and I have always laughed at your dramatics, but he's so sophisticated.... I'm not criticizing you, honestly I'm not. You should do just as you please in your own house. I was afraid he would think you were ... eccentric or something."

"He always has, Henry. You did make an awkward scene and you must learn not to put a guest in such a position. It was every bit as uncomfortable as my play-acting. I won't do that again with company. We have done it so much that I suppose I didn't really think about doing it with Mr. Rushton there. And he didn't seem to mind. But I never meant to ... embarrass you."

"I won't have you apologize to me, Selina!" Henry

exclaimed. "I was entirely at fault. Rushton was not the least put out; he said so."

"You spoke with him afterwards?"

"He summoned me to the study and gave me a proper raking down." Henry flushed to the roots of his hair.

"I see." She shivered and drew the shawl more closely about her shoulders. So Mr. Rushton had decided for himself that she was no longer able to manage her charge, and had taken on the necessary task of scolding him. The significance of such an action made Selina's throat ache, and she bit her lip to control its quiver. "This will probably mean your going to live with Lord Leyburn, Henry. I shall miss you dreadfully, but it will be better for you at your age to have a man to guide you. Perhaps you will come to visit me sometimes, or . . . or join me on a trip to the coast, or one of the spots we have gone to before. For a week or two. No one could object to that! I am, after all, your only relation. But you mustn't think it necessary! If you are happy and busy and haven't time to get away, I shall understand. Why, I shall be pleased for you. Your happiness is my only concern, dear Henry. You have not even seen Bromley Manor since you came here. To see your own estate . . . Oh, it will cause you some sadness, no doubt, at first, but you will be proud to think of the day it will be yours to run and to make into a home. Lord Leyburn's seat is no more than a few miles from it, I understand, and, though he has tenants there now, I am sure he can arrange for you to see it."

Henry sat stunned through this recital. Never had he envisioned such a punishment for even his most dastardly crime as to be sent away from Selina and Shalbrook. Lord Leyburn was, to his mind, the bogeyman. A dim shadow in his memory, with no features to fill in his face, nothing more than an angular script on a quarterly letter. The man who directed his future from afar, as though he were a puppet on strings. Henry found himself unable to utter a word.

"Henry dear, my head is aching unbearably. Would you mind very much if we talked more tomorrow? I can't seem to think clearly and there is so much I want to say to you. Have Alice bring me a drop or two of laudanum in water, will you, love?"

Desolated beyond anything he could remember, including the death of his family, Henry rose unsteadily and nodded mutely. He must, as Rushton would decree, bear his punishment like a man, at least in her presence. Tomorrow, oh, if tomorrow ever came, he would humbly ask for a reprieve, promise to behave better in future, assure her that he could and would respect her authority over him. To be banished from the warmth of her affection to the coldness of an uncaring stranger, surely that was more than he deserved. Even when one considered his various misdemeanors of the last few weeks, even then it was too much. How could Selina think it would be "better" for him to live with Lord Leyburn? Who would there be in that large family of unknown people to take his cousin's place? After giving Alice her instructions, Henry went numbly along the corridor to his room.

Certainly it was the longest night Henry had ever spent. While Selina succumbed to the first ministration of laudanum she had ever allowed herself, Henry tossed and turned in his bed, advancing and discarding arguments which he would offer her the next day. None of them somehow seemed sufficient. Henry did not doubt her love for him; it was that love that terrified him now, for Selina had indicated that she was proposing this course not in anger but out of her firm desire to see him happy, established where he would have the proper guidance. Rushton had said that awful thing about Henry's not acting like a gentleman. More than anything, of course, Selina wished to see her cousin instilled with those virtues, and if she thought Lord Leyburn could provide them where she could not, then she would, even if it made her desperately unhappy, send him to his guardian.

In spite of his resolve to bear up under this adversity, Henry greeted the dawn hollow-eyed and desperate. As he pulled on his buckskins and top boots, he began to formulate a plan in his mind, hazy but determined, to talk with Rushton. After all, Rushton had combed his hair about Henry's behavior, but he had also indicated his sympathy with the boy's growing pains. Henry donned a shirt and waistcoat mechanically before knotting a kerchief at his throat. Even if there was time to tie a cravat properly, he had not the patience. Shrugging into his riding coat, he made no attempt to see that it set correctly on his long arms and bony shoulders.

There were few people astir in the manor and he met none of them as he slipped out the back door onto the flagged path leading to the stables. The day promised to be as fine as the previous one, with the dawn sun already beginning to dry the dew, and the heady smell of newly-turned earth pervading Henry's nostrils. Such a day would be perfect for him to accompany Mr. Sands on his rounds of the estate. Henry gulped down the lump in his throat when he realized there might never be a chance to do so now. His pace quickened as he neared Catastrophe's box.

The horse whinnied as he was being saddled, and stretched out his stride as Henry directed him to the village. Only after leaving Catastrophe at the Horse and Hound stables was Henry checked in his hell-bent progress toward Mr. Rushton. The innkeeper, newly arisen from his warm bed, was issuing directions for lighting fires when he glanced around at the opening door. "Mr. Forrester! You're about early, and no mistake. No trouble at Shalbrook, I hope."

"No, no. I must see Mr. Rushton," Henry explained, running a hand through his tousled hair.

"At this hour? You can't do that, my good sir. I've never known him up and abroad before nine or ten, and that only once or twice. No, no, you mustn't disturb him. You can wait in the coffee room."

"But it is urgent!"

"Nothing is so urgent as to wake a man from his slumbers," Mr. Evans said severely. "Come and have some coffee. I dare say you've not even had your breakfast at this hour. We've pigeon pie, ham and a round of cold beef, or you might prefer the kidneys and rashers. Or a poached egg and toast, or muffins. No one in Leicestershire keeps a better table than the Horse and Hound."

"I know, sir, but this cannot wait. Mr. Rushton is in the rebuilt rooms, is he not? I'll not tell him I met you on the way," Henry promised as he skirted the astonished landlord and fled down the corridor toward the wing.

Mr. Evans considered the possibility of pursuit, but decided it would be undignified, unsuccessful and probably needless. The quality had their own ways, and far be it from him to try to understand them.

Although his single-minded purpose carried Henry to Mr. Rushton's door, once arrived there he hesitated. Nothing would change in the next few hours and Rushton would undoubtedly think him the greatest dunderhead for awakening him to pour out his problems. He would label Henry an unthinking, selfish child, as he had thought him the previous day. Henry decided that his best course of action was to wait at the door until he heard sounds of movement within, and then he would knock. After a while he tired of standing and sat down leaning against the doorframe, in which position he promptly fell asleep.

Rushton's valet, Victor, arose shortly after Henry's arrival and began to quietly light fires in his master's bedroom and the sitting room. From years of experience he chose the clothing he would propose for the day's toilette, laying the items lovingly over a chair in such a way that no wrinkles would result. A stack of cravats, neatly folded and glistening whitely, he left on the chest of drawers while he set out the shaving kit. It was too early to fetch hot water for his master, who lay sprawled on the bed unconscious of the movement about him, but Victor was never begrudged his own luxuries, so he made his way to the door with every intention of going to the kitchen to obtain a can for himself. If it had occurred to Victor that someone would be sleeping in the doorway, he would of course have carefully stepped over the recumbent form. Unfortunately, such a thought never occurred to him, and Henry had slipped down in such a way that he was practically invisible in the dark corridor outside.

Thus Victor stepped squarely on poor Henry's most tender part, and stumbled on his face in addition. The resulting commotion—Henry's scream of anguish, Victor's yelp of terror as he careened toward the gaping staircase—might have awoken anyone for some distance around, and it certainly woke Rushton. Unaccustomed to being startled from his bed by such pandemonium, he lept up in confusion and raced for the doorway in his nightshirt. The sight which greeted his eyes did nothing to alleviate his mystification, for Henry lay rolling on the floor and groaning, while Victor clung precariously to the bannister which appeared in imminent danger of giving way.

"What the hell is going on?!" Rushton cried as he attempted to pass Henry in an effort to save his valet from peril. Not particularly alert yet, he failed to notice that Henry was struggling to stand in his presence. Henry's head caught him at the back of the knees, throwing him forward against his hapless valet, and the bannister promptly gave way. Henry watched horrified as the two men disappeared from view.

It was a short stair, but neither of the victims was in any mood to rejoice at this lucky circumstance. The broken piece of bannister, under their combined weight, careened down the stairs and stopped abruptly at the bottom, where their momentum caused them to smash against the opposite wall. Momentarily dazed, Rushton did not notice that his nightshirt was caught up about his chest, but the bedchamber maid who was carrying fresh linens along the lower hall was struck by it first thing. She screamed, and, dropping her burden, fled in the opposite direction. Henry looked over the remaining bannister and groaned.

People began to converge on the scene of the accident with gratifying speed. Chambermaids, guests, and eventually Mr. and Mrs. Evans themselves stood staring at the two shaken men. Rushton was the soonest to regain his senses, and his concern was more for his valet than for the gaping throng. He felt for Victor's pulse and found it beating steadily, but there was a gash on his forehead and his fingers were bloodied. "Here, give me a hand with him," he rapped out to the innkeeper, who stepped forward immediately at the command, but, out of decency, first tugged down Rushton's nightshirt before laying hold of Victor.

By the time they had carried the valet up to his bed, past the shaking Henry, Victor's eyes were beginning to flicker open.

"Lie still," Rushton ordered, as he busied himself dipping two of his lawn handkerchiefs into the ewer and wringing them out. "His fingers will need professional attention. Will you send for Dr. Turner?" he asked Mr. Evans.

"Right away, sir," the man responded as he backed toward the door.

"And see to the boy. If he's all right, have him come here."

Henry, still shaky on his feet, had remained in the hall as the procession passed, but he assured Mr. Evans that he was fine and would go to Mr. Rushton. Unable to break himself from the grip of this nightmare, Henry stumbled uncertainly into the suite of rooms, where he could see Rushton bent over a bed in a small room off the sitting room. Carefully he placed one foot before the other to traverse the distance, but once he stood beside Rushton he couldn't think of a thing to say.

"Are you all right?"

"I . . . I think so. How is your man?"

"He'll do well enough," Rushton grunted as he finished wiping away the blood from the fingers. "The gash on his forehead is not serious, but some of his fingers may be broken. What happened?"

"I don't know, exactly. I fell asleep in your doorway and I think he stepped on me."

The valet, who had again opened his eyes at the sound of their voices, turned his gaze to Henry and whispered, "I am very sorry, sir. I did not see you."

"What the devil were you doing sleeping in my doorway?" Rushton demanded.

"I didn't want to wake you. That is, at first I thought I would, and I came here shortly after dawn. Then I was afraid you would think I was being a child again, and only thinking of myself, so I decided to wait outside your door until I heard you get up. But I didn't sleep much last night and I fell asleep just outside."

Rushton regarded him sharply. "Is there something wrong at Shalbrook? Is your cousin ill?"

"No, well, she wasn't feeling well last night but I suppose she'll be better this morning." Henry cast a glance at the valet. "I must talk with you but this is not the time. I never meant to cause any trouble." He shrugged helplessly. "This is what I get for trying to be patient. I should have woken you when I got here."

"I'd have wrung your neck," Rushton informed him casually. "Wait in the sitting room."

After half an hour the doctor came and went into the valet's room where he stayed for some time. Rushton showed him out and then returned to take a seat near Henry's. "Victor has two broken fingers which Turner says will heal without impairing his use of them." He fingered a sticking plaster on his cheek. "He also informed me that my own slight cut will undoubtedly leave a scar."

Nothing more was needed to complete Henry's desolation. If he had not been sixteen he would have burst into tears.

Rushton laughed. "When I was your age I wanted a scar more than anything else, I think. Romantic, you know. Of course, I visualized receiving it in a duel where I was the champion of a lady's virtue or a gentleman's honor. Well, who's to know how I received it?" he asked cheerfully. "I'd best get dressed. You can come in and tell me your problem while I'm at it."

Henry stammered, "I . . . I can wait until you're done."

"Lord, Henry, everyone in the damn inn has seen me naked this morning, so what odds? But please yourself. I thought you were in a hurry."

"Well, I am." Henry followed his host into the bedchamber and stood by the window looking out. The black depression settled on him again, so that he began to fear that even Rushton could not help him. "I'm frightfully sorry about what happened this morning. Tell Mr. Evans that I will take care of any damage. No, I shall tell him myself so he knows I'm responsible for the whole."

Rushton sighed. "I expect he will manage to take

me aside and ask if I don't think I would find myself more comfortable at some other hostelry. Imagine being thrown out of a country inn! It will be a first, my boy." He inspected the fit of his pantaloons and asked abruptly, "Am I likely to be returning to Shalbrook with you?"

"I hope so," Henry said fervently.

"Hmm. Then I'd best wear the Hessians. You have not come yet to your problem, young man," he reminded his guest as he tugged on one of the boots.

"Last night Selina said she would probably send me to Lord Leyburn. He's my guardian."

With a muffled oath, Rushton tossed the second boot back onto the floor. "Nonsense! There is nothing she wants less."

Henry turned around to face him. "That's true, of course, but she talked about it being best for me. She wasn't angry about yesterday afternoon. That's to say, she did reprimand me, of course, but she started to apologize for her acting. Fancy! When I made such a fuss, she apologized for embarrassing me. We were just sitting there discussing what had happened, when all of a sudden she said I should go to Lord Leyburn, and talked a lot of rubbish about how I would see my estate, and maybe I would come to visit her sometimes. I don't want to go!" Henry wailed. "I want to stay with her. I can't even remember Lord Leyburn. Don't you think she is being too severe? Couldn't you speak to her? Tell her that I am not so different from other boys? I promise I will do better! She shall have all the respect due her. I needn't learn about the farming after all, or at least, I could do so only after my regular lessons. And I won't complain about them, or say anything derogatory about Dr. Davenport. Only, please, help me to convince her not to send me away!"

"Now, hold on, Henry," Rushton advised, unaware that he had fallen so easily into calling the boy by his Christian name. "I want you to tell me exactly how all this came about. You say she wasn't angry with you. Did you try to excuse yourself?"

"No, I don't think so. But I did try to explain."

"Explain what?"

Henry flushed. "Why I was embarrassed. I didn't want you to think she was strange or anything."

Rushton's lips twisted awry. "And what did she say to that?"

"She said you always had . . . thought she was strange," Henry mumbled.

"Hmm, yes. And then what happened?"

"Oh, I don't remember exactly. She scolded me and told me my scene had been just as uncomfortable as her play-acting, but said she wouldn't do that again in company. I wouldn't let her apologize for it! I told her you'd said you didn't mind."

"Ah, now we are getting somewhere. What did you tell her about our talk?"

"Just that you had rung a peal over me. I didn't have a chance to say anything more. That was when she started to talk about my going to Lord Leyburn. You will speak to her, won't you? I know I am asking a lot, but yesterday you seemed to understand. If you would do this one thing for me, I . . . I would not hold you to the boxing lessons. That is, I would be so greatly in your debt that I should not wish to impose on you further. Just please convince her not to banish me!"

"Is she likely to be up yet?" Rushton asked curiously.

"Ordinarily she would be, but after last night . . . Still, we could go there, couldn't we, and see? I don't want her to have a chance to get it firmly implanted in her mind, you know. She can be very stubborn when she thinks she's doing the right thing. Did that sound as though I was criticizing her? I wasn't! Mostly she is right, anyhow. Would you come now? We could have breakfast after you talk to her."

"Or even before I talk to her," Rushton murmured.

Henry flushed again. "Of course. Before you talk to her."

"Very well. Go down and have my curricle brought round. I'll just have a look at Victor before I come along."

SIXTEEN

Selina was seated at the breakfast table when she heard the sounds of arrival in the courtyard. When she had heard that Henry was not in the house, and learned from the stables when she sent for word that he had gone out shortly after dawn, she had been somewhat alarmed. Counselling herself to patience, she had sat down to an array of delicacies which she did not find in the least tempting. Now that he was home, her appetite improved sufficiently for her to spread a glob of jam on her toast and pour another cup of tea. Her appetite deserted her once more when the breakfast parlor door opened, and she found not only Henry but Mr. Rushton standing there.

Even the most casual observer would not have declared her to be in looks. She was dressed in a dark blue morning dress that was unexceptionable, but her face was pale and drawn and her eyes, especially when they rested on Mr. Rushton, looked haunted. Her visitor appreciated her distress at a glance, and with one longing look at the sideboard heaped with a half dozen dishes, said curtly, "Have your breakfast, Henry. I am going to take your cousin for a drive."

Not disposed to argue this summary command, Selina promptly rose to her feet. Best that everything was settled now, rather than drag it out for any period of time. He had no right to order either of them, of course, but at this moment he wielded a power neither would dispute. "I'll get my wrap," Selina said.

The royal blue pelisse she chose only served to make

her face look more pale, but she was not aware of the fact. In silence they made their way to the stables, and waited while the curricle was once more prepared. Not until they were driving easily down the lane did Rushton speak. "Your cousin said you were talking of his going to his guardian. Did you think because I spoke with him yesterday that I would have him removed from your care?"

"Yes."

"Miss Easterly-Cummings, how could you possibly leap to such a conclusion?"

Surprised, Selina regarded him with enormous eyes. "Why else would you speak with him, except that you thought I could no longer handle him myself? And I suppose I can't," she said, her voice strangled. "There is no reason you should believe me capable. Not only did I put on a ludicrous show, but I had hysterics as well yesterday. The only thing you didn't see was my fit of temper when I could not mount Starlight with Scamp in my arms."

"How many times do I have to tell you that I don't wish to harm you?" he asked exasperatedly.

"It's not a matter of harming me, I know. You like Henry, and you want to see that he fulfills his promise as a man. I understand, Mr. Rushton; don't think I blame you."

"You don't understand anything, my dear Miss Easterly-Cummings. First, I spoke to Henry because I wished to save you the trouble after your exhausting bout of tears. Second, I don't know Lord Leyburn from a hole in the ground, have no intention of communicating with him, and don't believe he would benefit Henry in any case. Third, I *do* like Henry, but I would not presume to be the arbiter of his fate. All I ever intended was to offer you some advice. That was unwise of me, I now realize, and even then I realized it was presumptuous. Perhaps I was driven to it by my irritation with you, or by my concern for the boy. In either case, I should not have involved myself in any way. I ask your pardon."

Selina was regarding him with incredulity. "Henry can stay with me?"

"I have absolutely nothing to say in the matter. How can I possibly make myself more clear? I have no more influence in the matter than Penrith, McDonough or Mr. Evans, for God's sake! And if I did, I would certainly have the boy stay with you. Oh, Lord, you're not going to cry again, are you?"

Rushton drew in his pair and watched fascinated as her mouth quivered uncontrollably. It was too much for him, and, as much to his own surprise as hers, he caught her in his arms and stilled her lips with his own. His kiss was not comforting, or brotherly, nor was it excessively demanding, but he kissed her thoroughly, because she let him. He did not delude himself that at any other time she would have been so accommodating. Her release from the burden of anxiety she had suffered since the previous day found an outlet in his kiss. It was a moment separate in time, not to be construed in relation to the past or the future.

When he released her she said, "Thank you," in a very soft voice and he replied, with no trace of amusement, "It was my pleasure." He could see no sign of embarrassment in her as he gathered the reins and urged the patient pair forward. After a while she asked, "How did you injure your cheek?"

"An accident at the inn."

"You weren't boxing with Henry by chance?"

"No."

"I just wondered."

"Would you like to take a walk in the vale?"

"Another day, perhaps. I should go home and speak with Henry. Did he come to you because he was upset?"

"He asked me to convince you not to send him away. When he explained what had happened last night, I thought I understood."

"Yes, I see. He has a great deal of confidence in you."

Rushton laughed. "He offered to exchange my intervention for the boxing lessons. Staying with you was much more important than learning to box, you know. You must tell him that I will still come to teach him."

"You are generous, Mr. Rushton. The stable staff said that he left shortly after dawn. I hope he did not awaken you."

"Only incidentally," Rushton replied, his eyes on the road ahead.

Selina looked at him questioningly but he did not satisfy her curiosity. "How is Lord John coming with the plans? I hope we didn't keep him from them too long with our problems here. The flooding, I mean."

"I had a note from him saying they were progressing very well. He has taken on two apprentices to do the working drawings."

"Do you know when you'll be ready to build?"

"Sometime in April, I imagine."

They continued to discuss indifferent topics until they reached Shalbrook, when Selina turned to him and said, "You probably have not had breakfast. Will you come in?"

"Thank you, no. I shall have my meal at the inn."

Selina smiled hesitantly. "Yesterday I made you miss tea, today breakfast. Would you dine with Henry and me tomorrow?"

"With pleasure." He jumped down from the curricle and handed her out.

"We dine at six."

He nodded and raised her hands, one after the other, to his lips. "Until tomorrow."

The color restored to her cheeks, Selina hurried up the stairs and waved happily to Henry where he stood anxiously watching for her at the breakfast room window. Just as she reached the massive oak door, she glanced back at the drive where Mr. Rushton still stood at his horses' heads, his eyes following her progress. Behind her she heard the door drawn open, but before hastening through it, she made him a curtsey.

Henry raced into the hall and caught Selina's hands. "I can stay?"

"Yes, my dear. It was a misunderstanding. Though I may not be the best person to guide you, I have no intention of letting you go. We'll muddle through together."

"I *will* do better, Selina, I promise. You'll see. I shall be a model gentleman, and not keep distressing you the way I have been. Rushton said it was difficult for him, too, at my age. Don't you see what that means? There is nothing wrong with him now."

Her eyes sparkling, Selina patted his cheek. "No, there is nothing wrong with him now—except his occasionally autocratic behavior. I have invited him to dine with us tomorrow, and he says he intends to continue your boxing lessons."

"Really? Not for several days, I imagine, though. I dare say he is a bit bruised from his . . . accident."

"What did happen this morning?" she asked, her curiosity once again piqued.

"It was the most awful thing, Selina." Henry groaned before he relayed, in horrifying detail, the events at the inn. To his astonishment his cousin succumbed to gales of laughter, protesting that she was very sorry for all their injuries, but that it was the most amusing story she'd heard in years. Miffed at first, Henry eventually saw the more ridiculous side of the escapade, and joined in her laughter. "But don't go telling Rushton that we laughed about it. He's very dignified, you know."

"He would understand," Selina said with conviction, not sure whence the certainty sprang. "I must see to a menu for tomorrow, and I dare say you have studying to do."

Eager to prove his reformation, Henry immediately agreed and went off to the study. Selina remained standing in the hall for some time, now grinning at his story, and again lost in more serious thoughts. When McDonough asked if he might be of assistance she pulled herself out of her revery. "No, thank you. I shall be in the library."

JOURNAL. March 23. I am beginning to think Cathford's notion not so preposterous after all. Have I lost my wits? This is not at all what I envisioned, and I am not sure that it is what I want. Irrelevant anyway, in all likelihood.

From the wardrobe in a spare bedroom, Selina, with Alice's assistance, dragged forth all the evening dresses she had once worn but long since consigned to obscurity. She had begun to make forays into walking, carriage, riding and morning dresses she had worn when she was younger, though they were sadly out of fashion. Her perusal of the *Ladies' Magazine* had assisted her to update some of these creations, and others she had already worked on for her trips to Tunbridge Wells and Margate. In her own neighborhood, it was all very well to be an eccentric, but she had never carried the matter to extremes. When she traveled with Henry, she was always becomingly, if not entirely fashionably, dressed. There had been little call for the evening dresses, however, and she surveyed them with dismay. Not one of them had any distinctive color to it—pale primroses, pinks, and several almost entirely white.

Choosing the most presentable, she allowed Alice to assist her into it, and found to her chagrin that it did not even fit well any longer. She had filled out from her earlier boyish figure, and the gown pulled across her bosom and draped awkwardly over her hips. "It's these thin, revealing fabrics. It won't do at all," she complained.

"No, miss," Alice agreed with a shake of her head. "Shall we try another?"

None of them fit appreciably better. Selina turned dolefully to her maid. "Could you make any use of them, Alice? I daren't ever wear even the jaconet muslin. Oh, Lord, what am I to do? I've invited Mr. Rushton to dine tomorrow, and I cannot very well appear in a morning dress. It would be insulting."

If Alice had any comments to make on her mistress' lack of foresight in dressing so abominably for the last few years, she kept them to herself. "Mrs. Armstrong in Leicester might have a model which could be suitably altered in a day. Clara could help me, as she's frightfully clever with her needle."

"Leicester? That will take hours!"

"Yes, miss, but I can see no other solution. You might purchase fabric in Quorn, of course, though I can't see it would be much help. Even Clara couldn't turn out an evening dress in that short a time."

"No, no, of course she couldn't. What was I thinking of to invite him for tomorrow? To invite him at all," she murmured despairingly. "Very well, Alice. If you

172

will order the carriage around, we'll go to Leicester. And I had so many things planned to do today...."

Selina stopped at the study on her way out. "I have to go to Leicester, Henry. Is there anything I can get for you? Or did you wish to come along?"

"Why are you going?" he asked bluntly.

"I had out all my evening dresses and not one of them will do for dinner. It's the most exasperating thing! If I had known I would have to go to all this trouble, I'd never have invited Mr. Rushton in the first place," Selina said crossly.

"You're never going to buy a made-up dress!"

"I have no choice, Henry. It is either that, or crying off the dinner."

"Then I shall come with you. If there is nothing suitable, we'll have to postpone it."

"So you have become a judge of ladies' fashions, have you, young man?" Selina laughed. "I don't mind if you come, but do hurry. I've already ordered the carriage."

Mrs. Armstrong's shop in Leicester would not have disgraced itself on Bond Street in London. Her country clientele had the greatest faith in her claim that her fashions were the very latest, that she smuggled in designs from Paris, and that no one in the county was better equipped to outfit the Quality. Located on Peacock Lane not far from South Gate Street, the storefront was a study in Georgian elegance with no more indication of its function than the sign which read: *J. Armstrong, Modiste and Milliner.*

Selina had had no cause to visit Mrs. Armstrong for many years and felt disgruntled as the bell tinkled when she entered with her cousin and maid. The giddy excitement she had felt when she visited the establishment to order her first ball gown was long gone but she felt the stirrings of interest as her gaze fell on two evening dresses displayed near the three-sided mirror. One in pale blue silk, the other in russet gauze, they caught the early afternoon light streaming through the small-paned windows. Mrs. Armstrong came hastening from the nether regions, and her eyes widened perceptibly on sight of Selina.

"Miss Easterly-Cummings! What a delight to see you again. And in the best of health, if these eyes don't deceive me. How can I help you today?" she chirped in a merry voice, her face wreathed with smiles.

"I find myself in urgent need of an evening dress. Nothing elaborate! A demi-toilette, if you will. And something that I could take with me today. It can be altered at Shalbrook if necessary, but I must have it for tomorrow evening." Selina turned her gaze to the russet gauze, and cocked her head consideringly. "No, I think that color would not suit me."

"You like the gauze, though? I have something similar in an emerald green, but the lines are even more simple. Yes, that might be just the thing. Or the rose silk." Mrs. Armstrong bobbed her head and left them, to return a few moments later with three dresses over her arm. The silver crape over a gray sarsnet slip she displayed first.

Henry shook his head firmly. "Definitely not, Selina. You'd look like someone's mother."

Regretfully, Selina agreed. The other two dresses, held up to her, both took Henry's fancy and she agreed to try them on. The rose silk clung to her in an alarming fashion, and she would not have consented to exhibit it to Henry but for Mrs. Armstrong's insistence. Moderately high in the waist, it was astonishingly low over the bosom, and Selina entered the outer room protesting, "I would have to tuck a scarf in the neckline. It's not decent."

"Everyone is wearing their gowns just so, Miss Easterly-Cummings," Mrs. Armstrong protested. She turned to Henry for support. "It is elegant, is it not? Your cousin looks a very picture. The height of fashion. No, no, you must not slink down in it, my dear. That is just as it should be." She adjusted the neckline and tiny gathered sleeves with their fall of blond. "Just so, I promise you. What do you say, sir?"

"She'll take it," Henry declared with an impish grin.

"I suppose I could put a brooch right here," Selina mused as she turned to study herself in the mirror.

Although Mrs. Armstrong's face registered horror at the very suggestion, Henry only laughed.

"Try on the other one," he suggested.

"Yes, it might be more modest," Selina agreed. It was not. If anything, it was even more décolleté than the first. Mrs. Armstrong had even more difficulty urging her out into the front room where Henry waited.

"Admirable," he intoned in what he considered an imitation of Rushton's manner.

Selina flushed. "Don't be ridiculous. It is worse than the last."

"She'll take it," he repeated with a laugh.

"I won't! Henry, have your wits gone begging? What would our guest think of me?"

"He would think you dressed in the height of fashion, and strikingly beautiful. I had no idea, Selina, that you could look so well. Truly I didn't. Buy a shawl if it will make you feel any better, but you must certainly take both dresses. If you don't, I shall buy them for you, and it would make a considerable dent in my allowance."

"Wretched boy! A shawl won't make the least difference, unless I tie it round my throat and let it hang down in front."

"There is a shawl that goes with the dress, Miss Easterly-Cummings," Mrs. Armstrong assured her, aghast at the suggestion of such an improper use of that item, "but I am sure you would wish only to drape it about your shoulders."

"Of course she will," Henry declared stoutly.

"Haven't you anything less ... more modest?" Selina asked desperately.

Mrs. Armstrong frowned. "Anything more modest would not be fashionable, and I would not carry it."

"You see," Henry said triumphantly. "You'll be all the crack, Selina. You look grand, truly you do. I think I like this one even better than the other, but I insist on your taking both of them."

"You haven't a thing to say to it," she retorted. Catching her reflection in the mirror, she had to admit that the dress was vastly becoming. But she did not want Mr. Rushton to think that she had dressed so elegantly just to impress him. She sighed. Really, there was no choice. She had to take one of the dresses, or cancel the dinner. And she did not wish to be caught without the proper apparel again. "I will take them both."

SEVENTEEN

When Mr. Rushton was ushered into the drawing room, Selina knew a moment's embarrassment as his eyes rested on her in surprise, and then he grinned appreciatively. She had chosen the rose silk as the lesser of two evils, and had pinned a cameo brooch where the neckline dipped most grievously. Fortunately, she was not aware that this tactic served merely to draw the eye exactly where she did not wish. He was himself dressed more formally than she had previously seen him, having discarded his pantaloons or buckskins for cream knee-breeches, his riding coat for a longtailed blue coat of superfine with gold buttons. His cravat was elaborately arranged, which in turn elicited an amused glance from Selina, knowing that his valet was in no position to have contrived it for his master.

"I trust the downpour did not trouble you, Mr. Rushton," she said as she extended her hand.

"Not in the least. I would have weathered a blizzard for such a treat," he assured her as he pressed her hand.

"I have scrutinized the menu to prevent its including any fowls' feet or calves' ears, so I believe we can promise you no dishes which must be consigned to Scamp."

"That was not precisely what I meant, but never mind. How is your dog? Recovered from her scratches?"

"Yes, but it will take longer to restore her dignity. She is there under the sofa, but she won't even come out to eat most of the time."

Rushton could see a furry tail thumping beneath the sofa and he crouched down and called, "Come, Scamp," in his most peremptory voice. A black nose poked out inquisitively and he snapped his fingers. Scamp came bounding out and rushed at him in a frenzy of delight. Heedless of his consequence and his hose, she jumped on his muscular legs. With a muttered oath, he instructed her to sit, which she did, slavishly gazing up at him, but not before she had managed to snag his immaculate white stockings in her descent.

"Serves you right," Selina said softly.

"No one in this house has any respect for authority," he retorted.

"How can you say that? Scamp came when you called and sat when you told her to. I do not generally even allow her in company, you know, and would have put her in my room had I known you would insist on encouraging her."

Henry came forward to interject himself into what appeared well on its way to becoming another quarrel between the two of them. "Shall I put her in the library, Selina?"

"Not on my account," Rushton protested before Selina could speak.

Dinner was announced before any further discussion could be held, and Selina allowed Rushton to take her in on his arm. She was seated at the head of the table with the two men on either side of her. Determined to reverse the prevailing atmosphere, Selina smiled at her guest and said, "I think you will find, Mr. Rushton, that the stream which runs through the vale, for all its meager size, will provide you with some decent fishing."

"I'm glad to hear that. Trout, I suppose?"

"Yes, and some grayling. Henry has always had the most incredible success as an angler."

Happy to be on a neutral topic, Henry offered his observations on the fishing, and the two men discussed the subject for some time. When they left off, Rushton exerted himself to be charming, as he had on the previous occasion when he had dined with Selina, and she decided that all that was needed to improve his disposition was a good meal. For Henry's benefit, he described Astley's Royal Amphitheater and the Four-in-

Hand Club, for Selina's, the entertainments at Covent Garden, Drury Lane and Vauxhall. He had amusing anecdotes to tell them of people they had read about, and a knowledge of politics which indicated his close association with powerful figures in the government. His monopoly of the conversation was not offensive, as his listeners plied him with enthusiastic questions and remarks on his more astonishing revelations.

Selina rose at last to say, "Be leisurely over your port, gentlemen. I shall be in the green drawing room."

Although Henry would willingly have joined her immediately, Rushton chose to keep the lad with him for a small foray into information-seeking. "Your cousin is looking charming this evening, Henry. One would think her gown came straight from London, and yet I am sure she has told me that she has not recently been there."

"Straight from Leicester," Henry laughed, as he recalled the scene in Mrs. Armstrong's shop, "yesterday. Poor Selina! She literally had nothing to wear for a formal dinner. We've not gone anywhere or had anyone in for as long as I can remember. Other than tea, that is. And she was very silly about the low necklines, but I told her they were just the thing. I was right, wasn't I? Ladies do wear such low gowns, don't they?" he asked anxiously.

"Oh, decidedly." Rushton took a sip from the glass he was twirling between his fingers. "They don't even wear cameo brooches to ... ah ... disguise the fact. Is your cousin as retiring when you go to one of the watering holes?"

"Well, no, not really. Usually, Mrs. Morrow comes with us to act as Selina's chaperone, but we don't go out much in the evenings. Sometimes to a play or a concert, you know. Selina used to tell me she liked to dance, but I don't remember her going to any assemblies. I think she always wanted to include me in her excursions. But I didn't use to realize that, you understand. At Shalbrook, we do lots of things together and I didn't think much of it when we went on holiday. Next time I shall insist that she enjoy herself and not stick to me. I've been abominably selfish, I can see now, but I didn't know before," Henry admitted, shamefaced.

"She wouldn't have done it if she didn't want to."

Henry was not cheered by this reflection. "That's only partially true, though. Selina is a pretty woman. She should have married by now, and I have no doubt she would have, had it not been for me. Those years when she should have been caught up in the social whirl, she was reading to me and helping me learn to walk again. Now that I am old enough to understand, she's on the shelf. That doesn't seem fair, does it?"

Nearly choking on his wine, Rushton murmured a noncommital reply.

"Shall we join her? If she's in the green drawing room, then we can convince her to play for us, as the pianoforte is there. She's rather good, I think, and she has all the latest music sent from London."

Selina was already playing when they entered, but she stopped and rose.

"No, do play for us if you will," Rushton urged.

"Come and choose something you like, then. Nothing is more boring than hearing the player's favorites." She indicated a stack of music from which Rushton diplomatically chose the most worn sheets as likely to be those she not only enjoyed playing but played the best. God only knew if Henry had an ear for music.

Rushton needn't have worried. Her performance was far better than he generally heard in drawing rooms where mothers would insist on showing off their daughters' minimal skills. Several times she sang as well, in a clear sonorous voice. When Henry joined her, it was obvious that they often amused themselves this way, for they were blatantly unaware of their audience, caught up in the music. It provided an opportunity for Rushton to study Selina without her noticing, something he had little chance to do. Not as beautiful as Miss Longmead, to be sure, but much more animated. Not as haughty, but with an inherent regard for her position. More than that, a self-esteem based on something beside the accident of her birth. And eyes that laughed rather than snapped with intolerance and condescension. Miss Easterly-Cummings' anger was a spark of emotion, not the cold lash of disdain Miss Longmead summoned to her service.

There was the other side of the coin, however. Miss Easterly-Cummings *was* an emotional, opinionated, eccentric lady. To be sure, she kept her emotions under control most of the time, and her opinions were largely in agreement with his own, but it could be exhausting to be around such a woman for lengthy periods of time. Knowing that she felt things deeply would not make for an ease of mind in those around her. One would have to be on one's guard not to upset or hurt her. No such problem arose with Miss Longmead, whose self-conceit shielded her from slings and arrows of any description.

And there was the matter of social aplomb. Miss Longmead—all the Misses Longmeads who graced London Society—understood the London conventions, and would not for a moment have contemplated oversetting them in any way. They were trained, (like good hunting dogs), to do their job as members of the *ton*. Born and bred to a life in the highest circles, one could depend on them never to discompose one. The same could hardly be said of Miss Easterly-Cummings: totally unfamiliar with London, probably uncaring for the stiff formality which reigned there. The trouble was that Miss Easterly-Cummings had lived so long secluded, in the most modest country circles, that she had developed a definite style of her own. Rushton did not doubt for a moment that she could mold herself to his circles ... if she wished to. But it seemed cruel even to contemplate changing her, asking her to conform to a different mode simply because it happened to be the accepted one. What had he told her? That there were many acceptable behaviors? Well, that was true enough, but to tamper with the girl's spirit....

Eccentric. Was it merely an act? In some ways, of course, it had been. She had easily left behind the strange costume in which she had first met him. But she had not even had an evening dress to wear tonight! What other lady of his acquaintance would ever have been caught in such a situation? And it wasn't just the clothes. She had obviously been raised in some ways as a boy would be—given freedom, urged to a responsible attitude toward her dependents, taught to think for herself—to make decisions, to wield authority, to believe in her ability to manage for herself. How could you make a good wife out of such material? You might as well write "obey" out of the marriage ceremony. Possibly "honor" as well. "Love"? Rushton allowed his eyes to dwell on the animated face, the curls which were almost too tight because of the damp weather, the slender shoulders, the provocative figure. Oh, if she loved you, everything else would pale into insignificance. Her loyalty, her deep attachments, her sensitivity could not be doubted. Rushton sighed as the closing notes of the song filled the room. He had never before seriously contemplated a love-match.

"I'm sure that's more than enough music for Mr. Rushton," Selina said with amusement. "I think he's about to fall asleep on us, Henry. Shall we enliven his evening with some three-handed whist? Or would you prefer quinze, Mr. Rushton?"

"Whist will be fine, but I promise you I enjoyed every moment of the concert." He led her to the table set by the window, where the storm outside could be heard more clearly. "Will this occasion you more flooding?"

"I do hope not, but it's a possibility. We've moved the families from any of the endangered cottages, and I'm hoping the measures Lord John suggested will be effective. At least this will provide us with an opportunity to test them. Will you deal, sir?"

Rushton dealt their hands, but he found it difficult to keep his eyes and his mind from straying to her. She played thoughtfully, her face expressive of her reactions to her cards.

When she caught him staring at her he commented, "I think you would not be good at gambling, Miss Easterly-Cummings. Your face shows far too much."

"Henry says that, too, but I fool him sometimes."

"She's very subtle," Henry complained. "When she taught me brag, she completely fooled me. I was so used to her giving herself away that I completely muffed it. I know better now."

"Ah, I see. Your cousin can resort to her acting ability when she chooses," Rushton suggested.

Henry flushed at this allusion to his scene, but Selina patted his hand and laughed. "It all depends on how determined I am to win, Mr. Rushton. When Henry gets cocky, I am especially devious."

Recovering quickly, Henry said, "When we finish this hand let Selina try her skill at brag against you. I think she will astonish you."

"She frequently does," Rushton murmured, as he played a card. "I should like to match wits with her."

"A challenge!" Selina declared mischievously. "I accept, Mr. Rushton."

Within minutes the two were examining their cards while Henry looked on, alternating his gaze from one to the other. Rushton's face was totally impassive, while Selina's was more mobile, but Henry was not deceived. His cousin could be as misleading with her expressions as she was with an unmoved countenance. At first Rushton seemed duped by her wide eyes and quirked brows, but gradually he accustomed himself to her tricks and began a strategy of his own. He frankly allowed his eyes to caress her face until he could see the pulse beating in her throat. When she accidentally discarded two cards she had meant to keep, she protested shakily, "Your acting is far better than mine, Mr. Rushton. Let's have the supper tray in. There is surely no need for us to continue to prove that you are the winner." So discomposed that a nervous gesture made several of her cards fall to the floor, she bent over to retrieve them, only to feel their hands touch as he assisted her. His face was close to hers and as their eyes met she was reminded of nothing so much as his kiss of the previous day. And she could have sworn that he was remembering it, too. She straightened, a little out of breath, and turned to her cousin. "Would you ring for the tray, Henry?"

Mystified by the silent undercurrents, Henry did as he was bid with a perplexed shake of his head. "I think you were not at your best tonight, Selina. You had better cards than Rushton, you know. Perhaps you're tired."

"Not in the least," she said stiffly as she caught a glimpse of Rushton's laughing eyes.

"I shall allow her a rematch sometime when she's up to it," he offered generously.

"You are too kind," she retorted sweetly, waving a fan before her warm cheeks, "but I am willing to concede that you play brag better than I, which is as it should be. How is your valet after his accident?" Selina smiled at her adversary with mocking eyes.

Rushton darted a questioning glance at Henry, who shrugged helplessly. "Victor has very little discomfort, though he will be unable to use his hands for a few weeks."

"Poor fellow. Is there something I can send him?"

"I think not, Miss Easterly-Cummings."

"And will you be able to manage without his services? I know how difficult it is to do for oneself," she sighed, "and men *will* wear their coats so tight they need a shoehorn to be inserted. And the delicate intricacies of the cravat! I shudder to think of how exhausting that will be for you. But of course there will be a boot-boy to help you with your footwear. Perhaps Mr. Evans could suggest someone to assist you until your valet has recovered."

"I shall manage," Rushton retorted. "I had thought to apologize for playing unfair, but I see there is no need. My only hope is that you had a good laugh."

"Oh, she did," Henry interjected. "I can't recall when I have seen her so amused, and she continued to chuckle all day. I was annoyed with her at first, but she said you would understand."

"Did she?" Rushton sought Selina's eyes and held them for a searching moment. "You surprise me, ma'am. I wouldn't have thought you'd realize that."

Selina was spared the necessity of a reply by the arrival of the supper tray. In the bustle which followed, she was able to ignore the remark and turn the discussion to the weather, which appeared to be clearing. None too soon for her, he made his farewells and the oak door closed behind him.

Still perplexed by the strange interaction between his cousin and Mr. Rushton, Henry said hesitantly,

"Well, I think everything was fine this evening. I mean, he seemed to enjoy himself and all."

"Oh, he enjoyed himself tremendously," Selina responded with asperity. "Good night, Henry. You were an excellent host."

"Thanks, my dear. You looked lovely."

They parted at the head of the stairs and Selina hastened to her room, where Alice awaited her. Automatically she allowed the maid to divest her of her new gown and bundle her into a flannel nightdress before she climbed into the half-tester bed and pounded the pillow. How could he look at her that way, she wondered indignantly as she snuffed the candle. And all of it acting! Not that she wanted him to look at her that way at any time! Yes, she did, she admitted to herself in an excess of frankness. Oh, why did she always find herself attracted to the most ineligible men? Couldn't she fall in love with some retiring country squire who would share her interest in the land and the people?

It was true that Mr. Rushton had turned out to be not such a stiff, haughty man as she had first envisioned, but that did not negate the fact that he was from a different world than she. His life was devoted to his own entertainment, his companions from high social and political circles with which she was unfamiliar. They had very little in common. She would put such nonsense away from her. How could she even allow such thoughts to enter her mind? There was Henry to think of, and Shalbrook. Quite enough to occupy one's mind, and heart, she assured herself as she listened to the renewed tapping of the rain against the glass. And she would see him from time to time while he was building his house, and next winter when he stayed there to hunt. It was not as though he would disappear tomorrow or the next day, never to be seen again. In time they would be friends, as she and Pen were. The thought was not at all consoling.

EIGHTEEN

The rain continued through the night and into the next day. Rushton found a certain amount of humor in the necessity of his feeding his valet, who was mortified by such condescension on Rushton's part. "Don't fret, Victor. Miss Easterly-Cummings would find it marvelously amusing, and there is nothing I enjoy more than giving her a good laugh," Rushton assured him.

"But she won't know, sir."

"All the more poignant," Rushton replied as he speared another bite of sirloin. "Do you know where my writing materials are?"

"Certainly, sir. In the writing desk. I set them out as soon as we arrived."

"I should have known. Victor, would you prefer to go home for a few weeks? You'd be more comfortable there, and not on the fidget about what you couldn't do." Though the valet could not think of the proper words with which to accept this offer, Rushton clearly read the relief in his eyes. "That's what we'll do, then. I'll put you on the stage for London. Would you mind very much delivering several letters there for me before you go on?"

"I feel sure I can manage that," Victor said gruffly. "Thank you, sir."

Rushton sat at the writing desk for some time, his chin in his hand, contemplating the blank sheet. The letter to the housekeeper in Curzon Street was a simple matter: have the house ready for his arrival in two or three weeks. The one to Cathford was much more tricky, but Rushton had a burning curiosity to find out if he had indeed meant Miss Easterly-Cummings. Eventually, he managed to ease in the question between mentioning that Lord John was designing his hunting-box and that he had bought the land from Miss Easterly-Cummings. Very neat, he decided. No hint of more than philosophical interest. Of course, there was the possibility that Cathford would miss the question altogether, but then Rushton could ask him when he got to town. For a minute he considered destroying the letter, since he would be in town so soon, but the urge to have the answer before then made him set it aside to go with Victor.

The letter to Sir Penrith was the most difficult, especially stressing that the invitation must come from Lady Southwood as though it were her own idea. Nothing could be more fatal than to have Miss Easterly-Cummings think that he had engineered the whole thing. It would say more than he wished to at this point, and it might very well frighten her. There had been some talk, Rushton recalled, about Pen's sister Maria coming to town for Cassandra's Season, and of Maria being Miss Easterly-Cummings' good friend. Rushton suggested that this might be another avenue for Pen to explore. *Just see that she gets there, and I will be forever in your debt. I'll offer to have her cousin stay with me, so that she doesn't have to worry about leaving him here alone.*

On the whole, it was a very unsatisfactory letter. He was not able to tell Pen *why* he wished Miss Easterly-Cummings to come to London, though certainly the very request would stimulate the most rampant speculation in Pen's mind. Well, let it. There was no more Rushton could or would say on the matter right now. Fortunately, Pen was a patient man and not particularly prying, except perhaps in the case of Miss Longmead, and that had been more a matter of his inherent aversion to Rushton's leaving himself open to gossip.

The three letters were duly dispatched with Victor on the stage that afternoon. Although Rushton drove past Shalbrook on his way to and from Leicester, he did not venture through the gates. He did instruct that a bouquet of daffodils be delivered there, with his note conveying his thanks for the previous evening. It would not do to present himself there every day, even on the pretext of teaching Henry to box. Now was the time to proceed very cautiously.

Although he had not done so in some time, and then only for his mother's benefit, Rushton attended church the next day. Miss Easterly-Cummings and Henry arrived early and seated themselves in the family pew. Rushton arrived late and seated himself at the back. Bored as usual by the service, Henry saw him enter and excitedly nudged Selina in the ribs. She glared at him and would not allow him to whisper the startling tidings, so she did not discover for herself that he was present until the end of the service. There was a matter of parish relief which she had intended to discuss with the vicar, but Henry's tugging on her sleeve, and her own inclination, decided her to put it off for the time being. She would send him a note that afternoon.

"Dr. Davenport, I doubt that you have met Mr. Rushton. He's building a house on the Ashfordby Road," Selina said by way of introduction.

The two men exchanged polite greetings, but Rushton did not remain long in conversation with the vicar, a man for whom he had developed a severe dislike in the course of one lengthy, boring and intolerably condescending sermon. As Rushton walked off with Selina and Henry, he shook his head. "If that is a sample of his usual fare, I don't think I shall bother to return. No wonder Pen's family have asked him to speak to the man."

"Have they?" Selina asked with a smile. "I cannot think it would do the least good, though the gift is certainly in Pen's hands. Dr. Davenport is oblivious to criticism; he is, in fact, unaware of any. He's Henry's tutor, you know."

"Intolerable! Henry, you have my most profound condolences."

They had arrived at the end of the churchyard and Rushton looked about for their vehicle. "Didn't you drive?" he asked incredulously.

"We were driven here, but we prefer to walk home."

"But it's several miles!"

"I know. Usually it takes that long to regain my composure after one of Dr. Davenport's sermons," Selina replied seriously.

Henry said, "We have the phaeton when it rains, of course, but today appeared fair enough."

"Come with me to the inn and I will drive you back." Selina began to refuse, but Rushton continued, "Henry might like to take the ribbons."

A gleam appeared in Henry's eyes and Selina sighed. "Very well, Henry. You go with Mr. Rushton and I'll see you later."

"Nonsense. You are to come with us," Rushton declared.

Selina raised a disapproving brow. "Mr. Rushton, I wish to walk home, and, in case it has never been pointed out to you, a curricle will only hold two people."

"I had intended to stand up behind."

"Like a tiger?" Her eyes danced. "I would really have loved to see it, Mr. Rushton. Perhaps you will show me another day." With a casual wave of her hand, she turned and walked through the gate and down a path leading across the fields.

"Your cousin is the most vexing woman I have ever met," Rushton growled as he and Henry set out in the opposite direction.

"Well, you know, she's a bit stubborn and all, but I have always admired her for doing just as she pleases. If she wants to walk, she walks, and no amount of polite pressure will deter her. Sir Penrith often offers us a space in their carriage, but Selina is never one to accept out of a feeling of obligation."

"Do you really enjoy walking miles after church?"

"Not as much as Selina does, but I don't mind. At first, I was just so grateful to be able to walk that I would go anywhere. There's not much one can do on Sundays anyway, you see, so spending the time walking home is rather fun. Selina teaches me the names of trees and birds and such, or we play guessing games. But you mustn't think she minds walking alone! I've never known her bored by her own company. She says walking gives her a chance to think about things."

"She goes walking alone?"

"Scamp usually goes with her, and sometimes I do. Generally she stays on Shalbrook land; there's more than enough to make for good, long walks."

Rushton ended by allowing Henry to drive his team all the way to Shalbrook. They caught only the barest glimpse of Selina far across the fields, but Henry had a marvelous time. It was not at all the way Rushton had expected the day to turn out.

Courting was turning into a very heavy business, Rushton decided, as he drove the grays into the stableyard at Shalbrook. If he didn't know of Lord Benedict, and probably Geoffrey Haslett, as previous suitors of Miss Easterly-Cummings, he would have said of a certainty that she had never been courted before, and had no interest in being courted in the future. Probably the latter was true, anyway. It was just as well that he had the excuse of coming to give Henry a boxing lesson. The way things were going, Rushton was not the least certain that he wanted to court the young lady, after all.

Coming out of the stables to stand at the horses' heads, Morris greeted Rushton as a now familiar visitor. "Fine day, sir. Shall I unharness them and give them a good rubdown? I've no time for these public stables, though I will say Joe Evans runs one as well as could be expected. You'll be a while, then?"

"I expect so. Miss Easterly-Cummings and her cousin are at home, I take it."

"Yes. Out riding they was earlier, but unless they be walking, you're like to find them in the house."

"Thank you."

Rushton was ushered into the library, where he found Selina and Henry poring over a letter. His arrival was greeted with enthusiasm by the latter, and a warm smile by Miss Easterly-Cummings, who extended her hand to him. "We have just had a letter from Lady Southwood. What a dear woman she is. Actually . . ." She paused bemused, as he raised her hand to his lips. "Ah, actually it is rather a joint effort with her daughter Maria Franmore, who was my closest

190

friend when we were young. Cassandra is having the most delightful time in London."

"Well, tell him the important part, Selina," Henry said impatiently. "Lady Southwood has invited Selina to stay with them for a few weeks—to see London and be at Cassandra's ball."

"Isn't that kind of her?" Selina asked. "Imagine thinking of me, when she has so much to do in preparation for Cassandra's ball. I shan't accept, of course, but it makes me feel . . ."

"Not accept!" the two men exclaimed in unison.

"But of course you will, Selina," Henry protested. "You are not to stay here on my account. It is time you had some fun."

"I have promised to be in town shortly myself," Rushton told her, "and I had thought of inviting Henry to come with me. I shall only be a few weeks, and it would do him no harm to acquire some town polish. You could keep an eye on him," he suggested quizzingly.

Selina regarded him with astonishment. "Take Henry with you to London? Whatever for? He is far too young to attend parties, and gaming houses, and . . . and all the other places I am sure you frequent."

"I promise you I have no intention of leading him astray, Miss Easterly-Cummings. He is not too young to attend Astley's, or see the Tower, or explore the maze at Hampton Court," Rushton returned stiffly. "He would enjoy visiting Jackson's and Manton's, and seeing Westminster Abbey."

"Mr. Rushton," Selina said slowly, enunciating each syllable carefully, "I cannot picture you bear-leading a lad of sixteen in London. The imagination buckles under such an outrageous load. And I fail to see any humor if this is a jest. It is unfair to raise Henry's hopes by even mentioning such a scheme."

Somehow, it had not occurred to Rushton that she would see anything absurd in his taking the boy under his wing. He had, in fact, thought, when he had thought about it at all, that she would see it as a sign, perhaps more pointed than he wished to give, of his interest in her. To have the tables turned on himself in this way was hardly pleasant. Resisting a desire to shake those slender shoulders, he asked, "Would you deny Henry the treat of seeing London, Miss Easterly-Cummings? Of meeting the other boys who will be there on Easter holiday? Of viewing the world through other eyes than yours?"

"I deny Henry very little, Mr. Rushton. Take him with you! Show him the cockpits and the prizefights. Have an ice with him at Gunther's. Take him to a balloon ascent and a fair. You will have the most enchanting time. And don't forget to take him with you to Covent Garden or Drury Lane. I'm sure your friends will be most amused by your latest acquisition. Perhaps others will scout out their nephews and cousins to sport them about town, too. You can start a new fad."

"Selina," Henry said brokenly, "I am sure Mr. Rushton meant no harm. He didn't think of what a nuisance it would be to have a b-boy with him; he was only being kind."

"I thought so," Rushton remarked evenly, his temper well under control now. "At sixteen, I considered Henry old enough to amuse himself without my constant attendance. There will be other young men there, for him to explore London with and taste the delights that fellows his age find most intriguing. I had not intended to abandon him to his fate, *or* act as his nursemaid. I shall not be so preoccupied as to be unable to provide him with guidance, but if he isn't old enough to scout about town on his own, I would not consider taking him."

"He may go if he wishes, and if he feels capable of managing on those terms," Selina replied with a notable lack of enthusiasm.

"Won't you come and stay with the Southwoods?" Henry begged. "You have often spoken of all the things you would do if you ever got to London, and this is your chance."

"This is not the time to visit them, Henry. No one wants a house-guest when they are preparing for a large entertainment."

"But they've invited you!" Henry protested.

"Probably Maria is being impulsive. We have written of seeing one another this summer, and she is eager

192

to show off her family to me. But that can wait. She plans to return to Oak Park with Lady Southwood at the end of the Season." Selina laid a hand on Henry's sleeve. "If you wish to go, Henry, then you should go. I trust you will behave yourself and not cause Mr. Rushton any trouble."

Henry cast a despairing glance between his two elders, torn between a strong desire to visit the capital and an equally strong desire to please his cousin. This should surely be the time for him to keep his promise to show Selina respect, to accede to her authority. With a pathetic attempt to subdue his contrary emotions, he turned to Rushton. "It is very good of you to even think of taking me with you, sir, and I...I thank you most sincerely. I could not impose so on your good nature, however, and I shall have to decline."

"Oh, Henry, you gudgeon," Selina said mournfully. "I am not asking you to make sacrifices. Please go with Mr. Rushton. Impose on him! Eat him out of house and home! Use his horses and his carriages. Take up his time showing you about. He deserves to be repaid for all his thoughtful intervention in our domestic matters."

Rushton had just decided that he was crazy to have ever considered Selina as his wife. With a tongue like that, he would not have a moment's peace for the rest of his life. He caught a glimpse of her shaking shoulders as she turned away, and for a moment he thought she was crying again, but no, a gurgle of laughter escaped her, and soon she was laughing outright to both his and Henry's astonishment. When she had regained sufficient composure to face them she said, "Forgive me! On the surface it *is* a ludicrous notion, you know. Why on earth would Mr. Rushton want to be unnecessarily saddled with a youngster? And in London, of all places! I am not used to thinking of your acting on generous impulses, sir. It is really very kind of you and I am sure Henry will enjoy himself tremendously. And I don't think you would be unduly hampered by his presence. He's quite able to look after himself, as you suggested."

"And you think perhaps I would not lead him astray?" Rushton asked gravely.

"That I am not so sure of," Selina said wryly, "but, do you know, I feel I may trust you. Oh, you will take him places that I would not go, but that is not to say that Henry shouldn't. Did I . . . offend you, Mr. Rushton? I have a way of doing that, haven't I?"

"Yes, my dear lady, you do. Just once," he declared in imitation of her previous performance, "I would like to have an interview with you that did not consist largely of wrangling. Just out of curiosity as to whether it could be accomplished, you understand. If I were to present myself here tomorrow at two to take you driving, would you endeavor to satisfy my whim?"

Selina dropped her eyes from his. "Yes."

"Very well. You may expect me."

"You *will* have a good meal before you come, won't you?" she asked impulsively.

His eyebrows rose in wonder, but he merely shrugged. "Certainly, if you wish it. Henry, shall we get on with our lesson? Until tomorrow, Miss Easterly-Cummings."

JOURNAL. *March 30. Should have waited for the post before going to Shalbrook; Pen's letter warned me that Miss E-C would hardly consider it commonplace for me to invite Henry to London. I have urged the boy to convince his cousin to go to the Southwoods', but I see little chance of his success. The best-laid plans and all that . . . Lord John comes with the plans Friday.*

NINETEEN

"I thought I might show you my first endeavor in the vale," Rushton suggested as he handed Selina into the curricle. Although the sun shone, the air was chilly and she wore the scarlet mantelet which he thought delightful on her. "Shall I put the rug about you?"

"No, thank you. I'm perfectly warm. Have you done something in the vale already?"

"Yes, but I intend for it to be a surprise. I've been organizing for the construction, too. Lord John has given me a list of the various trades we'll have need of, and I have found a personable young man in Barton who has undertaken to arrange for the hiring. He has been instructed to use neighborhood people wherever possible, of course," he assured her.

"I'm glad."

"It was part of our agreement. His name is Drew Norton. Do you know him?"

"Yes." Selina watched his large hands as they lightly guided the pair through the Shalbrook gates and left onto the road. "If you had asked my advice, I would have recommended him."

"Hmm. It gave me great satisfaction to find him on my own," he retorted.

"I'm sure it did. Have you seen Lord John recently?"

"No, he's to come Friday. Construction will probably begin just when I am to leave for London."

"Should you not delay your trip?"

"I can't. Have you reconsidered going to the South-woods'?"

"No. Have you reconsidered taking Henry?"

"No, Miss Easterly-Cummings, I have not. You aren't really alarmed at the prospect, are you?" He watched her profile for a moment, since her gaze was toward the rolling hills.

"Of course not. It is just what he needs." She returned her eyes to the road. "I feel sure Pen would assist you if ... if you have other matters which will require your attention."

There was a strange note in her voice which drew his attention. Now what could he possibly have said to hurt her? The brown eyes would not meet his, and those provocative lips were ever so slightly turned down. He said softly, "I won't take him if you really don't want me to."

"But I do. I think it's a splended opportunity for him." Selina studied the vale as they approached. "Should I be able to see your surprise now?"

"No. We will have to walk beyond the trees. You won't mind, will you?"

"Not at all. Oh, you've made a gate, and had a drive started."

"There were a number of things which we could begin before the actual house construction. I fear I am a trifle impatient." Handing her the whip and reins, he jumped down to unfasten the new gate. "Drive them through if you will, and I'll close it again."

"Why not just leave it open for our return?"

"You'll see." He noted that she was as carelessly elegant in handling his pair as she had been in jumping her own fence with Scamp in her arms. As he climbed back in he asked, "Would you like to handle them for a bit?"

"Thank you. They're very fine animals."

The drive was still unfinished, and rough, but Selina had no trouble in guiding the horses through the first section of woods to the clearing. Here Rushton tied them and handed her down, explaining as he did so just where the house would be. "The glass room will be facing due south, over there, with the entry on the east. When Lord John comes Friday he'll start Drew with a list of the material requirements, so that we

196

needn't be unduly delayed over obtaining them. Come, let me walk you through the house."

His enthusiasm for their imaginary tour of inspection was infectious, and Selina smiled up at him. "And the stables? Where will they be?"

"Over there. No, you can't come out through there," he teased. "That's a wall." Pretending to guide her properly, he tucked her arm through his and led her out the door in the glass room.

"Have you decided what use you will make of it?"

"The glass room? Well, it depends. I prefer a billiard room, but under some circumstances I would be willing to use it as a breakfast parlor. I had intended a very masculine retreat, you understand." That was quite enough to tell her, he decided, as he grinned down at her.

To his surprise her face lost its animation and she said in a choked voice, "I see."

"What do you see, Miss Easterly-Cummings?" he asked, mystified.

Ever since he had said the previous day that he had promised to go to London, she had suffered from the most alarming thoughts. Had not Mr. Haslett told her that Rushton had offered for someone—a Miss Longstreet or Longmeadow? Of course Mr. Haslett had thought Rushton had been refused. Selina found that unlikely. Perhaps he had been, but the young lady had changed her mind. More likely, however, that they had arranged to meet during the Season and settle matters between them. Why else would Rushton speak of a promise? If he were going purely for his entertainment, he would not have said he "could not" delay his trip. He would not now be speaking of some unspecified change to his planned "masculine retreat." Selina brought her unhappy thoughts to an abrupt conclusion to say diffidently, "I see that your use of the room is still flexible."

Dissatisfied with her answer, he yet saw no advantage in pursuing his questioning. The only conclusion he could draw, and he refused to do so, was that she understood that he was contemplating offering for her, and the thought made her unhappy. He was not at all sure that she would accept him if he did offer for her, but there was no particular reason why his doing so should make her unhappy. If she didn't want to marry him, she wouldn't. As Henry had said, she very much followed her own course. Henry. Perhaps she thought he would not be willing to accept Henry along with her. Well, there was nothing he could say now to disabuse her of that idea, if he had not already done so by inviting the lad to go to London with him.

Selina continued to walk through the woods with him past the building site to the fields beyond, lost in agonizing thought. For some time she did not realize that he was speaking until she heard him say, "I thought there was no reason not to put the land to some use. Actually, I got the idea from Lord Benedict."

Suddenly she pulled her hand from his arm and began to walk hastily back toward the woods. "Where the devil are you going?" he called, but she did not answer, merely walking a little faster. Stunned by her precipitate departure, it took him a moment to realize that she had no intention of returning. With long, angry strides he caught up with her as she entered the forest path, and grasped her arm in a tight clasp. "Will you answer me?"

"I am afraid of cows," she gasped.

"Bulls, Miss Easterly-Cummings. You are afraid of bulls. No one is afraid of cows."

"I am," she whispered.

"For God's sake, don't be ridiculous. Half the land in Leicestershire must be used for grazing. No one raised here could possibly be afraid of cows."

Selina gave an involuntary shiver. "You needn't believe me, Mr. Rushton. It doesn't really matter. Please take me home."

"Now how in the hell was I supposed to know that you were afraid of cows?" he asked mutinously. "I've never met anyone who was afraid of cows. If you'd said so, I wouldn't have taken you to see them. For God's sake, slow down! They aren't chasing us, you know."

She sneaked a look behind her and forced herself to a more dignified walk. "I realize," she said stiffly, "that it is an irrational fear. No cow has ever so much as

198

harmed a hair of my head, so far as I can remember. They are, in fact, dear, sweet creatures of a rather placid disposition," she continued as though reciting a lesson. "I have never been chased by a bull, either. On the other hand, I have never gotten close enough to a bull for him to chase me . . . and I do not intend to."

"I haven't even gotten a bull yet," Rushton protested. "I'm having one sent from Farnside."

"How nice for you," she mumbled, climbing into his curricle without waiting for his assistance.

Thoroughly disgruntled, Rushton untied his pair and climbed up beside her. "That was my surprise," he said hollowly. "I thought you would be pleased to see the vale put to some use in addition to the house."

"A commendable project," she murmured.

"Until a few minutes ago it certainly seemed so. I could have a deer park instead. Are you afraid of deer?"

"No, I'm not afraid of deer, but don't be absurd. What does it matter if you keep cows? I will know better than to stray onto your land in future."

"But . . . I want you to feel free to come here, to walk in the vale when you wish."

"That is thoughtful of you, Mr. Rushton, though a bit unrealistic. Once your house is complete, no one will venture on your grounds for a simple country stroll."

"What I can't understand is how you can walk for miles around Shalbrook if you have this fear, Miss Easterly-Cummings. There must be cows everywhere."

"I am always aware of where the cows are on my lands, and Scamp is a wonderful warning system for the occasional mistake."

"Is Scamp afraid of cows, too?" he asked sardonically.

"No, she loves them. She doesn't like horses."

"You brought her home on your horse."

"Yes, and she scratched me severely for it," Selina grumbled as she pulled back her sleeve to exhibit the almost-healed wound. "I was very foolish not to accept your offer to wait for us."

"You don't like to accept help, do you, Miss Easterly-Cummings?"

"No, I suppose not."

"You should learn to. The pleasure you get from helping people is no different than they get from helping you. There is no disgrace in it, you know." As Rushton drew his pair in for the gate, Selina studied her hands intently. "I'm not scolding you, my dear," he said gently, "just offering another piece of unsolicited advice." When she still did not look at him, he laid a hand over hers and softly turned her face towards his. "I am not in the habit of interfering in other people's lives, you know. But we are ... friends, are we not?"

Her piquant expression struck him forcibly, and he touched his lips lightly to hers before forcing himself to silently hand her the reins and whip and jump to the ground. Selina watched bemused as he opened the gate and waved her through. When he was once again seated beside her, neither of them spoke, though the very air seemed charged with tension. Brief as it had been, the kiss had unsettled them both. It brought to mind their previous experience, that astonishing timeless adventure which promised nothing, and had yet served its purpose well.

Selina wondered if it had become less significant for a man to kiss a woman; when she was younger, only attached couples did so, and she could remember Maria blushing when she spoke of Franmore kissing her after they had agreed to be married. Or perhaps Mr. Rushton thought their ... friendship allowed of such a liberty. Surely it did not! Penrith was her friend, too, and yet she could not picture him kissing her so, even such a swift, light thing. He might, if he were moved by something, salute her cheek—though he never had. No, she decided indignantly, Mr. Rushton should not have kissed her.

Covertly watching her expressions, Rushton knew when she arrived at this conclusion. "It's too late to slap me, Miss Easterly-Cummings, so I hope you will forgive me," he said gravely, though his eyes belied any real seriousness.

"You think because I allowed you to kiss me that day I was upset ... I shouldn't have, I suppose, if it gave you the idea I was ... I'm not like that, Mr. Rushton. You are too accustomed to the morals of London

Society, I fear. In the country a more proper atmosphere reigns, I assure you." Selina twisted her hands agitatedly in her lap. "No, it is my fault. I gave you a mistaken impression and my actions will of course mean more than my words. I think perhaps I should not see you alone again."

"Don't be ridiculous," Rushton snapped, annoyed more with himself than her. "I am entirely to blame, and I promise you I have not received the wrong impression of your moral rectitude, Miss Easterly-Cummings. I won't attempt to kiss you again without your permission."

"There, you see? You suffer from the illusion that I would give you my permission. I won't! No more than I would give Frank..." A mortified blush splashed across her cheeks, and she longed to disappear from the moving carriage.

Although he strongly wished to know the conclusion of her unfinished sentence, Rushton guided his pair through the Shalbrook gates without a word. He drove around to the stables so that he could leave the curricle and walk Miss Easterly-Cummings to the house. Her color remained high, but she graciously took his arm and attempted, in a rather choked voice, to discuss matters of no importance. The walk up the terraces seemed endless to her but all too short to him. Rushton knew she would not invite him in.

"Won't you come to London to visit the Southwoods?" he asked in the middle of her comment on the daffodils poking up through the earth.

"Why, no, I can't do that."

"Lady Southwood won't notice one more person in the house, you know."

"They would try to entertain me, knowing that I have not been there before. And... and I have not the proper clothes for London," she admitted. "There isn't time to amass a suitable wardrobe, even for a short stay, and if there were time, what use would it be to me later?"

"The modiste in Leicester..."

Selina shook her head. "If there is one thing you might try to accomplish with Henry while you have him, Mr. Rushton, it is not to let his tongue wander off with him. He is far too frank, which is only to say he has no sense of discretion as yet. I would be infinitely grateful to you should you manage to instill a certain amount of reserve in him."

"I encourage him to talk about you."

Her eyes widened. "Whatever for?"

"You are more reserved than your cousin, Miss Easterly-Cummings. If it were left to you, I'd know nothing about you at all—except your problems in raising Henry."

"There is little to know about me."

"Patently untrue," he retorted, his mind locked on Lord Benedict and Geoffrey Haslett. Surely Benedict's name was Frank. . . . They stood before the door, and it was obvious that she intended for him to use the knocker, as she glanced toward it twice, but he could not allow their interview to end without assuring himself that it would not be their last. "May I call to take you riding on Saturday?"

Selina hesitated, her eyes searching his face. His regard was kindly, even affectionate. How could she refuse him when she might not have the opportunity of spending time again with him after his trip to London? What if he brought that Longstreet (or whatever) lady back to see the progress of his hunting-box? Yet how could she accept, when she had said they should not be alone together again? But he had promised not to kiss her, without her permission. And she had told him she would not give it. Was his intent perhaps to soothe over any misunderstanding between them? "I . . . yes, that would be fine, Mr. Rushton."

"Shall I have a good meal first?" he asked quizzingly.

"If you would."

"Certainly." He finally raised the knocker and tapped it firmly. "I shall call early, about ten, if that is satisfactory. Then I can have a session with Henry afterwards."

"He'll be pleased." The door opened and she smiled hesitantly before entering. "You don't have to eat a lot

202

if you're not accustomed to do so in the mornings. That would defeat the purpose, wouldn't it?"

Not knowing what the purpose was, he shook his head wonderingly as she slipped through the door.

TWENTY

Saturday morning arrived with a downpour of rain. Even half awake Rushton could hear the constant lashing of the drops against the window panes and he rose swiftly to draw back the garish purple draperies and survey the wet, gray world outside. He should, of course, send a message excusing himself, but he did not wish to miss the opportunity of seeing Miss Easterly-Cummings when it was but a few days before his proposed departure for London. The weather showed no sign of clearing; it would be impossible to ride with her. He *could* give Henry the promised boxing lesson. Purposefully he tugged off his nightshirt and began to dress himself.

The hood of the curricle provided little protection against the driving rain, and a mile out of Barton he regretted his decision. His driving coat was soaked through, his pair skittish on the slippery surface of the road and his temper none too placid from either circumstance. What would she think of his coming out on such a day? Surely it was as good as a declaration, and he was not prepared to offer for her as yet.

What was it Cathford had said in his reply?

How surprising you should remember my comments on Miss E-C! She is indeed the young lady to whom I referred, but that is years ago. I was so struck by her looks, her courage and her personality that I half fell in love with her myself. There was some talk of an attachment, to a soldier off in the Peninsula, but I would still have made a push for her had I thought myself equal to her spirits. A glorious girl, but you know me, Gareth—too reserved by half for such a one! She would need a sturdier hand on the reins than I possess. And I thought of you. What a pair you would make! Don't you like her? Sally has agreed to marry me in June.

A glorious girl, yes, but so alien to his way of life. She had not fallen in with his plan for her to appear on the London scene so that he could judge her ability to assume the role he was contemplating for her. Not that it was a test—surely he was not so presumptuous as to require of her that she prove acceptable to the ton! As the curricle slid dangerously close to a ditch at the side of the road, he gathered his wandering wits to steady his pair. Would he go through life perpetually distracted by her, he wondered dismally as the carriage regained the solid surface. And, yes, it was a test, his wanting her to go to London! If she could not enjoy the life there, then it was senseless to marry her, even if she was the most enchanting woman he had ever met. Perhaps she had seen the trap, and that was why she refused to go. Certainly her excuses were feeble enough. The Southwoods' hospitality was well known, and preparation for even so great an event as Cassandra's comeout ball was not likely to dim their reception of an old family friend. And from the example she had shown him of the Leicester modiste's expertise, there would have been no trouble in clothing her adequately in the time allotted.

A crack of lightning startled his pair no less than he himself. They bolted down the road, careening past the Shalbrook gates at just the moment he had started to rein them through. The subsequent confusion taxed his driving ability too far for his present state of mind. For a moment he thought mournfully that his distraction was going to cost him his life, as the light vehicle swung crazily against the bank with a consequent rending crack as the splinter bar gave way. Only with the deftness of long experience was he able to control the panic-stricken horses and bring them to a halt without further damage to themselves or the curricle, which hung from the cracked splinter bar like a broken toy.

Castigating himself for his carelessness, he leaped down from the carriage and went to his horses' heads, his calm voice reassuring, his hands searching their legs for any sign of damage. Relieved to find none, he expertly released them from the harness and began to lead them toward Shalbrook. His arrival at the stables caused a certain amount of concern, and Morris insisted he go straight into the house. "For you're wet to the skin, sir, and the lads and me can look after your beasts. No harm done, so far as I can see. No, no, we'll see to the curricle when the rain lets up a bit. Fancy your coming out on a day like this," he said with a disapproving shake of his head.

Rushton would gladly have returned to the inn, had he had the option, but since there was no longer any possibility of doing so, he made his way to the rear door he and Henry had used on the day Scamp had entangled herself in the brambles. His boots were muddy and rain dripped from the various capes of his driving coat—not for the world would he have presented himself at the front door. His knock was answered by a startled footman who instantly recognized him, but was at a loss as to how to handle the situation.

"If you would kindly inform Mr. Forrester of my arrival ... and my condition," Rushton suggested patiently, "I will await him here."

He was not to be allowed the consolation of appearing only to Henry, however. The footman, large with his news, found Henry with his cousin in the study and announced in grave tones, "Mr. Rushton has come to call and is at the rear entry, and I fear very much the worse for the weather."

Selina and Henry shared a startled glance and immediately proceeded to their very uncomfortable guest, who had deposited his soggy gloves and hat on the stone floor beside the door and was attempting, ineffectually, to wipe the moisture from his face with a soaking handkerchief.

"Good Lord!" Henry exclaimed at sight of him. "We had no thought that you would come out on a day like this, Rushton! Here, give Hooper your driving coat, and

I'll take you along to my room and see what can be done for you." He cast a helpless look at Selina.

"Have his clothes sent down to the kitchen where they can be dried, Henry," she suggested, stifling an impulse to laugh at the absurd picture Rushton presented. "You really should not have come, sir. When we rose to find the day so inclement, we did not even expect a messenger to be sent out on such a day." Her brows drew together in a tiny frown. "Surely you did not consider it a matter of keeping your word! You cannot be so inflexible as that!"

In a voice of icy sarcasm he rapped, "I could not deny myself the pleasure of seeing so welcoming a host and hostess. Seldom have I been told by both that my efforts were futile, and I had better not have made them. My curricle lies down the road with a broken splinter bar, my horses are undoubtedly shaken by their misadventure, I am soaked to the skin and likely to take an inflammation of the lungs, and the only greeting I receive is a disapproving shake of the head from your groom and a scolding from the two of you. I regret that I made the effort." He paused in the act of removing his coat, and shrugged his shoulders back into it. "If you will condescend to allow me the temporary use of a saddle, I shall have one of my pair prepared for my return to the Horse and Hound."

Although a flush of embarrassment spread over Henry's face, Selina was not the least moved by Rushton's pathetic monologue. "Stuff! You are just annoyed that your driving was not up to snuff today, my dear sir, and that your curricle will be out of commission for a few days. We're delighted you've come. Nothing is more tiresome than a rainy day. Come, give your coat to Hooper, and Henry will see that you are thoroughly dried out in no time. We would not wish to have you developing an inflammation of the lungs." The corners of her mouth twitched suspiciously as he continued to glare at her and made no effort to remove his coat.

"It would delight me, of course, to relieve your boredom, Miss Easterly-Cummings, but I fear I shall be more of an inconvenience than an assistance. Several hours would be needed for the drying of my clothes, and during that time I could hardly be expected to see to your amusement."

"Very stuffy he is today," Selina declared in a loud stage aside to Henry. "We will humor him, though, as he has gone to such lengths to visit us, and I myself would no doubt be equally irritable were I as wet as he." She turned to Rushton with an angelic smile. "There now, that is not the least problem. I have no doubt Hooper can look you out some suitable clothing. Henry's, I fear, would not do, but Hooper is more of your height."

Hooper obligingly murmured, "Certainly, ma'am. If Mr. Rushton will go along to Mr. Henry's room, I will be along in a trice with the necessary articles."

No further word of protest was forthcoming from Rushton, but he allowed Selina only a curt nod before divesting himself of his clammy driving coat, and following Henry up the back stairs to the latter's room. When the door was closed behind them, Rushton growled, "I thought your cousin had endeavored not to play-act any more when you had company."

"Did you think she was acting?" Henry asked stoutly. "Only teasing, I think. She should not have, of course, as you were not in the mood to accept it in the spirit offered."

"You think perhaps I should be?" Rushton asked indignantly, as he tugged at his muddy boots.

Henry kneeled to assist. "We meant no offense, sir. We didn't protest your arrival because we didn't wish to have you come, but because we didn't expect you. Selina was merely trying to cajole you out of the megrims."

"I do not succumb to the 'megrims,' as you call them, Forrester," Rushton retorted haughtily.

"Don't you, sir?" The second boot came off with a sloshing sound and Henry regarded it with dismay. "I'm afraid it may be ruined."

"Forget the damn boot," his companion rasped. "If I was rude..."

"Of course you weren't!"

"If I was rude, I apologize. Your cousin appeared to be laughing at me."

"I'm sure she never would. Well, she did, when she heard about what happened at the inn that morning, but you didn't seem to care."

This reminder gave Rushton pause. Why did he not mind her laughing at him for that ludicrous and painful episode, when he was so irate with her today? Perhaps because he had not been the principal figure in the comedy of errors, whereas he felt every kind of fool for having come out on such a miserable day to exhibit his eagerness to be with Miss Easterly-Cummings. It would not do to make so much of the affair, thereby only heightening his folly. He forced a laugh. "I suppose I must have looked like a drowned rat, and I admit to some concern for my horses. Your cousin was right, you know. My driving was not at its best today."

"Our roads are atrocious in the rain," Henry sympathized. "That must be Hooper with some clothes."

The footman entered majestically, bearing in his arms everything from drawers to cravats. Efficiently he stripped Rushton of his wet clothing and assisted him into the borrowed finery—Hooper's Sunday best, consisting of a red and yellow striped waistcoat and knee breeches of a bilious green, together with a coat of matching hue. Henry bit his lip as Rushton surveyed himself in the mirror. Not a muscle in the older man's face moved as his eyes traveled from his head to his feet, and he turned politely to the smiling footman. "My thanks, Hooper. You shall have your clothing back as soon as mine are dry."

"The coat is a little snug about the shoulders, sir, but never mind. We'll have yours ready in no time."

"I would be grateful," Rushton murmured as the footman departed with his wet clothing over his arm. Impassively, he turned to Henry and said, "I can only be thankful that Victor is not here. You needn't restrain your merriment, Henry. I would almost rather have retained my wet clothes."

In spite of having given his permission, Rushton was surprised at the very vigor of Henry's burst of laughter. Between gulps of amusement, Henry gasped, "You look...like a...Bond Street beau. Selina will... love it."

"Perhaps I should stay here until my clothes are dry."

"Oh, no, surely not! You wouldn't deny Selina such a treat."

"No, how could I when she was so kind as to afford me amusement by her own costume when first we met?" Rushton asked smoothly.

Henry's brows lifted in a query. "Would you remind her of that?"

"Of course not, and little she'd care if I did. Devil take you, Henry, you are putting me out of sorts again. Let's join your cousin."

After ordering a hot luncheon and leaving instructions for the care of Mr. Rushton's clothing in the kitchen, Selina had retired to the drawing room where she nervously picked up the fringe she was knotting. Undoubtedly, she had only managed to antagonize Mr. Rushton with her attempt at levity, and she was consumed with remorse. His approbation had come to mean more to her than she cared to acknowledge. She felt wicked for having pinched at him when he had gone to the trouble of visiting them on such an abominable day. In this chastened mood, she witnessed his entry into the room with a sort of despair, rising to say heartily, "Oh, good, they have found you dry clothing. I've ordered a warm meal, but if you should care for a glass of brandy now, you have only to say. Henry is convinced such spirits are a panacea for warding off all manner of evils."

Startled by her solicitousness, and her lack of awareness of his strange outfit, Rushton was at a loss to answer her. Henry looked no less dumbfounded, though he recovered sufficiently to say abruptly, "Yes, I'll have some brandy brought for you," whereupon he disappeared from the room.

"Won't you sit down, Mr. Rushton? Take the chair near the fire; you must be chilled still."

"No, I'm perfectly comfortable."

Selina seated herself awkwardly on the sofa and removed a feather that had escaped its pillow. Rushton continued to stand. "I . . . I hope your horses took no narm from the accident. Shall I send for word of their condition?"

"No, I'm sure Morris has matters in hand."

"He's very capable." Selina darted a glance up at his expressionless face. "Is your valet recovering?"

"I sent him home."

"Oh. I'm sure Henry would be happy to have his man serve you, since he was the cause of . . ."

"I don't want Henry's man."

"No, well, he's really only a boy in any case, though he is quick to learn."

Rushton made no reply but his eyes remained intent on her face.

Without looking up, Selina was yet aware of his regard and swallowed painfully. "I didn't mean to tease you when you arrived, Mr. Rushton. And I'm sorry you had an accident and were so very wet. Is there . . . a draft in here? I should not like to have you take a chill."

"I won't."

"No, I dare say you won't. But then, the most unlikely people do sometimes, you know. Mrs. Morrow was forever taking a chill, and blamed the dampness of the house. I don't notice it, myself. Not that Mrs. Morrow was an unlikely person to take a chill, for that is not the case at all. She is exactly the type of person one would expect to take a chill." Selina glanced anxiously to the door through which Henry had disappeared. "I wonder what is keeping him. You must be eager for your brandy."

"Not in the least."

"I see. Um, it won't be long until luncheon. I especially requested that I be informed as soon as the pigeon pie is ready. You do like pigeon pie, don't you?"

"Usually."

"Our cook makes a very fine pigeon pie. Don't you wish to sit down, Mr. Rushton?" she asked desperately.

"I would very likely split your footman's coat, Miss Casterly-Cummings."

"Oh. Take if off, if you like. I have no objection."

"I am not in the habit of sitting with ladies in my shirtsleeves."

"But this is a special circumstance, sir."

"Not special enough."

Her eyes flew to his and her chin came up. "Be uncomfortable, then. I'm sure I don't care. I didn't ask you to come in the rain. No one in his right mind would have come in the rain. You can't blame me for your folly."

"But I do," he said softly.

"Well, it's very unfair of you. I have tried to be agreeable. I have apologized for my teasing, and I have not so much as mentioned how ridiculous you look in those absurd breeches with that grotesque waistcoat. Even Hooper never looked such a quiz in them! He wears them to court the Southwoods' kitchen-maid, you know, and he is very proud of them. I hope you didn't embarrass him with any disparaging comments."

"I didn't."

"At least I can be thankful for that." Angrily she picked up the fringe and pointedly ignored him, her color high and her eyes mutinous.

Only the crackle of the fire disturbed the silence which fell on the room. Rushton picked up a magazine from the Pembroke table and casually flipped through the pages, but he paid no heed to the contents. He was no less aware of her presence than she of his, and he realized that whether or not he was in the same room with her, there was no chance that he would ever again be free from her influence. He was about to turn to her when the door opened to admit Henry, followed by Hooper with a silver tray bearing the finest brandy the Shalbrook cellars had to offer. Scamp managed to dart into the room and made straight for her rescuer. Alerted by her excited barking, Rushton hurriedly dropped the magazine and attempted to prevent her doing damage to his borrowed clothing. He scooped the dog up in her headlong dash at him, and held her at arm's length, her feet still scooting wildly in the air. Before Selina could make a move, she found Scamp deposited unceremoniously in her lap to the accompaniment of a rending tear as Hooper's coat, stretched beyond bearing by Rushton's broad shoulders, gave way. Hooper looked on with dismay while Henry murmured, "Oh, Lord."

His lips pressed in a tight line, Rushton said, "I will have it repaired or replaced, Hooper. Help me out of it, will you?"

Leaving the decanter on the side table, Hooper instantly performed this small service, though he eyed his coat with regret. "Shall I bring you another?" he asked skeptically.

"Thank you, no. Miss Easterly-Cummings will forgive my shirtsleeves."

"I said I would," Selina murmured virtuously, keeping a firm hold on the still energetic Scamp. As Hooper departed with the misused coat, she turned to Henry. "I feel sure Mr. Rushton is ready for his glass of brandy."

"I went with McDonough myself to choose the best we had, sir. Selina's father laid down some very fine brandy a dozen years ago." As he spoke, Henry poured out a solitary glass and handed it to Rushton.

"You don't join me?"

Henry flushed. "It makes me sleepy."

"You'll need to overcome that failing, and better here than when you come to town with me."

Obediently, Henry poured himself a glass and sipped at it as he and Rushton discussed boxing. Selina watched suspiciously as Rushton urged another glass on her cousin, but she said nothing. Henry had time to finish the second glass before luncheon was announced and, in honor of their guest, wine was served with the meal. Delighted by the light, heady feeling the brandy had given him, Henry consumed more than his share of the wine at luncheon, and under Rushton's prodding talked non-stop of his ambitions and interests.

The men adjourned to the drawing room some time after Selina, and she thought Henry much the worse for the unusual quantities of wine he had consumed. Rushton asked politely that she play an air on the pianoforte, and chose the most soporific he could find from the stack of sheets. By the conclusion of the piece, Selina looked up to find Henry slumped down on the sofa, fast asleep.

"He warned you that mid-day drinking makes him

sleepy," she said somewhat tartly. "And it is you who induced him to imbibe so freely."

"I know. He'll learn to handle it."

"Your teaching methods are rather unique, Mr. Rushton. He will also have the headache when he awakes."

"I'm sure you will see to his rapid recovery. He must learn not to be influenced by others to drink more than he can handle."

"So you admit you did it on purpose?"

"Not to teach him a lesson, my dear lady. I wished to have an opportunity to talk with you alone."

"You are an unscrupulous man, Mr. Rushton. If there was some matter you wished to discuss, you need only have asked for a word in private with me. There was no need to involve poor Henry."

"Poor Henry enjoyed himself enormously, Miss Easterly-Cummings, and you know it. Come and sit here with me."

Her eyes flashed with rebellion, but she responded to the note of command in his voice and his eyes. He stood waiting for her beside the sofa opposite Henry's, his hand outstretched. Approaching reluctantly, Selina impetuously seated herself in a chair close to the sofa before she reached him.

"Here," he instructed patiently, his hand still out.

"I . . . I am comfortable where I am."

"You will be more comfortable beside me." His compelling eyes did not leave her face.

She swallowed nervously and looked about as though for some escape, then rose hesitantly and placed her hand in his. It was lifted to his lips and brushed lightly before he allowed her to seat herself. The sofa was not a large one and she found that his shoulders touched hers, though she thought that was not strictly necessary. His being in his shirtsleeves somehow made their proximity seem intimate, and she began to twist the pillow fringe about her fingers. "You . . . wished to speak with me?"

"Yes." But he said nothing further, merely studied her profile, the nervous gestures of her fingers and the rapid rise and fall of her breathing.

"Are you still angry with me for teasing you?"

"No. I apologize for taking you amiss. You may have noticed that I do not possess the most benevolent of tempers."

"Well, I have, but then I am not precisely even-tempered myself. I . . . don't like you being . . . cross with me."

"I never am for long."

"No, I've noticed you regain your good humor when you have eaten well."

Rushton laughed. "Is that why you are forever enjoining a good meal on me?"

Her gaze remained intent on the fringe she was weaving between her fingers, but she nodded.

"Silly goose. I cannot excuse my irritability on the score of being sharp-set." He twined one of her brown curls about his finger and asked, "Does your hair curl so tightly because of the rain?"

In a strangled voice she said, "Yes, it always has."

"I like it."

"Th-thank you."

Rushton ran a finger along the line of her jaw and down to the pulse beating wildly in her throat. "On our way to London, I am going to take Henry to visit Rugby."

"You . . . think he should go there?" Selina forced herself to meet his eyes.

"Not necessarily Rugby, but it is closest, and will give him an idea of what such a school is like. My godmother's nephew is there and can show Henry about if we arrive before the Easter holidays." He took hold of her restless hands. "You don't object?"

"No, but I cannot speak for Lord Leyburn."

"He can't object to Henry visiting the school, and there is plenty of time to approach him on the matter later. You heard your cousin at luncheon. He's full of youthful hopes and dreams, but they have very little direction. The farming interests him, but he knows little else, Miss Easterly-Cummings. He's wistful about what other boys are doing and thinking and planning. He should have the opportunity to find out, and to have other young men as companions."

215

"I know," she whispered.

"Good. Now I should like to know why you would not sell the vale to Lord Benedict."

The question was so unexpected, so alarming, that she pulled her hands from his and rose precipitately. "I think that is not a matter of your concern, Mr. Rushton." She cast a hasty glance at the sleeping Henry.

"I understand you were once engaged to Lord Benedict," he said helpfully, retaining his seat in spite of her defiant stance.

"I don't see how that can possibly interest you, Mr. Rushton."

"But it does. Won't you tell me?" When she did not reply but stood staring at the fire, he asked, "Are the roses in the glass box from Lord Benedict?"

"How do you know about the roses?" she asked indignantly.

"You had me get a piece of paper from the drawer."

"Oh."

"Are you still attached to Lord Benedict?"

"Of course not."

"To Geoffrey Haslett?"

"This conversation is ridiculous, Mr. Rushton."

"Not at all."

"It is! How would you like it if I asked you if you were attached to Miss Longstreet?"

"Her name is Longmead, Miss Easterly-Cummings." Rushton regarded her speculatively. "Who told you about her?"

"She was mentioned in passing," Selina murmured, her chin up.

A slow smile spread over Rushton's face. "By Sir Penrith?"

"No. I'm sure Pen would never discuss your affairs."

"Haslett, then. What did he tell you?"

Selina kept her back stubbornly to him.

"Come now, my dear. I don't mind discussing Miss Longmead. Did Haslett think I had offered for her?"

"He said he thought she'd shown you the door," Selina quoted.

"She did."

Abruptly Selina turned to face him. "I'm truly sorry. Perhaps she will change her mind."

"I hope not," he laughed. "Did you think she had broken my heart? Or did you think about it at all?"

"I thought Mr. Haslett was probably wrong and that you were going to London to settle the matter," Selina admitted, her hands clenched until the knuckles became white.

"I see. Miss Longmead bruised my pride, but she never touched my heart. I think Pen was delighted that she wouldn't have me; he doesn't like her. He likes you very much."

Her startled eyes flew to his. "I . . . I'm very fond of Penrith."

"I envy him. Do sit down, my dear." He touched the seat beside him on the sofa and lifted a brow enquiringly. Selina moved forward without hesitation, and allowed him to take her hands when she sat beside him. He continued in a matter of fact voice, "I promised Penrith that I would come to town for Cassandra's ball. I have helped to send off his other sisters, you see, and he regards me as some sort of talisman, I fear."

"You are kind to help him," she said mechanically.

"His sisters don't need my help, if I have any to offer. They are all good-hearted girls with sufficient looks to do very well on their own. And Cassandra confided to me that she and Lord John have an understanding of sorts."

"She confided in you?" Selina asked, amazed.

"Not everyone sees me as an ogre, Miss Easterly-Cummings. I stayed at Oak Park for some weeks and we often fell into conversation. I see nothing unusual in it. She knew I would not misuse her confidence." He regarded her wistfully.

"You . . . want me to confide in you, too?"

"Just so that I will understand why you are afraid of me," he said blandly.

"But I'm *not* afraid of you," she protested, albeit somewhat nervously.

"Would you let me kiss you?"

"N-No. Why should I?"

Instead of answering her question he said, "I had Penrith arrange for you to be invited to London."

She regarded him helplessly, but could think of no comment to make.

"I enjoy the time I spend in London. I wondered if you would, too."

She pressed her lips together to keep them from trembling. "You thought I would not know how to act in Society."

"London is different than the shires, my dear. You have a habit of doing very much as you please."

"I could behave properly if I wished to."

"Precisely. But would you wish to? And would you find pleasure there if you had to conform to a lot of antiquated rules or be ostracized?"

"I would not have shamed Lady Southwood."

Again he twined a lock of her hair about his finger. "Why wouldn't you sell the vale to Lord Benedict?"

The red and yellow stripes of the waistcoat swam before her eyes. "Because he tried to seduce me there."

"When you were engaged?"

She nodded. "He offered to let me keep Henry with me if I would . . . As though Henry were a stray dog . . ." A quick glance assured her that her cousin was still asleep. "He didn't really care for me at all. He wanted Shalbrook, and the vale, and my . . . body."

"Why did you keep the roses?"

"They were from before he went to the Peninsula. I kept them on my vanity until that day. The roses are a reminder."

"Of what?"

"Of how easily I was deceived. He was so handsome, so attractive to me. I almost . . ." She attempted to draw her hand from his, but he held it firmly. "But he wasn't what I thought him at all. How could I be so blind?"

"And Geoffrey Haslett?"

"I met him only a few months later. He was so gay, so light-hearted. Everything had gotten to be too much for me, and he laughed at everything. I think he did care for me, after his fashion."

"And?"

Selina sighed. "I happened to overhear him tell

his . . . mistress that nothing need change if he married me." The red and yellow stripes were becoming a familiar pattern before her eyes. "He told me recently that everyone keeps a mistress, because wives are too fragile to be bothered all the time." She darted a questioning look at him.

"You don't appear very fragile to me," he assured her.

"I wouldn't like my husband to have a mistress."

"I doubt he'd have any need of one," Rushton retorted with a grin.

"Yes, well, the roses remind me that I have twice been mistaken."

He traced the oval of her face with a gentle finger. "I can't prove I am not like them, Selina. And you have only my word that I love you dearly. Will you let me kiss you?"

"Yes." Her eyes met his for a moment before she yielded to his embrace. As their first kiss had been, it was not in the least comforting, or brotherly, nor was it excessively demanding, but it was thorough. And he kissed her eyelids, and her nose, and her chin with a tenderness that contrasted delightfully with the obvious strength of him. She stared wide-eyed into his warm blue eyes when they drew apart. "I . . . know you are different than they were. I think I have always known it, but I was so afraid to trust my judgment."

"At least you know my faults from the start, my love. Will you marry me?"

"You trust me not to shame you, Gareth?" Selina felt unusually vulnerable as she searched his eyes.

"I have a profound respect for your loyalties, Selina. If you care for me . . ."

"Oh, I do. Sometimes so much that it hurts. And I want more than anything to marry you. But what of Shalbrook and the hunting-box and Henry, and . . ."

Rushton laid a finger on her lips. "We can work all of that out. The important thing is that you will marry me." As he made to take her in his arms, they heard Henry stir on the sofa opposite, and Selina clung fast to his hand.

Only partially awake, Henry regarded them owlishly. "I say, did I fall asleep? Forgive me! It was all that wine. Have I missed my boxing lesson?"

Rushton smiled at Selina as he addressed the young man. "We were just about to send for some champagne, Henry."

⊘ SIGNET REGENCY ROMANCE   (0451)

DILEMMAS OF THE HEART

☐ **THE AIM OF A LADY by Laura Matthews.** "Diana Savile has an interesting way of attracting a husband—she shoots him. Don't miss this one, it's a classic!"—Catherine Coulter   (170814—$3.99)

☐ **HEARTS BETRAYED by Gayle Buck.** The exquisite Michelle du Bois, who had broken so many hearts, risks having her own broken by a lord who shows no pity.   (168763—$3.95)

☐ **THE DUKE'S DAUGHTER by Melinda McRae.** Elizabeth Granford firmly resisted the Earl of Wentworth, and rejected his proposal of marriage. For she was someone who wanted nothing to do with wedlock, and even less with love. . . .   (169743—$3.99)

☐ **A CHRISTMAS COURTSHIP by Sandra Heath.** Beautiful Blanche Amberley knew she loved Antony Mortimer. She also knew she thoroughly disliked Sir Edmund Brandon. She was quite immune to the good looks and gallantry that made this arrogant blueblood the most eligible lord in the realm. But then Christmas approached and Cupid gave Blanche a gift that came as a most shocking surprise. . . .   (167929—$3.95)

☐ **THE DUKE'S DESIGN by Margaret Westhaven.** Miss Matilda Graham made it clear what she thought of the Duke of Arden's proposition. Yet how could she refuse this lord whose looks, wealth and charm won him any woman he wanted?   (169182—$3.99)

☐ **FALSE OF HEART by Elizabeth Hewitt.** A proud beauty follows passion's flaming path to love's shining truth.   (171233—$4.50)

☐ **DEVIL'S LADY by Patricia Rice.** Even as lovely Faith Montague was in peril of losing herself to the temptation of a lawless rake, and even greater danger threatened to overtake her. Love . . .   (169603—$3.99)

Prices slightly higher in Canada.

Buy them at your local bookstore or use this convenient coupon for ordering.

NEW AMERICAN LIBRARY
P.O. Box 999, Bergenfield, New Jersey 07621

Please send me the books I have checked above.
I am enclosing $_____ (please add $2.00 to cover postage and handling). Send check or money order (no cash or C.O.D.'s) or charge by Mastercard or VISA (with a $15.00 minimum). Prices and numbers are subject to change without notice.

Card #_____ Exp. Date _____
Signature_____
Name_____
Address_____
City _____ State _____ Zip Code _____

For faster service when ordering by credit card call **1-800-253-6476**

Allow a minimum of 4-6 weeks for delivery. This offer is subject to change without notice.

ⓞSIGNET REGENCY ROMANCE (0451)

NOVELS OF LOVE AND DESIRE

☐ **A CERTAIN MAGIC by Mary Balogh.** It was only after Piers Westhaven asked another to be his bride that the lovely young widow Alice Penhallow found that the way she needed Piers went beyond friendship . . . beyond propriety . . . to the very very brink of scandal. . . . (169166—$3.95)

☐ **THE SUBSTITUTE BRIDEGROOM by Charlotte Dolan.** Elizabeth Goldsborough was to wed the most handsome gentleman of the *ton*. But an accidental encounter with the arrogant Captain Darius St. John left her with no choice but to marry this man she barely knew . . . (168917—$3.95)

☐ **DOUBLE DECEIT by Emily Hendrickson.** Miss Caroline Beauchamp accepted the tricky task of seducing the handsome husband of her dearest friend to break the hold that an infamous beauty had on the vulnerable Viscount. But she also had to bedazzle the most renowned rake in the realm, Lord Rutledge, to keep him from making Mary his latest conquest. (168534—$3.95)

☐ **A REGENCY VALENTINE.** The joys and passions that surround St. Valentine's Day are captured in an extraordinary collection of all-new stories by five of the most highly acclaimed Regency authors: Mary Balogh, Katherine Kingsley, Emma Lange, Patricia Rice, and Joan Wolf. (168909—$4.50)

☐ **THE UNLIKELY CHAPERONE by Dorothy Mack.** Alexandra was supposed to be protecting her sister, Didi, from men. But now she was sorely tempted to protect men from Didi. One man, at least. the man whom Didi wanted as a victim . . . and whom Alexandra wanted in a very different way. (168933—$3.95)

☐ **FULL MOON MAGIC: Five stories by Mary Balogh, Gayle Buck, Charlotte Louise Dolan, Anita Mills, and Patricia Rice.** In this wondrous collection are tales of enchanted love sprinkled with moonbeams, where ghosts roam castles, spirits travel through the realms of time, and the unlikeliest matchmakers bring lovers together. (174577—$4.99)

Prices higher in Canada.

Buy them at your local bookstore or use this convenient coupon for ordering.

NEW AMERICAN LIBRARY
P.O. Box 999, Bergenfield, New Jersey 07621

Please send me the books I have checked above.
I am enclosing $_____ (please add $2.00 to cover postage and handling).
Send check or money order (no cash or C.O.D.'s) or charge by Mastercard or VISA (with a $15.00 minimum). Prices and numbers are subject to change without notice.

Card #_____ Exp. Date _____
Signature_____
Name_____
Address_____
City _____ State _____ Zip Code _____

For faster service when ordering by credit card call **1-800-253-6476**

Allow a minimum of 4-6 weeks for delivery. This offer is subject to change without notice.

⊘ SIGNET REGENCY ROMANCE   (0451)

ROMANTIC INTERLUDES

☐ **AN UNLIKELY ATTRACTION** by Melinda McRae   (170636—$3.99)

☐ **IRISH EARL'S RUSE** by Emma Lange   (172574—$3.99)

☐ **THE UNMANAGEABLE MISS MARLOWE** by Emma Lange (170458—$3.99)

☐ **THE HIDDEN HEART** by Gayle Buck   (172353—$3.99)

☐ **THE WALTZING WIDOW** by Gayle Buck   (167376—$3.99)

☐ **A CHANCE ENCOUNTER** by Gayle Buck   (170873—$3.99)

☐ **THE MOCK MARRIAGE** by Dorothy Mack   (170199—$3.99)

☐ **A WIFE FOR WARMINSTER** by Margaret Summerville   (169751—$3.99)

☐ **THE WICKED PROPOSAL** by Emily Hendrickson   (172345—$3.99)

☐ **A SCANDALOUS SUGGESTION** by Emily Hendrickson   (169921—$3.99)

☐ **THE DASHING MISS FAIRCHILD** by Emily Hendrickson (171276—$3.99)

☐ **A PERFECT PERFORMANCE** by Emily Hendrickson   (171047—$3.99)

☐ **THE BATH ECCENTRIC'S SON** by Amanda Scott   (171705—$3.99)

☐ **BATH CHARADE** by Amanda Scott   (169948—$3.99)

☐ **A LOVE MATCH** by Barbara Allister   (169387—$3.99)

Buy them at your local bookstore or use this convenient coupon for ordering.

NEW AMERICAN LIBRARY
P.O. Box 999, Bergenfield, New Jersey 07621

Please send me the books I have checked above.
I am enclosing $_____ (please add $2.00 to cover postage and handling).
Send check or money order (no cash or C.O.D.'s) or charge by Mastercard or
VISA (with a $15.00 minimum). Prices and numbers are subject to change without
notice.

Card #_____ Exp. Date _____
Signature_____
Name_____
Address_____
City _____ State _____ Zip Code _____

For faster service when ordering by credit card call **1-800-253-6476**

Allow a minimum of 4-6 weeks for delivery. This offer is subject to change without notice.

⊘SIGNET REGENCY ROMANCE   (0451)

LOVE IN THE HIGHEST CIRCLES

- ☐ **MISS GRIMSLEY'S OXFORD CAREER by Carla Kelly** (171950—$3.99)
- ☐ **THE IMPROPER PLAYWRIGHT by Margaret Summerville**
  (171969—$3.99)
- ☐ **A DASHING WIDOW by Carol Proctor** (170423—$3.99)
- ☐ **LORD BUCKINGHAM'S BRIDE by Sandra Heath** (169573—$3.99)
- ☐ **A CHRISTMAS COURTSHIP by Sandra Heath** (167929—$3.95)
- ☐ **LORD KANE'S KEEPSAKE by Sandra Heath** (172264—$3.99)
- ☐ **TALK OF THE TOWN by Irene Saunders** (170172—$3.99)
- ☐ **THE DOWAGER'S DILEMMA by Irene Saunders** (169581—$3.99)
- ☐ **LADY ARDEN'S REDEMPTION by Marjorie Farrell** (171942—$3.99)
- ☐ **AUTUMN ROSE by Marjorie Farrell.** (168747—$3.95)
- ☐ **THE ROGUE'S RETURN by Anita Mills** (172582—$3.99)
- ☐ **MISS GORDON'S MISTAKE by Anita Mills** (168518—$3.99)
- ☐ **THE UNOFFICIAL SUITOR by Charlotte Louise Dolan** (173007—$3.99)
- ☐ **THREE LORDS FOR LADY ANNE by Charlotte Louise Dolan**
  (170644—$3.99)
- ☐ **THE RESOLUTE RUNAWAY by Charlotte Louise Dolan** (171691—$3.99)

Prices slightly higher in Canada

Buy them at your local bookstore or use this convenient coupon for ordering.

NEW AMERICAN LIBRARY
P.O. Box 999, Bergenfield, New Jersey 07621

Please send me the books I have checked above.
I am enclosing $_____ (please add $2.00 to cover postage and handling).
Send check or money order (no cash or C.O.D.'s) or charge by Mastercard or
VISA (with a $15.00 minimum). Prices and numbers are subject to change without
notice.

Card #_____ Exp. Date _____
Signature_____
Name_____
Address_____
City _____ State _____ Zip Code _____

For faster service when ordering by credit card call **1-800-253-6476**

Allow a minimum of 4-6 weeks for delivery. This offer is subject to change without notice.